HOME  Second Nature

Lauren Roberts

Lauren Roberts

Illustrations By J`ne'

Lauren Roberts

Visit us on Facebook at Lauren Roberts Author
https://www.facebook.com/HappyAnimalTales/

Dedication

I want to dedicate this book to my love, my life, my Gary... again.
I thank the Good Lord every day for Blessing me with you.
You ARE my "M" and I your Harriet...
even though we both sometimes sympathize with
what M puts up with... Hmmm...
Thank you for loving all animals as much as I do
and for watching out for them and protecting them.
And for watching out for me and protecting me.
You have taught me to never say never.
You have taught me to always have Faith.
You have taught me anything is possible if you Believe.
You have enriched my life beyond my imagination.
And we know I have some imagination!
I love you!
You are my M92.
God Bless you!

Acknowledgements

Thank you, Lord
As always, Praise and Glory to our Heavenly Father and His Son, our Savior, Jesus Christ. He Guided me through this story from the day I woke up and had the first chapter in my head... with all the dialogue. And for Guiding me to the name of the book, Second Nature. I continue to acknowledge that I am so Blessed for all the people that He has Given me to Guide me to this peaceful and wonderful opportunity. For Blessing us with the amazing animals that we talk to every day. Thank you, Lord, for all of our loved ones here with us... and our loved ones that watch over us from Above. I am grateful and thankful for all of these Blessings!

SWFL Eagle Cam, Moderators, Zoomie and Hancock Wildlife Foundation
Thank you for giving us the opportunity to have a front row seat in the everyday lives of these majestic creatures. Thank you for sharing all your knowledge, for being a comfort when needed, and for sharing the joy of the eagles.

Vicki Ohsann and All The Photographers... And The Church Of The Nazarene
Vicki, thank you for your friendship, prayers, informative videos and your never-ending devotion to this eagle family and all wildlife. Thank you to the MANY photographers that capture the nest tree adventures. Desiree Deliz, Liz Grindstaff, Barb Henry, Kathy Kochanowski, Marie Lapointe-Chism and Marti Lord and many more. I apologize if I forgot to mention someone. Please know how much you are appreciated. Thank you to the Church of the Nazarene for graciously sharing the serene comfort of their property for us to enjoy the eagles.

Shawnlei Breeding, Florida Audubon Society Eagle Watch/CROW/Naples Conservancy/FL Fish and Wildlife/US Fish and Wildlife/Raptor Rescue/Raptor Center of Tampa Bay
I can never thank you enough for all you do. Thank you for all your guidance, knowledge, direction and dedication.

And Last, but CERTAINLY NOT LEAST! All of our friends and family
Thank you all! I tried to put as many of you in the book as possible, but although I added some new, I couldn't add all. If your name is in the book, please remember, the animal does not reflect your personality. I just needed to acknowledge you! Thank you all for your encouragement and support! And mostly, thank you for being there and for all your prayers! We love you all!

Table Of Contents

Lauren Roberts

Chapter 1 ... Precious E14

"Come on, Mama! Come on, Dad! You two are so slow! Come on! Catch me!" E14 laughed. E14 flew all around the nest tree and pasture.

"Slow down, E14," called M15 to his young male eaglet. Harriet flew alongside her mate. M looked at her in disbelief. "How can this be possible? He's too young! He hasn't developed his flight feathers. He can't be flying! He hasn't even branched yet! I don't get it!"

"I don't either, M. But look at both of us trying to catch up to him!"

Harriet and M15 flew at an alarming rate of speed to try to catch up to their precious E14 as he laughed and squeed high and low and all around them. E14 was as happy as he could be!

"Feel the wind! Woohoo! Watch me go real, real high!" E14 started to soar higher and higher in the sky. Harriet and M looked at each other in disbelief.

"How in the world...?" M questioned.

"WOOHOO! First one to the nest is the Grand Eagle Of All Time!" proclaimed E14. He swooped and swayed and landed in their nest. "Woohoo! I won! I'm the Grand Eagle!" he cheered.

"Okay E14, that's enough for today," said the familiar kind voice. "Come on, you know the rules."

"Oh, please...just a little longer..."

"No, not today."

"Okay," said E14 disappointedly, his head hung low.

"Don't be sad. You'll be back many times."

"Promise?"

"I promise."

"Okay," E14 smiled and squeed as he looked up at his Mom and Dad. "I love you, Mama. I love you, Dad. I'll see you again real soon!" E14 turned and grabbed onto the large wing that reached out to him and said, "Okay Ozzie, I'm ready to go home." There was an amazing bright flash of light and they were gone.

Harriet and M both bolted out of their slumber as they perched on the upper branch of their nest tree. They both shook their heads and looked around at the pasture and down into their nest.

Bewildered, Harriet looked at M and said, "I just had the oddest dream about E14. I've had a lot of dreams about him since... but this dream was like no other."

M's eyes opened wide as he said, "Me, too!"

Harriet started to explain her dream to M15. "E14 was flying and we were trying to catch up to him..."

M15 then continued for Harriet. "And he kept laughing at us and he kept telling us how slow we were..."

Shocked, Harriet added, "And he started soaring higher and higher..."

"Then he raced us to the nest..." M added.

Harriet continued, "And then an eagle's wing came into view. I don't know from where and I don't know how, but I saw it and I heard the eagle's voice. It was Ozzie's voice and E14 took hold of Ozzie's wing..."

"And E14 said he was ready to go home..." said M sadly.

They looked at each other with tears in their eyes and hope in their hearts.

Harriet quietly spoke. "You know what that means, don't you?"

M nodded and then said with a peaceful calmness, "Yes...it means he is alright. He is with Ozzie and he is healthy, happy and safe again."

Harriet softly smiled. "And he said he would be back and that he loves us." Harriet's voice cracked as tears started to roll down her beautiful face.

"And somehow," M added, "Somehow we were there to witness all of this. I mean, Harriet, we BOTH had the same dream!"

They both smiled like they used to smile before they lost their E14.

"So, it wasn't a dream!" said Harriet.

"It was real," said M. "We watched a real Miracle happen in front of us with our own eyes!"

Harriet and M both felt a peacefulness come over them and their nest tree. They knew their precious E14 was happy and would always be with them.

Harriet looked up to the sky and said, "Thank you, Lord. And thank you Ozzie for taking care of our baby."

"Thank you, Ozzie. You're a good guy!"

"Of course, he's a good guy!" Harriet teased M15. "I picked him!"

"Yes, you did! And you picked me, too! You have exceptionally good taste in male eagles!"

They both laughed... a much-needed laugh.

They hugged each other and remained in each other's wings as they gazed into the pasture reliving the Miracle they had just lived.

Chapter 2 ... Second Nature

Harriet and M15 now shared a greater bond after losing E14. But this bond was even stronger now that they shared in this Miracle! They spent the next few weeks like when they first met. They were inseparable. When one was there the other was not far behind. They went to the river for lunch. They soared high above the pasture. They watched the beautiful Southwest Florida sunsets perched side by side on their nest tree.

One night while watching the sunset, Harriet turned to M and said, "So, M... you know what eagles are supposed to do." M nodded. "So, I was thinking we should consider continuing this nesting season." M started to interrupt Harriet, but she stopped him before he could say anything. "I know... just saying it seems upsetting... and I still can't believe that our E14 isn't here anymore... but now that we know that he is always going to be with us and around us... I think we should do what we are supposed to do and let's try to have a second clutch."

M thought and looked at Harriet. He nodded his head and said, "I think you're right. My heart... our hearts... were so broken when we lost E14, but now I have such a peace about me and I know you do too. A second clutch just seems to be the right thing to do. It's..." M chuckled, "Second nature to us."

Harriet smiled and replied, "It certainly is second nature." They looked into each other's eyes and kissed.

"So..." M announced, "That means we have to get back to work quickly and get this nest back into egg laying condition. That means sticks and grasses. I'm on it, my Lady Love!" And with that M flew off of the nest tree. Harriet watched him in disbelief. M quickly turned around and flew back into the nest. "What was I thinking?" and he kissed Harriet.

"Now that's more like it," Harriet teased. M wiggled his eyebrows in M fashion and gave Harriet that irresistible M smile before he flew off again to gather nest material.

M flew around the pasture looking for the perfect sticks and then he flew back to the nest to place them in the perfect spot. Not to be outdone by her male eagle mate, Harriet started on her own nest material gathering mission.

One by one, the pasture animals started watching the two eagles.

"What do you think they're doing?" pondered Sandy as she waded in the pond with the other ducks.

"It looks like they're working on the nest," replied Waddles.

"I know that, but why?" questioned Sandy.

"I don't know," responded Waddles. "It's like they've lost their minds! That will do that to some animals, you know. Heartbreak can make you crazy. Heartbreak is like that, you know. One minute life is all happiness and roses and then the next minute your heart is ripped out of your chest and your mind just follows and you don't know what you're doing! THAT'S what it looks like to me. They are so distraught that they have completely lost their minds!"

Sandy rolled her eyes at Waddles. "I don't think you are right at all! They haven't lost their minds! Yes, they have suffered a terrible heartache, but Harriet and M are strong and resilient! They will always love and remember that sweet little baby of theirs." A tear ran down Sandy's face. She regained her composure and said, "But they also know that this is the circle of life and life must go on! Especially for eagles! They make sure eagles thrive. That's what they do."

"You can think what you want, but I think they went insane." And Waddles floated away from Sandy.

Sandy shook her head in disgust. She continued to watch the two eagles when suddenly Harriet landed at the pasture pond. "Good morning, Harriet," said Sandy as she floated closer to where Harriet was getting a drink of water.

"Oh, good morning, Sandy," replied Harriet.

"How are you and M doing," asked Sandy with great concern. "I can't express how deeply sorry I am to hear about your E14."

"We're okay, Sandy," Harriet said softly. "Thank you for asking. It has been such a shock to both of us."

"To all of us," added Sandy.

"Yes and thank you... thank you all. Everyone has been so nice and helpful. Even the humans. They placed flowers and items by the Church bench near the fence. I guess that is what humans do to express their sorrow and give their condolences."

"I saw that," said Sandy. "I was surprised that they did that. I thought they would have brought nest material or maybe a great big fish, but I guess what they left is what they do to show they care."

"Yes, I guess it is. It was very kind."

"So, if you don't mind me asking, what are you and M doing today? It looks like you're working on the nest."

"Yes, Sandy, we are doing nestorations."

"Really? Why?"

"Well, an eagle's goal in life is to have eaglets, teach them how to survive, and to continue the eagle way of life and have their own eaglets and on and on. That's what we do. Our hearts are so broken that we lost our E14, but now we know he is..." Harriet stopped in mid-sentence.

Sandy looked at Harriet and asked, "You know that he is what?"

Harriet didn't want to share the Miracle that she and M witnessed. Not everyone would understand. After all, they witnessed it and had a hard time understanding what they saw. Harriet thought quickly and said, "Just that he is in Heaven and will always be in our hearts."

Sandy had tears in her eyes. "Yes, he is. I don't know how you are holding up so well."

"I don't know either, but we both woke up today feeling life needs to go on."

"Well they say that eagles are resilient, but you two could be the poster eagles for resiliency!"

"Thank you, Sandy."

"So why are you doing nestorations?"

"We're planning on having a second clutch."

Sandy was surprised. "A second clutch?" Aren't you tired? Wouldn't you like a vacation or something... some time off?"

Harriet laughed. "That's not the eagle way, Sandy. It is still early enough in the season to think of having more eggs. So, we're going to try. And that reminds me, I better get back to getting sticks and grasses. Otherwise M will fill the nest with sticks that will go up to the top of the tree! I have to supervise otherwise the sky is truly the limit with him." Harriet laughed again and she thought it felt really good to be able to laugh... again. "

Sandy looked at the nest tree and said to Harriet. "I see your man working in the nest now. It looks like he might be starting a penthouse or a second story for your second clutch... maybe he misunderstood when he heard the word, second." Sandy and Harriet both laughed.

Harriet stopped laughing and said, "Why am I laughing? That's exactly what I'm afraid of." They laughed again. "Have a good day, Sandy!" and Harriet flew to the nest.

When Harriet got to the nest, she saw a collection of typical large M sticks scattered about the nest as he was deciding where to place them.

"Harriet! Look at all these great sticks!"

"Now M, remember we're doing nestorations to the nest. We're NOT building a multi-level condo."

"I know, I know. But we have to have high enough nest rails for the eaglets." Harriet watched and listened as M talked to himself as he went through the assortment of sticks he collected. "So, if we put this stick over here… and that stick… now where should we put that stick? Oh, it can go over there. Great! Perfect!" M continued to move the sticks to their designated spots as Harriet smiled as she saw her M15 filled with joy and purpose again. She was certain a second clutch was exactly what they needed. Yes, her M was right that a second clutch was second nature for them… all in the circle of life.

Chapter 3 ... Nestorations

T he days and weeks to come were filled with much dedication to having a second clutch. The mornings were full of constant stick and nest material gathering and placement. And that meant stick, "discussions."

Harriet flew to the nest with a large stick.

M rushed to help her. "Here my Lady Love, let me help you with that!"

"No, I have it, M. Thank you."

"No, I insist. Soon you'll be expecting eggs and I don't want you to overexert yourself."

"That's very sweet of you, M, but I'm perfectly capable of placing a stick... especially a stick that I found and carried to the nest all by myself in the first place."

"I didn't say you weren't capable. I just want to make sure that you stay healthy for our eggs that will be coming. I just wanted to help."

Without realizing that Harriet loosened her grip on the stick, M forcefully pulled it from Harriet causing him to fall onto the nest rail.

Harriet smiled and said, "Okay, if you insist."

M tried not to show his surprise that he lost his balance. He brushed himself off and said, "Great, no problem," and proceeded to place the stick.

This went on for quite a while and the "discussions" became more "spirited" as the days went by.

All the pasture animals had heard these "discussions" every season. This was nothing new to them. What was new was a second round of "discussions." They never saw a second clutch before at the nest tree so they were unsure of what this would entail. The pasture animals watched and learned... and listened.

Proudly M flew to the nest with a typical large M stick. Harriet was perched above the nest and just watched. She wasn't new here... she knew what to expect. But she watched the show as it unfolded. The large stick that M flew in with got caught on the nest rail and caused it to point straight up to the sky. Harriet turned her head away and smiled as she tried not to say anything. She then continued to watch. Poor M tried so hard to free the stick, but nothing worked. Harriet jumped down into the nest. At first the two of them silently moved other sticks... smaller sticks... without any arguing or name calling. But just as the pasture animals predicted, the "discussions" started... loudly.

"OW!" complained Harriet as M accidentally hit her with a stick. "Watch it, M!"

"Well, I'm sorry, but if you weren't in my way, you wouldn't have gotten hit with the stick."

Harriet picked up her own stick and turned to place it which caused the stick to hit M in the back of the head.

"Hey what was that for?" demanded M.

"What was what for?" asked Harriet.

"You know exactly what I'm talking about!" said M.

"No, I don't!"

"Uh-oh," said the Commander. "Sounds like the love birds are having a…"

"You hit me in the back of the head on purpose!" yelled M.

The Commander finished his sentence, "Slight difference of opinion." The pasture animals gathered near the Commander and listened to the "discussions."

"Well, if you weren't in my way like you accused me of being in your way, you wouldn't have gotten hit!" bellowed Harriet.

And so it began. They both bent over and picked up the same stick with their beaks. On opposite sides of the stick they faced each other. They looked each other in the eye. Both were determined to move the stick their way. Their eyes narrowed.

Harriet mumbled under her breath, "Frank Lloyd White Ibis!" Her gaze was piercing.

M groaned with equal determination and defiance. "Martha Screech Owl!" His eyes were ablaze.

They started their dance. They both walked forward. Neither letting go of the stick. Neither taking their eyes off of the other. Round and round they went. Then they stopped and just stared at each other determined to be the victor. Suddenly M let go of the stick and flew off. Surprised, Harriet watched. As quickly as he flew off, M returned… with another stick… a larger stick. To show he was the better nest builder, he smiled at Harriet and placed the large stick on the nest rails. But unfortunately, M ended up getting trapped between the nest rails and the impressive stick. Harriet laughed at M and went to show him how to place the stick. But in doing so Harriet now trapped herself. Her eyes opened wide in surprise and embarrassment.

"HA!" said M. "You think you know it all when it comes to building a nest, don't ya, Martha!"

The Commander's mouth dropped open. "Oh no, my man, not good, not good at all! Don't go there."

"Martha, the know-it-all…. SCREECH OWL!" yelled M.

"Yep, he went there…" said the Commander as he shook his head.

"FRANK LLOYD WHITE IBIS!" screamed Harriet.

But even though their "discussions" got heated, M was still a gentleman and moved the stick to free Harriet.

"Thank you, but I was perfectly fine and could have freed myself," Harriet said in a matter of fact tone.

"Oh, I didn't move the stick for you. I moved the stick because you put it in the wrong SPOT." M grinned. Harriet scowled at him.

Quietly, they both started moving sticks again. Each would peck at the back of the other's head.

"Oh sorry," said Harriet.

"Sorry," said M.

Until… again… they grabbed the same larger stick… and the dance started again. They stared each other down with narrowed eyes… again. And it started… again…

"Frank Lloyd White Ibis!"

"Martha Screech Owl!"

The Commander sighed, "Otherwise they are really an incredibly happy, loving couple. Maybe they should hire someone to work on the nest." The pasture animals laughed.

Soon things quieted down and the pasture was back to normal… Harriet and M continued day after day with their nestoration.

No matter how they acted during their nestorations, each day M would bring Harriet food. NutJob the squirrel noticed this loving gesture and he decided that he would like to do something nice for someone who was special to him. "Oh, THAT'S how you do it," exclaimed the little squirrel. So, the squirrel tried to find whatever he could to impress Twitch and make her happy the way M made Harriet happy. This was a tall order, especially for NutJob and his odd ways. NutJob went out and found something he thought Twitch would like. He planned his surprise. He quietly walked up behind Twitch and tapped her on the shoulder.

"AAAHHH!" Twitch screamed. She turned and saw NutJob looking very sweet and innocent standing behind her. She screamed at him. "What is wrong with you? Do you realize you could have given me a heart attack sneaking up on me like that and then tapping me on my shoulder?! Why I ought to..." Twitch suddenly stopped yelling at NutJob as he boyishly handed her a flower. "Oh my! NutJob... a flower for me?"

NutJob nodded, smiled and shyly said, "Yes!"

"Oh! It is so beautiful! Thank you! I guess you can be sweet... and good... at times. Thank you!" Twitch gave NutJob a kiss on the cheek which caused him to blush. Twitch placed the flower behind her ear and asked, "How do I look?"

NutJob replied, "Like a pansy!" Twitch furrowed her brow as she wasn't quite sure if she liked his response, but she quickly softened to a smile and shrugged it off. After all, the so-called compliment came from NutJob and only NutJob would be able to understand what he meant. "I mean you look pretty!"

Twitch smiled and batted her eyes and blushed. The two squirrels scurried off hand in hand and played amongst the trees and bushes. And now just like Harriet and M15, they decided to restore their home. NutJob was on a mission to win Twitch's heart. As the days went by, NutJob watched Harriet and M work together by bringing nest material and sticks to the nest. So NutJob continued to bring little gifts to Twitch, mostly flowers. Twitch would smile and she would give NutJob a little kiss. All went very well for the little squirrel Casanova. That is until one day Twitch caught a glimpse of NutJob on his gift finding mission. She saw the little squirrel as he snuck his way toward the front pasture. He jumped up on the fence that separated the nest tree area from the Church. He ran along the top of the fence rail with ease and jumped onto the Church property to a bench. A very important bench. A bench that was home to special gifts that were left by the humans in memory of E14.

Twitch's eyes narrowed. "Why that little thief!" she said under her breath.

NutJob had been stealing gifts for Twitch from the items to honor E14. This time NutJob had his heart set on one gift in particular, a small stuffed teddy bear. "Oh, she'll LOVE this!" He was so happy with his "shopping" excursion. Now he had to figure out how to carry the large stuffed animal back to their tree. The item was almost the same size as NutJob. He tried carrying it over his shoulder. He tried carrying it on his back. He tried everything imaginable. It looked like he was in a boxing match and he wasn't winning. Everything he tried looked so difficult. But he was determined to make his special someone happy. He finally somehow managed to wrap his arms around the teddy bear to carry it. He climbed up the fence and carefully ran along the rail and back to their tree without dropping the bear. Exhausted and out of breath, NutJob dropped the teddy bear at Twitch's feet and said, "Look what I got especially for you!" he proudly announced.

Twitch silently stood there with fire in her eyes and smoke coming out of her ears. Her arms were folded over her chest and she slowly tapped her foot. Furious with NutJob, she spoke in a slow and steady tone of voice. "What do you think you are doing?" she asked. Her words were like darts hitting their target as she said each word.

"I got you a present! Isn't it great?" NutJob smiled. He was so proud of himself. He had no idea what was to come.

"Do I think it is great? DO I THINK IT IS GREAT?"

Confused, NutJob asked, "You don't think it's great? You don't like it?"

"I don't like it? No, I don't like it! I don't like that you have been stealing gifts for me that were meant for E14's memory!"

"But..."

"I don't like that you gave me flowers from the bouquets that were brought here to honor E14."

"But..."

"I don't like that you are a thief and you stole all of the things you gave me!"

Sadly, NutJub replied, "But I wanted to make you happy, like M makes Harriet happy."

"Happy?" Twitch yelled. "DO I SOUND HAPPY TO YOU?"

NutJob lowered his head and softy replied, "No."

"That's right, I'm NOT happy! Now you pick up that bear and turn around and go back to that bench and put that bear back where it belongs!"

"But it's heavy."

"I don't care if it weighs a million pounds! Put it back where it belongs!"

"But..."

"NOW!"

Heartbroken, NutJob dragged the stuffed animal back toward the bench.

"And pick up the bear. You're getting it dirty!"

"And pick up the bear. You're getting it dirty! Blah, blah, blah!" NutJob mockingly repeated what Twitch said.

"I can hear you!" yelled Twitch.

"Well the whole world can hear you!" said NutJob. NutJob got the bear back to the bench and placed it gently next to a vase of flowers. "I'm sorry, Mr. Bear. I guess I did the wrong thing... again." The bear actually looked happier to be back on the bench. NutJob jumped onto the fence rail and slowly walked back toward Twitch. "I'm sorry," he said to Twitch. "I was only trying to do something nice for you." He kept his head lowered as he softly spoke.

"I know you were, NutJob, but you have to think before you do things. Those gifts weren't for you to take. None of it is."

"But no one's using any of it!"

"It isn't to be used. It is to honor and remember a precious baby."

"I didn't mean any harm and I didn't mean to disrespect E14."

"I know. Just please, try to think first, okay?"

"Okay, I promise."

"Thank you," said Twitch and they hugged. Immediately something caught NutJob's eye and he ran off. "Oh no," said Twitch. "Now what?" NutJob quickly ran back to Twitch with something behind his back. "NutJob..." Twitch's tone was somewhat annoyed.

"I got you something! And it doesn't belong to anyone! Here!" NutJob handed Twitch a pine cone.

"Oh..." Twitch thought, stopped and then smiled. "Thank you, NutJob."

"I thought it looked like you! See when you hold it like this it has a small head and a fat middle, just like you!" Twitch's eyes narrowed. NutJob was confused. He asked, "What? What did I say? Don't you like it?" NutJob ran as Twitch chased him.

"When I get you..."

And now the pasture was back to normal again!

15

Chapter 4 ... The Handsome Sub-Adult Comes Home

The days continued on with Harriet and M15 doing nestorations. M continued to bring Harriet food, all in anticipation of the arrival of a second clutch. The pasture animals enjoyed the weather and the pond. As for Twitch and NutJob... well they were always seen running through the pasture because of something that NutJob did or said that upset Twitch. Things were normal.

One day, M flew to the pond. As he landed, the Commander was returning to the stables after his walk around the pasture.

"Good day, my eagle friend! How are you today?" the Commander asked cheerfully.

"Very well, Commander! How are you?"

"I'm fine, my good man! Mighty fine! A good walk around the pasture always makes me feel good, especially when I see the stables because then I know I'm done walking around the pasture!" The Commander laughed at his own joke. M smiled as the Commander continued. "You know I just couldn't help noticing the past few days, maybe weeks, that you and the misses are busy working on your nest. Why we even got to hear a little of your... building discussions."

M chuckled. "Yes, Commander, we are restoring the nest."

"The buzz around here is that you and Harriet are thinking of having more eggs. Is that true?"

"Yes, sir, it is!"

"You can do that?"

M chuckled again. "Well that's what I've been told. We're preparing for a second clutch."

"You know how very sorry I am about E14. Such a tragic loss. I'm so sorry for yours and Harriet's heartache. He was a cute little guy sitting up there monitoring all of us down here in the pasture."

"Thank you. I still can't believe he is gone. I miss him so much. I'm sure you know that Harriet lost other eaglets, E3 and E5."

"Yes, I do know about that. I was here for both of them. She's a strong lady and she's been through a lot, but she is resilient. She would have made an amazing soldier! Oh, and you, too, M," the Commander added.

M gave an acknowleding smile. "This is what we eagles do and once Harriet makes up her mind about something there is no turning back."

"You two have had some nesting season. First you had that annoying Great Horned Owl hitting into both of you and trying to steal your nest."

"I know! Could you believe that guy? Who do those owls think they are? We put all the work in to build a nice, safe home for our eaglets and they try to steal it fom us. If I ever catch him!"

"Oh, I know, M. He wouldn't have a chance. You are such a good provider and protector for your family. That dumb owl is poking the wrong eagle." The Commander nodded his head in reassurance.

"Thank you, sir. Well I better get back to work."

The Commander laughed as he continued toward the stables. "I'm glad I'm retired," said the Commander. "Watching you and your bride work so hard is downright exhausting." They both chuckled. "Have a good day, M!"

"Thank you! You too, Commander," said M and he flew off.

All was fine in the pine on that beautiful day, but there was also something very special about that day. There was something in the air. Something remarkably familiar. An excitement that hadn't been felt in a while.

Suddenly an intruder arrived. A very handsome sub-adult intruder. A mighty shadow was cast on the pasture below and all the animals came out to see what was going on. The Commander heard all the commotion, turned and saw the shadow. He looked up toward the sun and squinted. He finally was able to focus on the figure in the sky.

"Well I'll be!" The Commander said in disbelief. "LOOK UP!" the Commander cheered loudly. "LOOK UP EVERYONE!"

All the pasture animals shielded their eyes from the sun as they looked up to the sky. They all gasped!

"It's him!" cried Sandy! Her mouth open in surprise.

"Oh, my goodness! It is him! How do I look?" Quacks anxiously exclaimed.

Twitch and NutJob ran to their tree to get a better view. Their eyes widened as the visitor flew past them.

At the pond Waddles and Maria swam into each other. Waddles pointed and said, "I see him! I see him!"

"Si! Si!" exclaimed Maria.

Waddles looked at Maria and replied, "I said, I see him!"

Again, Maria said, "Si! Si!"

"Stop telling me to see him. I said, I see him!" Waddles rolled her eyes at Maria and swam away.

Maria shook her head and then turned back to the visitor and waved. "Hola! Bienvenido a casa!"

Ben Rabbit watched behind a bush. Katie the Kestrel landed on what was left of the strangler fig tree that was knocked down after the hurricane came through the year "he" left.

Jett the starling flew to the snag tree. "Woohoo! Woohoo! I can't believe it! I can't believe it!!!" he cheered as he hopped up and down on the branch.

Jay the blue jay flew right up to him and said, "Hey, E9! Welcome home! What are you doing here?"

"Hey, Jay! I was in the area and I thought I would stop and see my Mom and Dad and all my friends."

"Aww, you missed us," teased the blue jay as he hit into the handsome eagle. "I bet you miss me hitting into you, don't ya?"

"Well to tell you the truth Jay, you and your relatives are all alike. So, trust me when I say sometimes it feels like you are always around."

"That's so sweet! Wait, I think you meant that as a compliment... or did you? Hey wait up!"

E9 flew faster and flew straight to his friend, the Commander. The handsome eagle landed right in front of the mighty horse. Standing tall, proud and majestic E9 stood at attention and saluted the huge horse and said, "Sub-adult E9 reporting for duty, sir!" He smiled and winked at his friend.

"E9..." the Commander said softly with love and respect in his voice. "My God it is good to see you, son. You look so grown up... so big and strong. How are you, son?" E9 was still at attention and was still saluting. "Oh, at ease, son, at ease." The Commander chuckled.

"I'm well, sir! Life can be tough, but my Mom and Dad taught me well so I'm doing okay. When I was young, I always cheered, 'Life Is A Toy'. But as a sub-adult, I see that you can still have fun, but life isn't always a toy. How have you been, Commander?"

"Still enjoying my retirement and trying to keep up with the events that go on in the pasture." The Commander looked at E9 again and said in a happy and bold voice, "Oh I am so glad to see you, son!"

"Me too, sir! Me too!"

"It is great to have you back home!"

"Thank you, sir, but it is only a visit. I can't stay. The rules... you know."

"Yes, I know about your eagle rules. But we all really needed to see you."

"Sir? Is everything alright? My Mom and Dad? Are they okay?"

"They're fine, son... but this season has been a tough one for them."

19

E9 still had that E9 pose when he didn't understand something and tilted his head to the side. "Sir?"

"They had an owl picking on them. He tried to steal their nest. He would hit into them while they slept. He tried real hard to take their beautiful nest away from them. One night, your Mom got hit really hard and your Dad was hit multiple times."

E9's eyes were on fire as he listened to what his parents had endured. "Are they alright?"

"Yes, they're fine. Then some moron human flew a drone over their nest. What is wrong with humans? But you know your folks, nothing and no one will ever harm or take their loved ones or home away from them. They are the epitome of love and family. Eventually the owl gave up. In a way you couldn't help but feel a little bad for the pain in the butt." E9 looked surprised at the Commander. The Commander explained, "I'm not defending the owl. What he did was wrong and nasty, but look over there..." The Commander pointed toward Yonder Pond.

"Oh, no! Yonder Pond... what happened?" asked E9.

"Humans. That's what happened. They tore down all your trees, especially where you went as a family. They tore down your feathered friends' homes. And they are building homes for themselves. So as much as the owl was very bad to your parents, I bet he must have lost his home and now needed to do what he had to do for his family."

"Wow," E9 said softly. "And owls don't know how to build their own nests. And let's face it, Mom and Dad can build better than any of us! They should be in Nest and Garden Magazine or on Lifestyles of the Feathered and Famous." E9 smiled.

"Absolutely," the Commander replied. Then the Commander opened his mouth, but stopped before he said anything.

"What Commander? You looked like you were going to say something. Do you have more to tell me about my parents?"

The Commander hung his head down and then he looked E9 in the eyes. "Your Mom and Dad only had one eaglet this season. And just like you, he had an egg sibling, so we all called him Eggbert2... and like you, he became friends with his egg sibling."

E9 laughed, "That's great! I can't wait to meet the little guy and Eggbert2! So, this sibling must be E14, right?" E9 was so happy. He smiled.

But as the Commander looked at E9, tears filled his eyes. E9's smile quickly disappeared.

"E14 passed away a short while ago, son. I'm so sorry... your brother has left us."

E9's heart broke. Within seconds he found out he had a new brother and then just like that he heard he was gone. E9 looked upset and confused. His eyes filled with tears as he searched the pasture and asked, "How? Why? What happened?"

"His wing somehow got hurt while in the nest. One of his feathers that was growing broke. We later found out he also had rat poison in his system."

"Rat poison?" E9 questioned angrily.

"The rat poison made it impossible for his feather to heal and he didn't survive. These HUMANS!" The Commander got angry as he spoke. "They have no clue how their actions, their selfishness affects others.... how they hurt wildlife. How they destroy lives and families! They think just because it is called Rat Poison that it only kills rats! They don't get it. It kills the rat and then someone else eats the rat... and the same happens to that animal. And THEY'RE supposed to be the smart ones on the planet."

"My parents always warned me about the humans." E9 slowly paced. "The poor little guy. I wish I was here to help him."

"There was nothing you could have done... there was nothing anyone could have done."

"I could have been there for Mom and Dad."

"They needed time, E9. They would never want you to see them hurting. And they're okay. They are amazing. I know your Mom lost two other babies. But this was the first for your Dad. But they are getting through it together." The Commander smiled, "But I have to tell you something... the little guy reminded me of you. The way he would look over at me from the nest. Sometimes I still look up there," the Commander looked at the nest tree, "and I could swear I still see him in the nest... watching me." The Commander's voice trailed off. E9 followed the Commander's gaze to the nest. "BUT..." the Commander said to change the subject, "But now you are here and it is a joyous day! The magnificient E9 is home!" E9 smiled, although his heart ached for his brother and for his parents. "I see your little girlfriend is over there straining her neck to get a glimpse of you." The Commander winked at E9 and gave him a big smile.

"Wow! She's prettier than I remember." E9 just stood there looking at Quacks.

The Commander then said, "Well then what are you still doing here talking to an old horse like me? Go on! Say hello to her!"

"Yes, sir!" said E9. "I'll see you later, Commander, sir!"

"Not if I see you first," chuckled the Commander. The Commander walked to the stables. "Man, I am so happy to see him!"

E9 flew off toward the pond. Quacks quickly turned away from him so he wouldn't see that she was watching him.

E9 landed at the pond. "Hi, Quacks! Remember me?" E9 smiled that E9 handsome smile of his.

Quacks blushed. "E9? Is that really you?"

"It's me alright!" E9 flapped his mighty wings. The other ducks swam closer to greet E9. "Hello ladies!"

Before they could say a word, Quacks gave them all a look to go away and they reluctantly did. "So, E9, what brings you home?"

"I'm trying to see where I would like to settle down someday... after all I am over three years old now. In less than two years I'll be ready to start a family of my own." Quacks smiled as E9 spoke. "You look great, Quacks! But you always did." Quacks blushed again. "What have you been up to?"

"Not much really, just the usual. Have you been to many places, E9?"

"Oh, wow, yes! I feel like I've been all over the country! I've seen the White House... DC LOVES anything that is an eagle... New York City, the Chesapeake Bay, so many places I can't name them all! But my favorite place is the place I miss the most... HOME."

"Have you seen your parents yet?"

"No, I haven't... and I heard they lost E14," E9 said sadly.

"Yes, E9. I'm so sorry. But please know your parents have been so loving and supportive of each other. We all felt their pain and heartache, but they have been together day and night. They are just an inspiration to us all."

E9 looked at Quacks with pride. "Thank you, Quacks. I know they are the best parents in the world."

Mr. Duckerson swam up to E9 and Quacks. "Well, well, well! Hello, E9! What a wonderful surprise! How are you?"

"Hello, Mr. Duckerson. I'm fine, thank you."

"Are you here to stay or just visiting?"

"Just visiting for now."

"Well it is wonderful to see you again, but I'm sorry I have to steal Quacks. Her Mother and I are taking her on a special outing today. You are welcome to join us... if you like." Quacks' eyes lit up.

"Thank you, sir. But I haven't seen my parents yet so I want to stay around the nest tree."

"I understand," said Mr. Duckerson. "Shall we go, Quacks?"

"Yes, Daddy. Bye, E9. I hope I get to see you again."

"I hope so, too," said E9 and Quacks and her Father swam away.

E9 took a sip of water from the pond and then he also took a refreshing walk through the water. He looked around at what he would always call HOME. He flew to the nest tree and landed on the attic branch. His heart raced. He was HOME! He hopped down into the nest. He was so excited! He looked around and took a deep breath. Everything in the nest brought back a flood of memories. His eyes filled with tears of joy. He thought of his Mom and Dad and his wonderful eaglet childhood. He stood there tall, strong and proud. A stick caught his eye and he immediately started rearranging the nest. He looked closer at the floor of the nest and smiled. But his smile quickly disappeared.

"For a minute there I thought it was you Eggbert." E9 made a little smile. "I sure do miss you." E9 looked up and saw the webcam. "Well, well, well!" E9 tilted his head in E9 fashion. "I forgot all about you! Hey good-lookin'!" E9 backed up and then moved closer to his reflection in the camera lens. "Whoa! I look different!" E9 turned his head to the left and then to the right as he admired himself in the lens. "Wow! I'm even better looking now!" He wiggled his eyebrows like his Dad and smiled. He looked at the pasture and took a long, deep cleansing breath. Yes, he was HOME and it filled his heart, mind and soul with joy. He smiled and his smile got bigger as he looked at his snag tree and saw a familiar face. Without hesitation, E9 flew to the snag. "Jett!"

"Hi, E9! How are you! I saw you flying way up high and the Commander yelled out, 'Look up' and I did and there you were! I couldn't believe it! I just couldn't believe it! It's you! It's really you!" Jett spoke so fast and he hardly took a breath. He rushed over to E9 and hugged his leg... after all that was all he could reach.

E9 laughed, "Slow down, little buddy, slow down!" He smiled at his little friend.

Jett moved away from E9's leg so he could look at him and said, "I'm sorry, E9! I'm just so happy to see you!" He ran back to E9 and wrapped his wings around E9's leg again.

"That's okay, Jett. I understand! I'm really happy to see you too! I really missed you!"

"You did?" Jett asked excitedly.

"Of course I did! So tell me, how have you been? What's new?"

"I'm good E9... Oh! WAIT! Look what I can do!" Jett flew high and proud over the snag tree.

"Whoa, little man! Look at you!" cheered E9.

Jett landed next to E9 and said, "That's all because of you, E9. You taught me to be sure of myself and you told me all I had to do was believe in myself and I could do anything! Thank you, E9!" He hugged E9's leg again, "Thank you!"

"You don't have to thank me, Jett. That was all you! You did an amazing job! I'm so proud of you!"

"Thank you. So, tell me, E9, you must be doing amazing things! I wish I could go with you!"

"I wish you could, too, Jett. But it isn't all that much fun out there. It's a LOT of work and it's very lonely and sometimes it's scary."

"It is? I can't belive you would be scared!"

"Oh trust me, Jett, I get scared... many times. And the only thing that keeps me going is I stop and think of my parents and all the lessons they taught me. Without their guidance, I couldn't survive... Plus..." E9 stopped and smiled at his friend, "I pray A LOT!" They both smiled.

"Jett! Jett, honey!"

"That's my Mom. I have to go." Jett turned to answer his Mother, "Coming, Mom!" He turned back to E9 and said, "We built a nest under your parents' nest. They said it was okay."

"Wow, that's really cool!"

"Yeah, I just wish you were still here though. It would have seemed like we were nestmates!

E9 laughed, "That would have been fun."

"Jett!"

"Okay, Mom!" Jett said to his Mother. He looked at his friend and said, "I better go, E9. Thank you. I miss you. Please take care of yourself and I hope we see each other again. I love you, my friend."

"I love you, too, Jett." And E9's little friend flew to his Mother.

E9 stayed perched on the snag tree... HIS snag tree. He thought about days gone by. He looked so natural and happy. He truly looked like he was home... like he never left. He started humming and then he started tapping his feet. The pasture animals all gathered close to the snag tree. Once again, the pasture came alive with E9 music, magic and fun... and of course, they all joined in. They all cheered. E9 took a bow and quickly turned when he felt someone next to him.

"DAD!" E9 said. M15 and E9 wrapped their wings around each other, tears filled their eyes.

"E9, my son... my little buddy!" M15's voice cracked. It was obvious that this was a much-needed hug for both of them. And it felt good. They let go and faced each other. "It's so good to see you, E9!"

"It's so good to see you, too, Dad!"

"How have you been?"

"I'm good. It's tough just like you and Mom said it would be. But I could never have done it without everything you taught me... thank you."

"Obviously, you've been eating."

"Yes, I have been."

"You look really good. You're getting older," M smiled teasingly. "And I see those good-lookin' genes of mine are coming through just fine."

E9 smiled. "How could I lose? I'm yours and Mom's son!" They both laughed. "So where is Mom?"

"I'm not sure, but I'm sure she's watching. NOTHING gets passed your Mother." Knowing it was the truth, they both laughed again.

"Dad, I heard about E14. I'm so sorry."

"Thank you, E9. I still can't believe it. He was fine one minute and then it all happened so quickly. Your Mom and I stayed in the nest with him. Then I went to guard the tree and your Mom..." M's voice cracked, "...your Mom never left his side."

"I'm so sorry, Dad."

"He was a cute little guy. Very much like you and he even had an Eggbert2. So, seeing you today means the world to me. I really needed to see you. This is a true Blessing. We always wonder about you and worry about you. We say a prayer every night for you and all the kids. But seeing you now, it does my heart good. I've missed you so much, E9. We both miss you."

"I miss you, too, Dad. And I miss, Mom. I was in the nest before. Are you and Mom rebuilding it?"

"We're going to try to have a second clutch."

"A second clutch?" E9 asked, his head tilted, of course.

"We're going to try to have more eggs this season."

"WOW! That's great!"

"So, we've been very busy."

"Well, if you need any help with the nest, I'm here."

"Thank you, E9. But you know the rules."

"I know, I know. But I just want you to know that I'm around if you need me."

"Thank you, son."

"And I know I should probably go. I was really hoping I would get to see Mom too."

"She'll be so upset that she missed you."

"Please tell her I love her and I was hoping that I would at least see her wink."

"I will." M and E9 hugged. "Be safe, my son."

"I will, Dad. You and Mom be safe, too."

"I love you, E9."

"I love you, Dad." And E9 flew off of the snag. He circled around the stables and pond. He saw the Commander and called out to him. "Commander, I have to go for now. You take care of yourself."

"Okay, good soldier. You be safe. God Speed."

E9 tipped his wings to the Commander and saluted, "Thank you, sir!"

And once again, E9 flew out of their lives. But for a short period of time on that day, the pasture was full of E9's love, fun and magic.

As the day was ending, Harriet and M perched side by side while they watched the sunset. Harriet noticed that M seemed quiet, preoccupied. "M, is everything alright?" she asked.

M looked at Harriet. "It's been quite a day. I was having a tough time today." Harriet lovingly listened. "I keep thinking of E14. I just can't believe he's gone."

"I know, M. His memory sneaks up on me a lot. And I lost E3 and E5, but it is never easy. But remember what we saw."

"I know and I think of it all the time. But today I just couldn't stop thinking of him. I pictured when he first hatched and how cute he was with his little attitude." M smiled. "I started thinking of when he bonked me or tried to bonk me. I couldn't believe how this little eaglet grabbed my head feathers with all his might and twisted and pulled to knock me out! He actually thought he could bonk me!" They both gave a soft laugh picturing E14. "He had that sweet twinkle in his eye with so much hope and excitement looking forward to the future." A tear ran down M's face. "And how he would use that HUGE crop of his as a pillow and how he would hold onto his buddy, Eggbert2. All this then reminded me of E9 and how he was very much like him. So, then I started thinking and worrying about E9. And as I was thinking of all of these things I flew back to the pasture. And the weirdest thing happened…" Confused, Harriet looked at M as he continued. "I heard music and all the pasture animals were dancing and singing." Harriet smiled. "I saw someone on the snag and out of curiosity I landed next to him." M looked at Harriet. M took a deep breath. "It was E9!"

"OH, M! REALLY?" Harriet couldn't contain her happiness.

"Yes!" they hugged.

"Oh, I can't believe I missed him! How is he? How does he look? Is he eating? Does he know I love him? Where was I? Why didn't you call me?" Harriet slapped M's wing teasingly.

"Ow!" M said jokingly. "Okay let me see if I can answer all of your questions… Hmmm, let me see… Fine… Amazing… Yes… Yes… Who knows…?" M purposely did not answer Harriet's last question.

Harriet narrowed her eyes at M. "M, come on! Tell me!"

M laughed, "Okay, okay… He is fine. He looks amazing! He's very good-looking. In fact, he looks just like me when I was his age," M wiggled his eyebrows and smiled.

Harriet giggled, "Alright, go on."

"He's eating. He knows you love him and he loves you. I didn't know where you were. He was upset that he didn't get to see you. He said he was looking forward to at least seeing your wink."

"Awww… my sweet baby." A tear rolled down Harriet's beautiful face. She wiped it off with her wing and then said to M, "You forgot to answer the last question!" She looked at him sternly.

"The last question. No, I answered it, I didn't know where you were."

"That wasn't the last question."

M sat and thought for a minute. He knew he was in trouble. He was just buying time. "Gee, I don't remember the last question," he said innocently.

"Well then I guess I'll remind you… WHY didn't you call me?"

"WHY didn't I call you?" M tried to think of something, but he couldn't, but he tried anyway. "I did, but you didn't hear me." Harriet's eyes narrowed again. "No, not buying that, huh? Okay… Okay I didn't call you because…"

"I'm waiting…"

M took a deep breath and said, "Because I honestly didn't think of it. I know that sounds terrible, but we were so busy talking and the time just flew by and then he was leaving and we talked about you, but I just didn't think to call out to you… I'm sorry. I just got so caught up in the moment of seeing him… I'm sorry."

Harriet saw that M was telling the truth and it was just an honest mistake. "I understand," she said.

"You do?" M asked, shocked.

"Oh M, I just can't believe I missed him!"

"Well he knows the rules, but this is E9 we're talking about and we know now that he is in the area… so we never know if he might show up again soon."

"He looked good?" Harriet asked.

"He looked great! After all…" M wiggled his eyebrows again, "…I am his Father and he is my son!"

"He's happy and healthy?"

"Yes, Harriet, he is." M reassured Harriet. "I told him about E14. He felt so bad to hear what happened. I also told him about the second clutch and he is happy for us." Harriet smiled. M continued, "So he knows he has to stay away. But like I said… remember, this is E9."

They both smiled. Harriet rested her head on M's head and they both stared off as the sun set. Their hearts were full of love for all of their eaglets. And they were hopeful for a second chance.

Chapter 5 ... Number 3 And Number 4

The days started to fly by. The nest rails got higher and higher than they ever were. It almost seemed as if they were being even more careful in preparation for the second clutch. Maybe they blamed themselves for E14 that they needed to over-compensate for their loss. But hopefully that wasn't it because that wasn't true. For this was all in God's Plan and they found comfort in knowing E14 was happy and healthy with Ozzie. Harriet's and M's bond was strong if not stronger.

Valentine's Day arrived and M found the perfect fish for his Lady Love. Harriet saw M as he approached the nest.

She called out to him, "Good morning, M!"

M landed in the nest with his gift for his Harriet. He pulled Harriet close to him, kissed her and said, "Happy Valentine's Day, Harriet. I love you!"

"Happy Valentine's Day, M! I love you, too!" She kissed her mate and then looked at him and added. "You know, M, you look so handsome with your white shoulders... very distinguished!"

M smiled and wiggled his eyebrows in typical M style. "Well thank you, my Lady Love! And you are always beautiful!" he replied.

Harriet smiled and giggled. She then saw what M had brought for her. Her eyes opened wide when she got a good look at the huge fish. She couldn't be happier and she enjoyed her present.

Throughout the days Harriet and M would both make changes in the nest and they would analyze the stick placement to make sure each stick was in the perfect spot. They would take turns as they tested out the nest bowl and cup in anticipation of more eggs.

One day after they stopped working and sat perched above the nest, M grabbed Harriet's wing and said, "Come with me." And they flew off. They flew higher and higher. They both soared! They both enjoyed the feeling of just being up high and free. They felt the wind, the quiet, the peaceful solitude of soaring. This was a much-needed break for both of them. They soared for quite a while before they returned to the nest.

Harriet looked at M and smiled, "Oh thank you, M! That was exactly what I needed!"

"You're very welcome, my love. We BOTH needed it. We have been through a lot and we are now willingly going to put ourselves through starting the season up again. So, we needed a break. We needed some time just for ourselves."

They both sat perched, side by side as they enjoyed the calm and peace within.

As the days went by, Harriet and M15 started to get anxious hoping a second clutch would come true for them. The nest rails were good and high and the nest was comfy and cozy for the anticipated eggs. And M had kept his Lady Love nicely fed. All things were in place to start up the season again. Now they just waited...

One February afternoon, Harriet felt the feeling she knew so well. "This is it!" she calmly said. She remained in the nest over the cup. She looked up and said, "Thank you, Lord!" She got up and looked at their new egg... their third egg of the season. She smiled and took a deep, soothing breath. She started incubating the new egg. Soon thereafter, M returned with grasses.

"Hello, my love! I have a special delivery for you!" M started to place the newly collected grasses in the nest.

Harriet moved away from the cup and replied, "And I have a special delivery for you, M!" Harriet threw back her head and cheered, "Look, M, look!"

M cautiously looked in the cup. He took a double take at the egg and said, "WOOHOO! WE DID IT! We have a second clutch! We have a second chance!" M started doing a happy dance around the nest. "Oh yeah, we did it! Oh yes, we did!!!"

Harriet laughed and did a little happy dance of her own. Not as flamboyant as M's dance, but she did a mild tail wiggle and hop. She looked at M. She loved seeing the happiness on his face and how his eyes twinkled as he looked at the egg. "I'll be right back... I just need to stretch my wings," said Harriet as she flew up to the attic.

M immediately shimmied down to incubate the egg. "Hello little egg! I'm your Dad, M15. Well, I'm going to be your Dad. You could possibly be E15." M smiled. He was so happy and proud! "You could be a mini M! Wouldn't that be cool!?" Harriet soon hopped back down into the nest. M wasn't too eager to get up so Harriet started putting grasses on him. "Okay, okay, I get the hint."

M got up and rearranged grasses and aerated the cup all under Harriet's watchful eye. She moved toward the egg and M moved off the nest and flew off of the nest tree.

"Okay little one, now we do some more sitting and waiting for you to hatch! I hope your Dad comes back with some food. Laying an egg makes me hungry!" And like magic, M appeared with a fish to celebrate their new egg. "Oh, M! Thank you! I was starving."

"Bon appetit, my love." M gave Harriet a kiss. She moved toward the fish and ate and M incubated the egg.

The coming days would be very similar. Now the question was, would there be a fourth egg for the season? Harriet always laid two eggs each season, so now they would see if she would lay two eggs for the second clutch. Although second clutches were not unheard of, this was all new territory for them.

Then three days later... "Oh, my! It's happening again!" Harriet knew the feeling well. This time it was early evening and M was already perched on his nightly post. "M! M, look!" said Harriet as she moved away from the nest bowl.

M15 looked down from the upper branch. "Is that...?" he asked.

"Yes, M... number four!" Harriet smiled. "But M, I'm really tired and I'm going to get settled in for the night and incubate the eggs and get some sleep. I'm sorry. I promise first thing tomorrow you'll get to meet egg number four!"

"I understand..." M was disappointed, but he knew this was a lot of work for Harriet. He would make up for it in the days to come. They both needed rest.

Morning came quickly and it came with rain.

"Good morning, M," said Harriet.

M quickly hopped down into the nest as Harriet moved for him to meet the fourth egg. M's heart melted. He was so happy and proud as he smiled at their two new eggs. Harriet looked at her loving mate, kissed him and flew off of the nest tree.

"Hello number four! I'm going to be your Dad. But until then I have to keep you warm and dry." M shimmied down over the eggs to protect them from the rain.

Harriet and M let the pasture animals know that two little eggs were in their nest. But they didn't go overboard in spreading the good news. They wanted to take things slow and quiet this time. It was unchartered territory for all. In the days to come, both Harriet and M would take turns incubating the eggs. Being such good, caring parents they both loved incubating the eggs. Sometimes it took putting grasses AND sticks on each other to get the point across that it was time for the changing of the guard. But they were pros at this by now and they worked it out just fine.

One day, late in the afternoon, while M was incubating the eggs, Harriet was perched in the attic. Suddenly a sub-adult landed in the nest tree.

"E9!" Harriet gasped.

"Mom! Hi, Mom! I've missed you! How are you?"

"E9! Oh, my E9... you can't be here! We have eggs. You can't visit," Harriet said anxiously.

"I know, Mom. Being I missed you when I was here the other day, I just had to see you and say hello and that I love you."

"I love you, E9, but please, you know the rules and you know what I have to do. So please... GO!" Harriet's tone had gotten stern. Harriet started to alert M of the so called "intruder." M flew up next to Harriet and they sounded the alert to chase E9 away.

"I'm going. I love you both!" And E9 flew off of the nest tree. He turned and looked at his parents. Harriet strained her neck to see him. That's when E9 saw it! "YES! The WINK!" E9 cheered out loud. "I saw the wink! I love you, too! WOOHOO!" And once again E9 flew out of sight.

Harriet hung her head. Her heart was full. M put his wing around her. "Oh, M... how that breaks my heart to chase him away."

"I know, Harriet. But he knows and understands the rules... and he saw your wink!" M winked at Harriet. "And that's all that matters."

"I know, I know," she replied. Harriet sat and thought as she looked in the direction that E9 flew toward. She smiled and said, "He looks majestic, doesn't he?"

"Of course, he looks majestic!" M said teasingly. "Hello!" and he pointed to himself.

Harriet laughed. "Oh, that's right! It's all about you! I had nothing to do with his good looks." She stared at M to make him nervous, which she enjoyed.

"Well.... MAYBE... you had a little to do with his good looks, too." They smiled and laughed.

"Well I better go incubate the eggs. Before we know it, it will be bedtime. So, I'll say goodnight now, M, in case I fall asleep."

"Okay, goodnight Harriet." M looked at the nest as Harriet hopped down into it. He smiled and said, "Goodnight little eggies!"

In the days to come, Harriet and M kept up their wonderful teamwork with incubating, taking breaks, nest maintenance and eating. One day while M was incubating the eggs, Harriet took a break over at Yonder Pond. She caught a fish and enjoyed her meal. But sadness came over Harriet's face as she looked around her surroundings.

"How could they?" she softly said. "Look what you've done!" she cried out loud. "We don't destroy your homes! So what gives you the right to destroy ours?" Harriet shook her head in disgust. She took a quick drink at the pond. She then decided to dunk her head in the water so the refreshing water would cascade over her beautiful feathers. She then flew back to the nest to relieve M of incubating time. As she started to get settled in, she finally noticed all the small feathers that came off of her and M while they molted. "Well, it adds to the comfort of the nest," she smiled. As she went to incubate the eggs, she noticed the tiny feathers had attached themselves to her beak and head. She sighed and said, "Really?" She shook her head to get them off without much success, but she knew she was beautiful no matter what. Just as long as M didn't have a remark to make about them. But he was getting better at not "upsetting" her over some things... Better, not perfect.

The days were getting closer and closer to when they should see a pip. The pasture animals were all doing their own thing. Jett and his Mom were completing the finishing touches on their nest below the tremendous eagle nest. Harriet was stretching her wings when she saw E9's little friend, Jett, on the edge of their nest.

"Good morning, Miss Harriet!" said Jett.

"Good morning, Jett! How are you today?"

"I'm fine, Miss Harriet. Thank you so much for letting my Mom and I live beneath your nest. I sort of feel like E9 by being so close to HIS nest! I talked with him the other day. Did you see him?"

"Yes, I did, Jett." Harriet smiled as she pictured E9 in her mind's eye.

"He looks great! I miss him though."

"I do too, Jett. I do, too."

"Well I better start my chores. Thank you again, Miss Harriet!"

"Have a good day, Jett!" And the little starling went on his way. Suddenly a brave Muscovy duck decided she was interested in the nest tree too. She landed on one of the nest branches. Harriet looked at the duck in disbelief. "What is this? Just because we let the starlings build a nest in our tree doesn't mean that we are opening a boarding house!" Harriet said out loud.

"Oh! I didn't know this was occupied. Sorry!" Harriet flapped her enormous wings and the duck flew off.

Harriet shook her head. She looked toward the pasture pond. There was so much activity going on. Maria the anhinga was swimming in the pond and then flew to one of the pylons to dry off and preen her beautiful, outstretched wings. The snowy egrets were also at the pond enjoying a beach day.

Harriet also noticed one of E9's friends, Kelli the turtle. Harriet tried to get a better look at what Kelli was doing. "Oh!" Harriet said in surprise. "She's laying eggs, too! Good luck, Mama Kelli!" Harriet called out.

"Thank you, Miss Harriet! The same to you and Mr. M!" And with that Kelli ran into the pond.

The anticipation of a pip was getting closer and Harriet and M were both getting extremely anxious! M brought Harriet an air plant to entice her to let him have time with the eggs. And it worked. Harriet flew off so M could take over incubating the eggs. He rolled the eggs and then smiled thinking of all the great things to come. He rearranged sticks to make the nest safe and then he shimmied down over the eggs. Or in M's case maybe it wasn't a shimmy. Maybe it was more of a dance. Either way, he was such a good Dad-to-be and such a good Dad.

Harriet was perched on the snag and she watched M and his "nestcapades."

A dove named Lisa landed next to Harriet. "It must be getting close to pip time, right Harriet?"

"That's right, Lisa. We can't wait!"

"Good luck to you and Mr. M."

"Thanks, Lisa." And the dove flew off.

Slick the crow came by Harriet and hit into her. "So, I see that you and M15 have two more new eggs this season."

"That's right, Slick. So get lost!"

"Now why are you being like that? I'm being neighborly and you are being rude."

"Neighborly? You hit into me! I didn't hit into you. So, beat it!" demanded Harriet and Slick flew off. Harriet shook her head. "Well I guess I should get back to the nest." Harriet gracefully and swiftly flew to the nest. "Okay, my turn."

M looked at Harriet. He heard Slick give her a hard time so he made sure he didn't upset her. M quickly moved away from the eggs and kissed Harriet

35

on the head. Harriet positioned herself over the eggs and M15 flew off of the nest tree. He quickly returned with a gift for Harriet... food.

"Oh, M, thank you! I was hungry. Thank you, you read my mind."

"Anything for my Lady Love," and M flew off to the pond to cool off. He walked into the water. "Oh, that feels great!" He took a deep breath and splashed the water all over his body and enjoyed the refreshing water. He floated around a little and then he stopped. He narrowed his eyes. "What is this? A stick? In the water? A stick in the pond that is pointing to the sky?" The stick stood straight up and out of the water. M examined the stick with great interest. "Hmmm..." he said. So, he grabbed the stick with his beak and he pulled on it with all his might. But the stick did not budge at all. "Hmmm..." he said again. Even though there was no reason to move the stick, it was just extremely intriguing to M... after all it was a stick! AND it was in the water! He kept trying, but he wasn't having any luck getting it to move. M decided he would continue to bathe. He slowly moved away from the stick, although he kept his eye on it the whole time. He then slowly went back to the stick as if to sneak up on it. He tried again. He bit it, he pulled on it, he moved around it, he splashed it. He did everything... but get it. The ducks and birds watched in amazement as M waged war against this stick. Exhausted... not defeated... never defeated... M hopped out of the water and went to the snag to dry off. He continued to watch the stick. He mumbled under his breath, "This isn't over. You might think you have won, but if I decide that you will be mine, you will be mine. I just haven't decided if you are worth my time. Just know... I'll be watching you."

Chapter 6 ... A Pip

The days seemed to go on forever waiting to see a pip develop. The Muscovy duck had her ducklings and they were already playing and floating around in the pond. Yet Harriet and M continued to wait for their first pip.

Harriet and M started each of their days with hope.

"Good morning, Harriet!" said M as he gave Harriet a kiss on her head.

"Good morning, M," Harriet replied. "I need to stretch my wings a bit. This double nest duty this season is making my joints stiff and achy. I'm looking forward to sleeping on a perch again when the little ones are old enough to sleep alone."

M laughed, "We have a LOT to go through before that happens."

"I know," said Harriet. "But I can dream, can't I?" she smiled. "But in the meantime, let me go do some morning stretches. I'll be back soon." And she flew to the snag.

"Good morning, Mrs. M15," said Jett's Mother.

"Good morning! But please, call me Harriet."

"Okay, Harriet. And please call me Gladys."

"Okay, Gladys!"

"Jett and I are so appreciative of you and M letting us set up our nest under yours."

"It is our pleasure! Actually, we hardly know you are there," said Harriet as she did her morning stretches. "I hope we aren't too noisy above you."

"No, not at all! We enjoy the added security of living near raptors. I'm an overprotective mother and I worry about my Jett. Especially with the crows, the blue jays and the grackles around. They are such bullies! I feel safe with Jett under your nest."

"Well we enjoy having you both there. Jett is such a good boy and so well-mannered. He and our E9 were good friends. We also enjoy hearing the two of you singing. It is so nice to hear throughout our day!"

"Thank you! We love to sing!"

Harriet laughed, "So does my M!" Harriet stretched one more time and said, "Well Gladys, I better get back to the nest. M needs to get us some breakfast so I need to get back to incubate the eggs."

"How many little ones in this clutch?"

"Two, God Willing."

"You're both wonderful parents." Gladys then sadly added, "We're so sorry about E14. He was an adorable baby."

"Thank you. It just seems so surreal. But it was God's Plan." Harriet paused and then said, "Well I better go. It was nice talking with you. Have a good day!"

"You too, Mrs., I mean, Harriet."

Harriet flew back to the nest. "Okay, M, I'd like a nice big fish for breakfast."

M looked at Harriet, kissed her cheek and said, "I will do my best. Your wish is my command!" and off he flew. That was pretty much how the mornings went. All pretty typical.

Until Sunday morning. Harriet had gotten up to roll the eggs and stretch her wings. When she looked down, she saw it! "A pip!" she softly exclaimed.

M was just waking up. "What Harriet?" he asked as he stretched his wing.

"We have a pip!" she said as she smiled.

"YES!" said M. He looked up and said, "Thank you, God!" M sighed. "I'll go get some breakfast."

It was a heat record-breaking day on that day in March in Southwest Florida. The temperature was a scorching 90 degrees and it was even hotter in the nest. M15 flew back to the nest with breakfast.

Harriet looked at the item and questioned, "What is that?"

"Ummm…" M thought and replied, "It's a bone of some sort."

"From what?" asked Harriet. "A dinosaur?"

"I don't know. I thought you might like it." Displeased, Harriet looked at M and sighed. But it was all he could find.

They were so hot and there wasn't a breeze to give them any relief. They took turns incubating the eggs. Harriet flew to the pond for a refreshing drink of water and then flew to the snag where she relaxed. But as soon as break time was over, she headed back to the nest. She flew to the upper branch. "I'm back," she said to M. M got up, rolled the eggs and then continued to incubate them. Harriet watched his every move. Every time M got up Harriet asked him, "What are you doing?"

"I'm rolling the eggs," said M. Harriet didn't respond and M went back to incubating the eggs.

Soon M got up again and Harriet asked him, "What are you doing now?"

"I'm aerating the nest," M replied and went back to incubating the eggs.

M got up one more time. Annoyed, Harriet asked in a stern voice, "NOW, what are you doing?"

"I'm looking for buried treasure! What do you think I'm doing? I'm not new at this. I know I haven't done this as long as you have, but I have done it for a few years now and I know what to do. So, stop questioning my every move! I know you are hot and uncomfortable. I am too. But stop picking on me!"

Harriet knew he was right and she felt foolish. "I was only asking."

M got up and said, "Okay your turn. I'll let the expert take over. After all I'm just the Father and Mother knows best." The heat had gotten to both of them. M's feelings were hurt and he let Harriet know it.

"I'm sorry, M. You are right. BUT! I'm glad that you admit that I know best!" She looked at M and smiled. They both laughed. "I'm truly sorry. Forgive me?"

"Of course!" replied M and they kissed.

Harriet incubated the eggs and M stood guard on the upper branch. It was a long and hot day that turned into a long, hot night. Every time Harriet started to doze off to sleep, the egg with the pip would move and wake her up. This happened all night long. Every little move woke Harriet up. Meanwhile, M slept peacefully above the nest. He snored and dreamt of the eaglets to come. The proud Dad-to-be smiled as he slept while Harriet longed for a few minutes of undisturbed sleep.

Morning came quickly.

"Good morning, my love!" said M in a chipper voice. Fully rested he said, "Isn't it a beautiful day!?" He took a deep breath of fresh air. "Ahhh! Smell that clean, fresh morning air! Look at the beautiful blue sky! Hear the beautiful song of the songbirds. See the…"

Harriet interrupted M's description of the "beautiful" day. Very upset, Harriet said, "See ME going to the pond to get a drink of water. I am exhausted! Every time I closed my eyes, our little pip egg decided it would try to break through more. I didn't get five minutes of sleep last night."

"Really? I slept like a newly hatched eaglet!" Harriet gave M a very stern look. "Oh, I'm sorry," M said quickly. "Why didn't you wake me? I would have switched with you."

Harriet's tone got louder. "Well I knew if your SNORING didn't wake you, I would never be able to wake you. So now I am completely EXHAUSTED!" She took a deep breath and softly said, "I'll be right back," and she flew to the pond.

M hopped down into the nest. "Your Mom thinks that I snore loudly. I don't snore loudly. Do I? You have no problem with my snoring, do you? No, of course you don't." M then looked to his left and then he looked to his right. When he saw that Harriet wasn't close by, he looked at the eggs and whispered, "I think your Mom is just a little cranky today."

Harriet had returned to the attic. "I heard that."

"No, I meant that in a good way," said M with a nervous laugh.

"Oh, you did, did you?"

"Yes, I did!" M said confidently.

"So, tell me, how did you mean I am a little 'cranky' in a good way?" M stood there silently. "M?... I'm waiting."

"WAIT! I think I hear someone peeping!" M listened to the pip egg. "What? What was that?" he asked the egg. "Oh yes, your Mother is very beautiful! What? Oh yes, you are so right! She is very smart, extremely smart! And you would like what? Oh... you would like her to sit with you. I'm sure she would love to sit with you too! Wouldn't you, Harriet?" M looked so sweet as he tried to soften Harriet's heart. Harriet looked at M and just gave him a small grin. She hopped down into the nest. "Here she is, you lucky eggs! Here's your wonderful Mama!" M smiled at Harriet and he quickly flew off.

Harriet called out to him, "Good one, M. Nice try. And don't forget I might still be 'cranky' when you get back." She lowered her voice and said to herself, "Cranky, I'll give him cranky." She continued to incubate the eggs and the pip egg continued to hatch some more. All she could do was sigh.

Harriet stayed with the eggs most of the day. Just before evening, M came to the nest to relieve Harriet. She was no longer cranky.

"Okay, Harriet, it's my turn. You need a break."

"Thank you, M. The heat is unbearable. Usually at this time of year the eaglets are flying around the pasture and we have more freedom. But the nest is so hot this March."

"I know. So, go. Relax, cool off. I've got this."

"Thank you, M." She kissed M and she flew off for some Harriet time.

"Okay eggies! I'm in charge! So, you know what that means? It means... fun time!" M started to sing to the eggs. "My love and I have two eggies... soon instead of shells they'll each have two leggies... right now just one has a pip that we see... and before you know it, we'll be a fam-i-ly! Oh, yeah! I should write that down. That was pretty good!" The pip egg continued to crack more as the little one inside pushed harder and harder to get out. M looked down at the little egg that was desperately trying to hatch. M looked to his left and then he looked to his right to see where Harriet was. Nowhere in sight, he then looked at the egg. "Okay, let me just get this one small, annoying piece of shell out of your way. DO NOT tell your Mother... EVER!" M removed the small piece of the shell. He also aerated the nest and moved a palm frond.

Harriet returned to the nest. "I'm back, M. How is our little one coming along?"

"Still hatching," M couldn't look Harriet in the eye.

"Well, I'm back and I'll take over now." Harriet looked at the egg and noticed the opening was larger now. "M, you're not helping it hatch... are you?"

"No, of course not," he said still not making eye contact with Harriet.

Harriet gave M a stern questioning look and simply asked, "M?"

"No, I just moved a piece of the shell that was bothering it."

"M!" Harriet yelled.

"It's okay! I didn't do much of anything!"

Harriet sighed in disbelief. "M, you are just a big eaglet at heart." M looked at Harriet. He knew she was right. "Please, let the soon to be hatchling hatch on its own. Okay?"

"Okay..." M said sadly.

"Goodnight, M. I love you."

M smiled, "Goodnight, Harriet. I love you, too!" M looked at their eggs and said, "Goodnight my little eggies... yes, you are my little eggies... oh yes you are... yes, you are!"

"M! Goodnight already! Let's go."

"Alright, alright. I'm going." M hesitated and looked at the eggs again and said, "That's right, I'm going... yes, I am... yes, I..."

"M!!!"

Softly and quickly M whispered, "Am..." He flew up to the upper branch for the night.

Harriet sighed heavily and said, "Okay, you two. Let's try to get some sleep tonight." She moved the palm frond that M moved earlier and said, "NOW, it is in the right spot." She smiled and closed her eyes.

Chapter 7 ... M Jr. And Princess Harriet

H arriet was able to get more sleep that evening. On March 31st before sunrise the first little Blessing showed up! E15 made her way out of the shell and into Harriet's and M's heart.

"Hello, my little one! Welcome! I'm your Mama! Your Dad is above us guarding the nest." M snored loudly and Harriet looked up at him. She then looked back at E15 and said, "Your Dad is also sleeping while guarding the nest." Harriet smiled and giggled. "But I'll keep you comfy and safe!" E15's little head bobbled back and forth as she smiled at her beautiful Mommy. She then quickly closed her eyes and went to sleep while she was protected by her Mom and her sleeping Dad. The sun soon woke up the pasture and E15 was ready to check out her home. "Good morning, sweet baby," Harriet said and smiled. E15 still couldn't control her head movements, but she smiled at her Mom. She was so happy!

M15 woke up, stretched and looked down into the nest. "Good morning, Harriet! How are... HEY! Is that???" M asked excitedly.

"Yes, M! Come meet your daughter, E15!"

M quickly hopped into the nest. He puffed out his chest and had a majestic eagle look on his face as he looked at his namesake. Harriet had been anticipating what type of reaction E15 would spark in M.

"Hello! Hello, E15!" M hugged his daughter. "I'm your Dad!" M announced proudly. "YOU are my Junior! M Junior or 15 Junior." M was so excited! M flew back up to the upper branch and called out to the pasture animals. "Hey everyone! Junior me, I mean, M Junior, I mean 15 Junior..."

Harriet cleared her throat and said, "E15."

"Right, right... I mean E15 is here!!!"

The pasture animals all cheered. The Commander chuckled and said, "Oh my! This little one is going to have some big talons to fill. Dad is either going to be very forgiving of what Junior does or he's going to be very critical. Either way, this is going to be interesting." He chuckled again, "Poor Harriet."

"Okay, M. Let E15 rest."

"I do like the sound of Mini M! That's one of my favorites!" M then stopped and thought. "Hmmm, but maybe it should be something spectacular... more eagle like... more regal... something ... I GOT IT!!! M15 the Second!" He was so proud and so proud of himself with his idea.

Harriet just looked at M and said, "Or E15..."

Disappointed M replied, "Yeah or E15... that's okay, too. We'll work on it."

They looked at the other egg. "Oh my!" said Harriet. "Seems we will be going through the other hatching soon... very soon!"

They both looked closer at the egg and saw the newly developed pip. They looked at each other and smiled. E15 smiled too and knocked herself over and she fell back into dreamland. The two new parents took turns brooding E15... or Mini M... or whatever her name would be... and they continued to incubate the pip egg.

When it was M's turn to brood and incubate, he was so excited that instead of rolling the egg, he rolled his protégé. E15's eyes opened wide with surprise. "Oh, I am so sorry, Junior." M looked around nervously for Harriet hoping she didn't see M's mistake. E15 looked up at her Dad and wrapped her little wings around her Dad's legs and hugged him as if to say that she was okay and she knew she was safe. M's heart melted as tears of love and pride filled his eyes.

Harriet flew to the nest. She saw the tears in M's eyes. "Are you okay, M?" she asked.

M quickly wiped away his tears and said, "Me? I'm fine. Just trying to think of what to call E15. Hey... how about J.R.?"

"Or how about E15?" Harriet reiterated.

"Yeah, there's that name too." M looked at his daughter as she peacefully slept. E15 stirred as she dreamt of fun adventures she would eventually have. She soon woke up and looked at her parents. "Well, I better go get us some food." M kissed Harriet, winked at his daughter and then flew off.

Harriet looked at the dinosaur bone that was still in the nest and tried to see if E15 would eat it. She brought a piece of the mystery meat to E15's beak and she just looked lovingly at her Mom, but she wasn't interested in the food... whatever it was.

"I don't blame you. I thought the same thing," she said to her daughter.

The nest was quite active with E15 being so cute while she tried to control her head and her newly strengthening neck muscles. At one point, her head went in circles so fast that she knocked herself over onto the remnants of her egg and the pip egg. "WHOA!" she said. But the little hatchling promptly propped herself up and smiled.

Harriet laughed. "Be careful, 15. You look like you're on a carnival ride and the nest is just one big amusement park. Remember it is YOU that is moving, not the nest." Harriet laughed again causing E15 to smile and squee. The nest was full of love and happiness again.

E15 slept well that first night and so did her Mom. She also slept most of the new day. She attempted to eat although it was the usual challenge as she tried to master food and mouth coordination while her head was going in all directions. But she managed to get some food in her mouth. But no matter what, she was happy. She kept her wing around her future sibling's egg. And the egg's pip was getting larger.

Now two days old, E15 ate more. She was getting big fast. She was also very curious and was already trying to imitate her parents' actions. The palm frond in the nest was a popular attraction. She watched her Mom and Dad move it around the nest… so she tried to do the same. She tried with all her might to get her eye/mouth coordination together so she too could move the frond. It took a while, but she finally got to bite the frond, not move it, but it was success to her! But eating, growing and trying to move palm fronds took a lot of energy, so E15 slept a lot. She settled down next to the pip egg and got ready for her nap. She hugged the egg when suddenly she felt someone hug her back!

E15's eyes opened wide. "Who's hugging me?"

Harriet watched and laughed. She asked, "Is everything alright, sweetheart?"

"Ummm… everything is fine, Mama." Her little voice didn't sound very convincing. Harriet smiled and watched. E15 felt the hug again. She quickly turned and still saw no one there. "What is going on? Who is hugging me?" she softly said. She looked all around and then she saw it. Someone waved at her. Her tiny eyes opened wide and got big and round. "MOM! MOM! IT'S ALIVE!" One of the wings of the soon to be hatchling had broken through the egg and was moving around to break through. Harriet giggled. E15 examined the egg. "How does it see me? I couldn't see out when I was in my shell."

Harriet laughed. "Your sibling hears your voice. So, it knows you are nearby."

E15 went closer to the egg and spoke into the enlarged pip, "Hello in there. Can you hear me? I'm your sister, E15." E15 rested her ear on the shell and waited for a response.

Harriet watched in disbelief. "M, is right, this is HIS Junior!" She giggled.

E15 spoke into the pip again. "Can you hear me?" and she quickly put her ear back to the shell in hopes of hearing a reply. Sadly, she didn't hear anything. "I don't think he or she can hear me."

Harriet tried to control her laughter. This little one was definitely just like her Father looking for the fun and laughter in everything. She reassured her adorable eaglet. "I'm sure your sibling can hear you. But just like when you were trying to hatch, your sibling needs to take breaks and rest to get strong enough to break through the shell. So, I think he or she is resting now."

"That makes sense. I'll hold his or her wing so when they wake up they'll know I'm with them."

Harriet's heart smiled with love for her E15. "You are so sweet and adorable, E15! You're a wonderful sister." E15 smiled. So proud of herself.

The day went on and Harriet and M tended to the pip egg and fed little E15. And they also continued to move the palm frond in the nest. The pip got larger throughout the day and the little one inside tried desperately to join the family as its wing frantically waved to get out.

M fed Harriet and Harriet fed E15. While doing so, M kept an eye on the egg. Suddenly M started laughing. "Wouldn't it be funny if the other wing came out of the other side?" Harriet looked at M and just listened. M laughed more and continued, "And then if both legs popped out of the bottom and the egg ran around the nest. It would be a real egghead!" M laughed a good hardy laugh. Harriet just stared at M, her big eaglet. M looked at Harriet and saw she wasn't amused by his comments so he stopped laughing. He cleared his throat and said, "No, I guess that wouldn't be too funny." He put his head down, looked at E15 and winked. E15 squeed with joy!

That evening, the soon-to-be hatchling tried and tried to break through its shell. Like a mighty little fighter, the wing swung to break free. Soon the little one inside of the egg gave a mighty kick to the shell and it finally hatched! Harriet was feeding E15 when it happened. E16 managed to position herself right on E15's back. She was in line for food. Harriet watched E16 in disbelief. "Oh, my goodness," said Harriet. "You JUST hatched! And you are looking for food already!" Harriet continued feeding E15. E15 was too concerned about food to notice or acknowledge her sister. She just kept eating. But E16 did not like being ignored. So, she started biting the back of E15's head feathers and she tried with all her might to bonk her sister, but her head bobbled too much. She managed to steal a bite of food. "E16! You just got here! How is this possible?"

M flew to the nest and met their feisty newborn. "Hello, E16! I'm your Dad!"

E16 looked at her Dad to see if he had any food for her and when she saw he didn't she simply said, "Hello," and she went back to trying to bite E15's head feathers. She then saw the popular palm frond and tried to bite that without much success.

Both Harriet and M flew to the upper branch. "WHAT was that about?" M asked.

"I know! You won't believe this one! You don't know what you have missed. I was feeding E15 and suddenly she popped out of the shell and she maneuvered herself onto E15's back. She wasn't tired like a normal hatchling. She just joined in. She kept biting at the air for food. She did get one bite. But she kept biting E15's head and tried to bonk her! E15 really didn't feel anything... But M! She just hatched and took over! She wasn't even a minute old! Oh, she's feisty this one. She's going to be a handful!"

M listened to every word Harriet said. He then carefully responded with, "Hmmm... do they remind you of anyone?" Harriet looked at M unsure of what he meant. He explained, "Well 15 is obviously just like me." Harriet nodded. M continued, "But the feisty one that thinks she's in charge... that's mini YOU!"

"Me?"

"Yes, YOU! She thinks she's in charge..." M thought quickly and added, "But she'll soon find out she isn't and you are!" Harriet smiled. He continued. "But she showed up on her terms and with her rules. I'm not saying that's a bad thing. I'm just saying that is just like you!" Harriet smiled again. M muttered, "Poor 15."

"What, M?"

"Huh? Oh, I was going to say..." M came up with a quick response, "She knows she's a princess right now, but she also knows that she is in line to be a queen like her Mother someday."

They watched their two little ones in the nest below. E15 was sleeping and E16 was sitting up. Her little head started going in circles causing her to fall backward. She woke E15 up. Both started clumsily moving around and E16 fell into her partial shell face first. E15 pointed and laughed.

Both Harriet and M laughed too. They couldn't help it. Harriet looked at M and asked, "So should we say something? I'm sure they are all curious to know."

M said, "YES!"

"Okay on three... one, two, three!"

Both Harriet and M cheered out as loud as they could to the pasture animals, "WE HAVE TWO EAGLETS! WOOHOO!!!"

One by one the pasture animals gathered at the base of the nest tree and expressed their well wishes. It was a long and exciting day. And now they could all sleep peacefully knowing that E15 and E16 had hatched.

And now the fun could begin. Well maybe not fun for Harriet and M. Everyone slept well. M got up early and saw Harriet on the upper branch. He was surprised that she wasn't with the kids.

"Good morning, all!" said M. No one answered. M looked at Harriet. Surprised by no answer he repeated, "I said, good morning, all."

"Oh, I know what you said. I'll just say, 'morning' and you can decide if it is good."

"I don't understand," M said confused.

"I think you'll understand when you see what is going on in the nest."

M hopped down into the nest to see his two little eaglets and started to give them some food from the nest pantry. "I said, good morning."

In unison the two eaglets mumbled "Good morning" to their Dad. They were too preoccupied to care about anything than what they were up to.

M watched in disbelief! E15 and E16 were fighting. They weren't bonking. They were actually fighting.

"Hey, hey, hey, you two!" M said sternly. "Stop fighting!"

Mockingly, Harriet rolled her eyes and said, "Oh that's a good idea! Why didn't I think of saying that?"

M attempted to feed the eaglets, but they didn't want to have anything to do with food. They only wanted to fight.

"I liked you better when you were an egg," said E15 to E16.

E16 answered toughly with, "HA! I never liked you!"

"Hey! Knock it off! BOTH OF YOU!" M demanded. Both eaglets ignored their Father and continued fighting. M flew up to the upper branch and landed next to Harriet.

"I told you," said Harriet.

"I can't believe this!" M said, shocked.

"It started as soon as they woke up." Harriet and M continued to watch in disbelief. Annoyed and fed-up, Harriet said, "Okay, I've had enough of this!" She hopped down into the nest and stood between E15 and E16. Their little wings punching her legs while trying to punch each other. "ENOUGH!" Harriet yelled. They continued to fight. "I SAID ENOUGH!!!" Harriet opened her massive wings and created a threatening shadow over the nest. Scared, the two eaglets stopped fighting. "YOU!" Harriet pointed to E15, "YOU go over there! And YOU!" Harriet pointed to E16, "YOU go over there!"

E16 being E16 spoke back to her Mother. "But I don't want to go over there!" she said defiantly.

"Uh-oh! Someone is going to learn their first lesson real fast," said M.

Furious, Harriet bent over and leaned in close to her youngest eaglet. "What did you say?" Harriet asked calmly.

Annoyed that she had to repeat herself, E16 sighed as she looked Harriet in the eyes and answered, "I SAID, I don't want to go over there!"

Harriet gave a grin to her little girl. Very sweetly Harriet said, "Oh, I'm sorry. I didn't realize that you were in charge here and that whatever you say goes. How silly of me to not realize that." Harriet smiled and said, "Can you ever forgive me?"

E16 grinned feeling victorious! "Well I will this time, but don't let it happen again!"

Harriet batted her eyes and then in less than a second bellowed, "MOVE OR I'LL MOVE YOU MYSELF!" Harriet was furious!

Visibly shaken, E16 softly said, "Yes, Mama. I'm sorry, Mama." And she moved.

Harriet smiled and said, "That's my girl." Harriet moved to the center of the nest and said, "You two stay away from each other until you can act civilized. We know eaglets bonk. But there is a difference between bonking and fighting. NO FIGHTING! And the next time you disrespect your Father, I will deal with you. And trust me, you don't want that." She looked toward E16, "Right little girl?"

"Right, Mama."

"Now have I made myself clear?"

"Yes, Mama," the two eaglets responded innocently and sweetly.

"Good! Now let's have breakfish!" said Harriet.

M fed E16 and Harriet fed E15. They ate and did normal bonking, which was fine with Harriet and M. E15 bonked E16 and E16 fell onto E15... and then E15 fell asleep on top of E16. Harriet and M looked at each other.

"AH! Peace and quiet!" Harriet said. M smiled.

And the day went on with feedings... but the fighting continued. But after they finally calmed down and fell asleep, M turned to Harriet and asked, "So is this what second clutches are like?"

"I don't think it has anything to do with them being a second clutch," said Harriet.

"But they're not normal! They're like two boxers fighting in a ring. A left, a right, an upper cut, a shot to the breadbasket. I feel like I should be saying, 'In this corner weighing three ounces and four inches tall'... it's not normal!" Harriet laughed. "Harriet, we have to face facts..." M hesitated. "Our children are insane." Harriet continued laughing. "I've got it! I have the perfect solution!" Harriet listened. M continued, "When E9 comes back to visit, why don't we give them to him!" Harriet raised her eyebrow at M in disapproval. M thought and added, "Okay, how about this... E9 can at least babysit... at least until... until they... fledge!" They both laughed. That was when they looked down into the nest and saw it. E15 and E16 were sound asleep with their wings around each other. And suddenly it was worth all the craziness.

Chapter 8 ... Growing Up Fast

The fighting started to turn into bonking. Not exactly a fun thing to watch, but possibly less brutal looking than fighting... possibly. So now E15 and E16 acted more like typical siblings.

One day, M was taking care of E15 and E16 in the nest. E16 decided to bonk E15. Enraged that her younger sibling had the nerve to bonk her, E15 got up. She attempted to get her sister back and tried to bonk her, but missed. Frustrated with herself, E15 grabbed and bit at the closest thing to her which just so happened to be her Dad. She bit her Dad's feathers and pulled on them while twisting her head in a fury.

M15 looked down at his namesake and sarcastically asked, "What are you doing?"

Upset with herself even more now, E15 started swinging her wings and hit her Father's legs. "ARGH! She is just so annoying!" E15 said trying to catch her breath.

"So why are you taking it out on me?" asked her Dad.

E15 stopped, thought and said, "I don't know why. I guess because you are the nearest thing to me." E15 put her little head down. "I'm sorry, Dad."

M15 rolled his eyes and sighed. E15 then laid down, hugged her Dad's legs and fell asleep. M's heart melted.

Later that day, M brought a huge fish to the nest. Harriet was thrilled. "Oh, M! You outdid yourself with this fish!" M wiggled his eyebrows in M15 fashion and smiled.

"Thank you, my lady," and he bowed.

The two eaglets saw the fish and tried to quickly get in line for food. Standing and walking was still something they needed to master. But they were young and it was quite normal. While being fed, E16 stood up and fell backward. E15 pointed and laughed at her sister while she was on her back and her toes grabbed at the air.

"Good one, twinkle toes," E15 teased.

"Shut up!" demanded E16. "Leave me alone!" The feisty eaglet tried to roll over, but all she did was tire herself out and gave her sister reason to laugh. She stopped trying and she relaxed. She took a deep breath and regained her strength. She gave it another try and suddenly she was standing. She looked at E15 and said, "HA! In your face, 15!"

"Okay you two... enough!" said Harriet.

"She started it," E15 defended herself.

"I did not! You did!" replied E16.

"What did I do?" questioned E15.

"You laughed at me."

"That's because you're a spaz and you're funny looking!"

"You're funny looking!"

"ALRIGHT! ENOUGH!" Harriet yelled. "Please!"

They could be a handful and quite exhausting at times. They started to attempt walking. It seemed more like a belly crawl. They looked like sea turtles trying to get to the ocean's edge while their wings moved back and forth like a turtle's flippers. E15 would start to walk and E16 would be right behind her.

"Stop copying me!" demanded E15.

"I'm not copying you!" responded E16.

"Then stop following me!"

"I'm not following you!" replied E16.

E15 stopped to stand up and yell at her sister when suddenly she started to fall backward. E16 was so close to her that she was able to put out her wing and catch her.

"Thanks," E15 said softly to E16.

"You're welcome."

In shock, Harriet stopped and stared ahead. It was as if she didn't want to move in fear that it would disturb the peace that just happened. *Thank you and you're welcome?* Am I in the right nest?" They finally took a break from arguing and bonking and they took a nap. E15 put her wing around her little sister as they slept. Harriet looked at her two little... angels?... and said, "Aww, they are so sweet when they sleep!" She smiled.

Now five days old, E15 was getting restless and wanted to explore the nest. Harriet and M had taken a short break and the eaglets were by themselves in the nest. E15 turtle walked toward the nest rails.

E16 opened her eyes wide and said, "I don't think you're allowed over there."

"Said who?"

"Said me!"

"Well you're nobody."

"I am too somebody! I'm E16! I'm your beautiful sister, and I KNOW you're not allowed over there!"

"Why not?"

"Because we're too young!"

"I'm not too young. I'm older than you! You're not allowed over here!" E15 got closer to the nest rails. "I DID IT!" E15 cheered as she held onto the very bottom of the rails.

Harriet flew to the nest. E16 smiled when she saw her Mother and she seemed to sing the words as she spoke to her sister, "You're gonna get it! You're gonna get it!"

"Okay, little girl, what are you doing?" asked Harriet.

"I'm just exploring the nest," E15 innocently replied.

"Very good, but now go back to the nest bowl."

"HA! I told you!" said E16.

Harriet looked at the feisty child and said, "I don't need your help, E16. I've got this. I'll let you know when I need your help, thank you."

"Okay, Mama!" E16 smiled at her sister. "Mama will let ME know when she needs MY help!" She gave a defiant look to E15 before she put her beak in the air and turned her back to E15. She felt victorious.

Everything in the nest was a lesson. Whether it was about food, caring for the nest, prey, or relationships, the eaglets watched and learned.

One morning they heard a new sound. They heard a human voice.

"What is that sound?" asked E16.

E15 looked bewildered. "I don't know. I've never heard that animal before."

Still unable to look over the nest rails, they stayed still in the nest and listened.

"Congratulations you two on both of your eaglets! You did it! I'm so proud of you and M! So proud! They're growing up so fast and you're teaching them well. Hopefully in a couple of weeks, we'll be able to see them over the nest rails. We'll see. You built them pretty high."

E15 and E16 looked at their Mother. They seemed uncertain and a little scared.

Harriet smiled and said, "Don't be afraid. That is our friend, Vicki. You'll see her when you get older. She's a human."

"A what?" asked E15.

Harriet laughed, "A human. We'll teach you about them as you get older. Right now, you have more important things to learn. You have to eat and grow. Those are the most important things you need to know right now."

E15 and E16 were confused and looked at each other. E15 raised her wings and narrowed her eyes to frighten E16 and said, "Humans! MAHWAHHH!"

"Oh, please!" said her feisty sister as she rolled her eyes. "Nothing could be scarier looking than you!"

"Thank you! That's a good thing! I'm an eagle and we are supposed to look threatening and scary!"

"Well you don't scare me!" and E16 bonked E15 and E15 bonked her right back. But 16 got right back up and they sat there beak to beak staring at each other. The bonking went back to brawling which seemed to always end up with E16 face down in the nest. "You wait until I get big like Mama! You'll see! I'll bonk you right off the tree!" threatened E16.

"Oh, I'm scared, pip squeak!" E15 laughed.

"ALRIGHT! What is wrong with the two of you? Can't you be nice to each other at least when you first wake up?"

"She started it!" cried E16.

"I didn't start it! You started it!"

"QUIET!" Harriet screamed.

The two siblings quickly closed their beaks and sat quietly with their eyes wide open. Harriet shook her head and sighed.

While Harriet was having a stressful time with the kids, M was in the pasture and saw Felix the great blue heron flying around at the pasture pond.

"Hmmm... I am hungry," said M quietly as he watched the heron. "And I know Harriet and the kids must be hungry, too." M quickly flew toward Felix and as soon as the heron caught a fish, M flew up to him and stole it.

"HEY! M, I've had enough of you stealing my food!"

"Ah, come on, Felix! We have two new eaglets and they are always hungry. And they love the way you catch fish!"

"Don't try to flatter me, M15! I have to eat too, you know!"

"I know... but thanks, Felix!" M15 said as he flew away with the heron's fish. "You're the best!"

As the two young eaglets sat quietly in the nest... almost being good... M flew to the nest with the fish.

Harriet was thrilled when she saw the fish. "Oh, that looks good!" M immediately started feeding Harriet. "Oh, my goodness! That's delicious! Did you do something different to it?"

"No, I stole it from Felix the great blue heron the way I normally do."

"Well it is delicious! Please tell him I said so when you see him next time."

M laughed and said, "Oh, I'm SURE he'll love to hear that!"

M continued to feed Harriet. E15 and E16 looked at each other as they watched and waited. The more M fed Harriet the more she wanted. "Oh, this is just so good!" The two eaglets looked at Harriet. They were really hungry. "I should really feed the kids," said Harriet. E15 and E16 both swiftly nodded their heads while still being quiet. Harriet hesitated and said, "Maybe one more bite..."

The eaglets' eyes opened wide. M laughed as he gave her another piece. Harriet looked at M flirtingly as he fed her. They kissed in between bites as the little ones made faces during their parents' romantic meal. Little did E15 and E16 know they had learned a lesson. The close bond of loving mates. And even though the young ones made faces and rolled their eyes, they would remember the closeness of their parents forever and they too would have happy, loving relationships with their mates.

But for right now their parent's affection for each other was, "Yuck!" said E15.

"Gross!" said E16.

M and Harriet laughed. "Okay, you two. We've tortured you long enough. Hey, wouldn't that be something if the two of you learned how to be nice and loving to each other?" asked Harriet.

E15 and E16 looked at each other as they thought about what their Mom just asked. In unison they both replied, "NAW!" and they laughed and laughed.

Harriet fed the two eaglets and when feeding time was through, she treated herself to her favorite part of the meal... the tail! All under the watchful eyes of E16, Harriet put the fish tail in her mouth and gulped it down.

"WOW!" E16 said in amazement. "That was so cool! I'm going to do that someday. I'm going to be just like Mama!"

Yes, all sorts of lessons were learned in the nest. And this was just the beginning... the basics.

But some lessons were even learned by the parents...

One morning, Harriet flew to the nest with a very large catch for the eaglets to eat. She was so thrilled. She started to defur the food while the eaglets slept.

"Oh, they'll be so excited when they wake up!" Harriet smiled. But soon she seemed to have some difficulty with preparing the food.

E15 and E16 woke up. "Good morning, Mama!" They both sweetly said in angel voices.

"Good morning, my babies!" Harriet continued to defur the animal.

"What's that?" E15 asked as she moved closer to get a better look.

"It's squirrel, E15."

E15 just watched as she waited to try the new food item. Harriet continued to work hard on preparing the food.

"This is so odd. It doesn't look right at all. It seems to be all fur and weird stuff." Harriet's eyes opened wide. "Uh-oh! OH, NO!" She quickly looked around to see if M was anywhere nearby. "Where's M? He'll never let me live this down if he finds out I brought a stuffed animal toy, a fake squirrel to the nest as food." She looked at the toy and shook her head. She quickly moved the stuffed animal to the other side of the nest while E15 and E16 were taking it all in.

"Aren't we going to eat?" asked E15.

"No, honey. Not now. This squirrel doesn't taste good."

"But I've been waiting. I don't care how it tastes. I'll eat it!" exclaimed E15.

"NO!" said Harriet "Just leave it alone!"

Just then M15 flew into the nest. "I have a treat for my wonderful family!"

"Yay, Dad!" the eaglets cheered.

"What is it?" asked E16.

"It's SQUIRREL!" Dad said proudly.

"Squirrel?" E15 questioned. "That's what Mom brought in, but she said it doesn't taste good... it tasted bad."

"No, E15..." and Harriet shook her head at her daughter.

"But that's what you said!" E15 sounded confused.

"I know what I said!" snapped Harriet.

"But...?" E15 started to question.

M interrupted and asked, "Bad tasting squirrel? I don't understand." Both E15 and E16 pointed to the toy. Defeated, Harriet put her head down. M looked at what the kids pointed to. His eyes opened wide and he raised his eyebrows. He laughed and jokingly asked... "What in the world?"

"NOTHING!" Harriet said abruptly.

M continued to laugh which caused the kids to laugh, even though they really didn't know what was actually going on.

M laughed and said, "I'll say 'nothing'! That's not..."

Now Harriet interrupted M, "That's not for discussion!"

"But that's not even a real…" M stopped immediately when he saw Harriet narrow her eyes at him.

"It's not a real what, Dad?" asked E15.

M slowly thought up an answer, "It's not even a really good-looking squirrel." Harriet gave M a little smile. "Here, try this." M gave Harriet a taste of the real squirrel. "I'm sure it tastes better than Stuffy the Squirrel." The two kids laughed.

"It is very good, M. Thank you," said Harriet. She was embarrassed, but tried not to show it.

M knew this was BIG! This was his Get Out Of Jail Free card. This was what he could use as leverage the next time he and Harriet had their spirited stick "discussions." He softly muttered and chuckled under his breath… "Eagle eye, HA!"

"What was that, M?" Harriet asked as she fed E15 and E16 their meal.

"Huh?" M thought quickly again… he was getting good at that… "Oh nothing. I just said, 'my eye. OW!' I have something in my eye." And he smiled at Harriet and together he and Harriet fed the kids.

Harriet looked at the toy. "Well, now they have a cuddle buddy. Maybe they can use him as their sparring partner instead of boxing with each other."

M just smiled and dreamed of days to come.

Chapter 9 ... A Mother's Love

The two E's slept, ate and grew…. and slept, ate and grew some more. And yes, there was still a lot of bonking going on. But it was bonking, not fighting… usually. But regardless it was still E16 that got the worst of it. At feeding time, E15 would let E16 know it was her food and she would bonk E16. But E16 quickly learned that if she would just submit and stay away from the food while E15 was eating, she could avoid being bonked. There was one day that E16 spread her wings and blocked E15 from getting close to the food… but that was one day… and at one feeding, but she was learning.

During the nest visit by Vicki, Harriet's human friend, the two siblings were seen through the nest peepholes while their Dad was feeding them breakfast.

"There's a baby! Hi! There's another! Hi you two! Oh, look at you! Oh boy! I see you! Look at you!" Vicki was so excited that she was able to get a glimpse of E15 and E16. "Good little eaters! It's so good to be able to see you, little ones." Harriet flew to the nest tree and looked at her friend. "Thank you for letting me see them. I'm so proud of you and M15. You never gave up! And now we have two new eaglets… E15 and E16! Happy days! I'll be back in a few days. Bye E15 and E16. Enjoy your day! I love you all. Be safe and be careful." And Vicki packed up her car and went home. The two eaglets ate the entire time Vicki was there. They were now full, but still curious.

"Mama, who and what is a Vicki?" asked E15.

"She is a human and she is my friend," replied Harriet.

"So, what is a human?" asked E16.

"That is the type of animal she is. They are called humans or people. They are supposedly the smartest animal God created."

"Well then you know that 16 isn't human," E15 jokingly teased her sister as she pushed E16 with her wing. E16 pushed E15's wing away and narrowed her eyes at her.

"But you stay away from humans!" M said sternly.

"Why?" asked E15.

"First, because I said so. And second because they can't be trusted."

"Even Mama's friend?" asked E15.

"No, not my friend. Vicki would never harm you or any animal for that matter. But we know Vicki and we don't know the others," explained Harriet.

M continued, "They only think of themselves and…"

Harriet added, "So it is best to just stay away from them. Okay?"

E16 quickly answered, "OKAY!" and smiled.

"Good girl, 16!" Harriet smiled.

"Yes, good girl, 16! And 15 you stay away from them, too." M waited for a response. "FIFTEEN!" M yelled.

"Okay, I'll stay away from them. Geez, keep your feathers on." E15 answered in an annoyed tone.

"You made Dad mad. That wasn't smart. So, we KNOW you aren't human!" E16 laughed.

"Oh, you're real funny," said E15, still annoyed. E16 laughed louder. "And you're funny looking, too!" mocked E15.

"Not as funny looking as you," E16 continued to laugh.

Upset, E15 pushed her sister and she fell over. E16 struggled to right herself, but managed to and moved over to Harriet to get away from E15. She rested under her Mother which also kept her out of the hot sun. Harriet smiled at her sweet eaglet. E16 quickly fell asleep as she reached out and held onto her Mother's foot. While E16 rested, Harriet noticed E16 moved a lot in her sleep. E16 abruptly woke herself up.

"Are you okay, sweetheart?" Harriet asked E16.

"Yes, Mama. Just a bad dream," replied E16. Harriet watched E16 with concern as her little one went back to sleep.

Easter morning quickly arrived. And the way the two eaglets awkwardly walked, they looked more like bunnies hopping around the nest than eagles.

M15 flew into the nest with a delicious Easter meal and announced, "Happy Easter, family! Let's celebrate!"

E15 rushed over to her Dad and M15 started feeding her. E16 waited to the side to avoid her sister's bullying. As E15 enjoyed her feast, E16 scurried over to the fish her Dad was feeding her sister and she sat on it. M15 pulled on the fish and soon it became a carnival ride for E16.

"WOOHOO! I'm a cowgirl... or a fishgirl! Ride 'em fishgirl!" E16 happily cheered.

"Oh brother," said E15 as she fell into a food coma.

Both siblings enjoyed a wonderful meal. Their crops and bellies were full and they were ready for a nap. Even Harriet enjoyed a delicious meal as she moved sticks and nest material around. She found a yummy surprise... a fish tail nestled amongst the nest material. Her eyes opened wide and she smiled with sheer delight.

"Oh, this is like being on an Easter egg hunt and I found the BEST Easter egg... shaped just like a yummy fish tail!" Harriet picked up the tail and in one gulp it was gone. "Yum! That was good!" she said as she feaked her beak.

Later that day, M15 brought in another fish. "Incoming!" M announced.

E15 immediately went to her Dad. "Yay, Dad! I'm starving!" M smiled and started feeding E15.

"I'm starving, too," said little E16.

"I know, but I have to feed E15 first."

"Yeah, wait your turn, pip squeak," mocked E15.

"I'm NOT a pip squeak and you're mean!"

M15 and E15 both ignored E16. Harriet flew to the nest and saw that M was only feeding E15. Harriet grabbed a nestover fish from earlier and she started to feed E16.

"Here baby," said Harriet to E16.

"Thank you, Mama. I'm hungry."

"I know baby," replied Harriet as she looked at M with disapproval.

But the fish was picked over and there wasn't much left to give to E16. Again, Harriet looked at M.

"Would you like some?" asked M.

"I don't want any. I want some for E16."

M heard the tone in her voice and it wasn't a happy one. "Oh right! Of course!" M fed Harriet the pieces of fish and Harriet fed them to E16. Then Harriet did the unthinkable... she gave little E16 the fish tail.

E16's eyes opened wide. "For me?" she gleefully asked. Harriet smiled and nodded. E16 grabbed it and gulped it right down! E16 enjoyed her meal. Tummy full, 16 soon was very tired. With sleepy eyes, E16 looked at Harriet and said, "Thank you, Mama... I love you," and she fell asleep right next to Stuffy the squirrel toy.

Harriet smiled at her sweet E16 and said, "You're welcome, baby. I love you, too, sweetheart. Goodnight. Sweet eagle dreams."

Yes, it means so much... a Mother's love!

Chapter 10 ... We're Always With You

The two siblings were over by the nest rails. They were actually being good. Until...

"Stop it!" cried E16.

"I didn't do anything!" replied E15.

"You did to! You touched me!"

"I didn't touch you! But if you want I will," taunted E15.

"Don't lie! You pulled my tail!"

"I wouldn't go near your tail!" yelled E15.

"Then who pulled my tail?"

"Maybe you're insane. That happens you know when you're in the heat too long. It fries your brain and it wouldn't take long because your brain is so small to start with," E15 laughed.

"It is not! You're mean!" yelled E16.

Harriet was perched above the nest preening her feathers as she listened to her children bickering. She saw that 15 did not touch 16's tail and 15 had told the truth. So, Harriet didn't understand what all the arguing was about. She continued to preen when suddenly a feather floated in front of her. She grabbed the feather in her beak and transferred it to her talons. She leaned over and looked at the beautiful eagle feather. She studied the feather. It certainly looked like a normal feather, but it smelled different... a familiar smell. And although it looked like any other feather it had a different beauty to it... a glow about it. She enjoyed holding it. Harriet looked all around.

She stopped and looked up and said, "Ozzie?"

E15 and E16 stopped bickering for a moment and in unison they responded, "Yes, Mama?"

"Oh, no, babies, I was just... talking to myself," Harriet replied.

"See, E16," E15 whispered to her sibling, "Just like I said. It's the heat. It makes everyone insane." E15 got up and rested her large crop on E16.

"Get off of me!" demanded E16.

"You're such a whiner," said E15 as she moved away from E16.

E16 did a poop shoot and it hit E15 in the back of the head. E16's eyes opened in surprise and with a little fear. "Uh-oh," she quietly said.

"Did you feel something," asked E15.

E16 turned to look at E15. "Like what?" E16 asked innocently.

"I don't know... like rain or something."

"No, I didn't feel anything." E16 turned away from E15 and opened her mouth and silently laughed. "Maybe it's your brain melting from the heat," she said and smiled.

Mockingly, E15 repeated, "Maybe it's your brain melting from the heat. You're such a child."

"That's because I am a child, brainiac."

"Okay you two... enough!" said Harriet.

"She started it," E15 said quickly.

"Did not... you did!" responded E16 loud enough for Harriet to hear.

"ENOUGH!" yelled Harriet. And they both FINALLY sat silently.

M15 flew to the nest tree and landed next to Harriet. "Little ones acting up?" he asked.

"When aren't they," answered Harriet. They both smiled.

"Why are you holding a feather?" asked M.

"It's not mine," replied Harriet.

M looked confused. "Then who's feather is it? Who is he? I'll tear him to shreds!" M smiled.

Harriet giggled. "Calm down, lover boy. It floated in front of me while I was preening. Doesn't it have a slight glow to it?"

M replied, "Yeah, it does. I think you're right."

"Now don't think I'm crazy..."

"It's a little too late for that," M laughed. Harriet gave him a typical Harriet look of disapproval. "Oh, sorry," M said seriously. "Go on."

"Well 16 thought that 15 pulled her tail and I was watching and I saw that 15 didn't touch 16. And of course, they argued. I was preening and suddenly I saw this feather float in front of my face." M listened as Harriet continued. "Well after the dream that you and I shared... I know this couldn't be, but... I thought what if E14 pulled E16's tail and what if this is Ozzie's feather?"

M wasn't smiling anymore. "Wow, I would never have thought of that."

"I know it's crazy."

"No. No, it isn't. We both had the same dream and we know we weren't crazy with that. So, this could really be true. You could be right." said M.

"Ozzie said in the dream that E14 would be back to visit. And I'm sure Ozzie would come here with 14."

"I don't doubt anything anymore."

"So, maybe this is their way of showing us that they are here... a feather... a touch." They both looked into the nest and then at each other. And then they just sat in wonder.

That night M left his post and dropped into the nest while the kids were asleep with Harriet.

Surprised, Harriet asked, "What's wrong?"

"Nothing," replied M.

Harriet quietly giggled. "So why aren't you on guard perched above the nest?"

"Well I thought I'd stay with you and the kids in case you had a late-night visitor."

Harriet was confused. "A late-night visitor? Who?"

M hesitated. "I don't know... maybe... Ozzie... maybe?"

"Ozzie?" Harriet was shocked. "Are you jealous?" Her eyes were opened wide.

"NO, I'm not jealous!" M quickly snapped. Harriet looked away and smiled. M continued, "I'm just concerned that he might show up and frighten the kids."

"Oh, he might frighten the kids."

"Yeah, you know how kids are."

"Have you met our kids?" Harriet teased. "I'm sorry... Yes, I do know how kids are. But thank you. I think they'll be fine."

"Well, I don't want him to frighten you."

"Ozzie would never frighten me."

"Yeah, I kinda figured that."

"You're not afraid of him, are you, M?" Harriet asked.

"Me? NO WAY! Please!" M softly mumbled, "Afraid of an eagle that isn't here anymore," he laughed. "Yeah, right."

"Okay! Well then goodnight."

M hesitated and then kissed Harriet and said, "Goodnight," and he flew back up to stand guard over his family.

Harriet smiled. She couldn't help but love her M.

Chapter 11 ... She Needs You

The kids were getting bigger every day and their pin feathers started to emerge. The sibling rivalry continued. Even while sleeping they would have to do something to the other one. E15 would give E16 a kick and E16 would return the gesture with a wing punch to E15's face. But the good thing was they continued to sleep. So, it wasn't too brutal.

The temperatures in Southwest Florida were reaching record breaking numbers. E15 and E16 would look to find shelter under their parents to get relief from the blazing sun. But their Mom and Dad weren't always in the nest.

One day while sleeping and growing, E15 and E16 were cuddled together. E15 woke up and started allopreening E16.

E16 woke up. "Stop it!" she demanded.

"You're such a baby, 16," said 15. And then as if talking to a baby E15 said, "Oh, yes you are! Oh, yes you are!" E15 continued to allopreen 16.

"I said, STOP it!" yelled E16 and she jumped up and spread her wings and accidently slapped E15 in the face. "Uh-oh," said E16, her eyes widened as she expected the worst. But E15 surprised her and didn't say a word. E16 moved clumsily to the nest rails. She stretched her wings. "Ahhh! Feel the wind," she sighed. But soon the breeze knocked E16 over and she tumbled back over to her sister. E15 put her wing around E16 and continued to allopreen her. E16 closed her eyes and shook her head.

There were other times that E15 and E16 would relax by the nest rails and one of them would put their wing around the other. They were capable of being good and nice to each other. And they were even known to give each other a hug.

As the days went by, they tried their best to imitate their parents. They enjoyed moving sticks and nest material around the nest like they had seen their Mom and Dad do. They adored their parents. Both of their parents were so loving and devoted to the two of them. Their Mom was the epitome of strength, beauty and grace. Harriet was the backbone of their family. M15 was strong, loving and devoted... and sometimes a little awkward or quirky, but that made M15... M15!

But Harriet started noticing something about M that upset her. She knew that the first hatched was always more aggressive and eagles know to survive you must be aggressive. They taught all of their eaglets that lesson. And usually the aggressive eaglet would be fed first and sort of catered to. But Harriet felt that M15 was being too attentive to E15 and actually ignoring E16.

She hoped she was just overreacting, but it was bothering her. So, one evening before sunset while the kids were asleep, Harriet went to the upper branch and perched next to M.

"Looks like it is going to be another beautiful sunset tonight," said M as he faced the west.

"Yes, it does," replied Harriet. She took a deep breath and said, "M, something is bothering me."

"What's that?" asked M.

"I'm probably just being overly protective, but I wanted to mention it to you."

"Uh-oh, what did I do?" M asked.

Harriet rolled her eyes. "I know you love both of the kids."

"Yes, I do."

"But sometimes when I see you with them," Harriet hesitated. "I don't like what I see." M sat quietly as he listened. Harriet continued. "You feed 15 and I get it, first hatched, more aggressive, I know all of that. But sometimes you feed 15 and then you just feed yourself."

"No, I don't!"

"Oh yes you do! I've been watching you. And then you just fly off. You completely ignore 16."

"I do not!" M said defensively.

"You do too," Harriet said firmly. "And I don't like it!" Now Harriet was getting angry. "The other day you fed 15 and you walked away from them. But you walked into 16 causing her to fall over. It's like she isn't even there! Like she's invisible to you! Something is going on in your head that is making you act like this."

Annoyed, M responded, "NOTHING is going on in my head!" Harriet smiled and let out a small laugh. "Ha, ha... very funny!" M said.

Harriet's tone quickly became more serious, "Well, something is causing you to be different then you were with 7 and 8, 10 and 11, and 12 and 13. You are showing favoritism."

"I am NOT!" M said loudly.

"Lower your voice!" Harriet whispered. "You'll wake the kids and they'll hear what we are talking about."

"Sorry," M said softly. They sat silently together. M looked around the pasture. "Okay... you want to know what it is?"

"Yes, I do!"

"Well I'll tell you! Yes, 15 is the first hatched. Yes, 15 is more aggressive. And yes, E15 is my namesake. So, there is that connection.

"Okay and you were really close to E9. He was your buddy. But I don't get it! You were able to be close with the others too... E7, E8, E10, E11, E12, E13, and E14."

"And E14..." M said quietly, "...14..." M hung his head. "I miss him, Harriet."

Harriet grabbed M's wing. "I know, M. I miss him, too," she said softly.

"But we were getting so close and then..." Harriet and M both sat and looked at the branch they were perched on. Then M continued, "And then he left. And I..." M stopped.

"M?"

"And I can't get close to 16 because I'm afraid she'll leave too. I look in her eyes and I see 14's heart. That twinkle in her eye. That happy playfulness that he had."

"Oh, M..." Harriet's heart broke with M's words. "M, you can't think like that."

"Well, I do."

"But you shouldn't. E16 needs you. She loves you. She looks up to you and wants to be like you and wants your approval. She looks just like you! She is trying to take care of the nest like you... moving nest material and sticks. She just wants to please you. But I see the hurt in her eyes when you push right past her as if she wasn't even there." Harriet stopped. She saw the pain in M's eyes as he heard her words. "She needs you, M. She needs to feel her Father's love." Harriet and M looked into each other's tear-filled eyes. "E14 will always be with us. But E16 is here with us now. She's here, M. And she needs you." M hugged Harriet. He knew she was right.

The next morning, M sat perched on the upper branch of the nest tree while he watched Felix the great blue heron at the pasture pond. Felix slowly inched his way to a tasty fish. M watched closely. "Ah... Breakfish!" he said under his breath. M swiftly swooped down to the pond and with precise artistry stole the heron's fish.

"M!" Felix shouted. "That's mine! This better stop!"

"Thanks, Felix! The kids are really hungry!"

Maria, the anhinga, watched the events unfold as she leisurely floated in the pond. Suddenly she saw M flying toward her with the stolen fish held tightly in his talons. "Ay Dios mio!" she cried before she quickly went under the water for safety.

M flew to the nest with the fish. "Breakfish!" he announced.

"Yay, Dad!" cheered E15 and E16.

Then the usual happened. E16 stayed to the side to avoid getting bonked by E15 while their Dad fed 15. M attempted to give 16 some food, but E15 didn't agree with that plan. So E15 ate, but this was a big fish. So as soon as E15's crop was full, she walked to the nest rails to take a nap. Most of the fish was leftover. M15 quickly started to feed E16.

"Is it good, E16," M asked the little one.

"Yummy, Dad! You make a great breakfish!"

"You'll have to thank Felix for that," M replied.

"Who's Felix, Dad?" asked 16.

"He's a great blue heron friend of ours. He caught the fish and... and I took it!" M smiled at 16 and 16 gave a great big smile to her Dad.

M15 continued to feed E16. They sat side by side. Such a beautiful sight to see a Father and daughter as they sat together and enjoyed each other's company. They looked like they were at a movie sharing popcorn. M tried not to bend to give the food to E16. He let her reach for it. He felt it was a good exercise in eye/beak coordination and it also helped strengthen E16's muscles. E16 didn't care what the reason was... she was having breakfast with her Dad! E16 squeed with delight with every bite.

Harriet landed in the attic. "Well look at the two of you enjoying breakfish together!" M looked at Harriet and Harriet smiled with approval which made M proud. "Don't forget, the tail is mine!" and Harriet flew off.

E16 kept eating like a bottomless pit. Soon only the fish tail was left. M looked around to see where Harriet was.

E16's eyes opened wide in anticipation. "Oh, boy! The tail!" she said with a big smile.

But Harriet was watching from somewhere nearby and she swiftly returned to the nest. She moved in front of M15, grabbed the fish tail and ate it. "Mmmm! Very good!" she said. She smiled and flew off again.

E16 and her Dad looked at each other and shrugged their shoulders. There would be plenty more fish tails to come and more importantly more special moments shared with her Dad.

"Hey, 16. I've been meaning to say something to you. I hear you singing in the nest sometimes."

"Oh I love to sing, Dad!"

"I do too... would you like to try writing a song with me?"

E16 was thrilled! "I would love to!" she replied. "But how do we write a song together?"

"Well one of us will start a line and then the other will do the next line. Let's try it out and see how it goes, okay?"

"Okay!" E16 paused and said, "Dad I sometimes sing this when I go to sleep at night. I don't sing it out loud. I sing it to myself so E15 won't make fun of me. Can we maybe try that song?"

M laughed to himself. He didn't want to make his E16 feel bad. He quietly thought, "What could a little eaglet possibly write that could be a song?" Regardless M said, "Sure 16! That would be great! Go ahead and I'll add on after you start."

E16 cleared her throat and softly started to sing. "I'm your girl and you're my Dad. You're the best friend I ever had. Eagles may come and eagles may go, but my Dad's the best male eagle I'll ever know."

M stood silent. His heart full of love for his little 16. "Sixteen... I don't know what to say. That is beautiful and your words..." M started to get choked up and took a deep breath. "Oh 16..." M hugged his little girl.

"I'm glad you like it, Dad!" E16 was so happy and proud. "Okay, now it's your line."

"Right, right... you're a tough act to follow," M laughed. "Okay..." He cleared his throat. "You're my girl." He stopped again and tried to stop from getting emotional.

"And you're my Dad," added 16.

M then sang, "My heart skips a beat and I'm so glad."

"I took your wing," sang 16.

"And you stole my heart," sang M.

They both sang, "In your eyes I saw this love start."

Proud as could be, M suggested, "How about we take it from the top and see how it all sounds?" E16 smiled and nodded.

"I'm your girl and you're my Dad. You're the best friend I ever had. Eagles may come and eagles may go, but my Dad's the best male eagle I'll ever know."

"You're my girl."

"And you're my Dad."

"My heart skips a beat and I'm so glad."

"I took your wing."

"And you stole my heart."

Together they harmonized, "In your eyes I saw this love start."

M hugged his little girl. "Oh E16... I love you... thank you."

"I love you, Dad... thank you! This has been the best day ever!"

Harriet was perched close by and heard the entire thing. Tears rolled down her beautiful face. Tears of joy, happiness and love for her family. This moment would never be forgotten and it would live on in their hearts forever.

Chapter 12 ... Kids Will Be Kids

The two siblings had an extremely busy schedule. They ate, slept, learned lessons by watching their parents, they played and observed each other sometimes with love, sometimes with curiosity and sometimes with mischief in mind.

They both waddled toward Stuffy and cuddled with it. It certainly was a source of comfort as any stuffed animal is to a child. As they relaxed, E16 looked over E15's feathers. Intrigued, 16 started to play with her sibling's feathers. Surprisingly, E15 just calmly watched 16. Suddenly, 16 "beeped" 15's beak. E15 then did the most shocking, out of character gesture she could possibly have done! E15 kissed E16 on the beak.

E16 jumped up, "YUCK! Get away!" E15 sat up and laughed. She didn't get mad, she didn't have a quick comeback, she just started preening herself and while doing so she almost fell over... causing E16 to laugh. "Ha! Ha!"

But still no reaction from E15. So E16 started moving nest material and while doing so she found a white feather and started playing with it. E15 watched E16. E15 tried to see what the feather toy was about, but quickly lost interest. They were actually being quite good and pretty quiet. They moved to the nest rails and seemed to do synchronized watching. They watched the birds in the sky, the pine needles, the clouds, the cars... whatever they could see. And as if the same neck turned each head, when one looked one way, so did the other. But they were still young and required that much needed sleep while they grew big and strong. They soon fell asleep. Only this time, E16 fell asleep with E15's toe in her mouth. E15 woke up and was still being good and didn't complain or get angry with 16. E16 then woke up and decided that E15's toes were good enough to nibble.

Finally, E15 asked, "What do you think you're doing?"

"Nothing," replied 16 as she continued to nibble on E15's toes.

"Well, it LOOKS like you're doing something."

"I found a chew toy," replied E16. She only stopped chewing to answer E15.

"A chew toy?"

"Yep!"

"Did you happen to notice that YOUR chew toy looks just like MY toes?"

"Ha! Imagine that!" E16 said innocently and continued to chew on 15's toes.

"Can you please tell me WHY you think it is okay for you to have my toes in your mouth?"

"Because they taste good," teased 16.

"Well, eat your own toes!"

"I don't want to! I need them to walk!"

"Well, I need mind too!" E15 was getting a little annoyed, but not as annoyed as she normally would.

"Don't worry, I'll leave you some."

E15 shook her head, "Why couldn't I be an only child?"

"Because then you wouldn't have me as your adorable, beautiful, intelligent sister!"

E15 sighed and rolled her eyes. She knew deep down inside she loved her sister no matter how much she annoyed her.

But typical of kids the "chew toy" toes became old news and E16 wanted something else to chew... food! She walked over to a fish in the pantry and started to try to feed herself. It was difficult, but she managed a few bites on her own. She proved that she was strong, determined and a survivor.

E15 watched E16 and asked, "NOW what are you doing?"

E16 replied again with, "Nothing."

"You always say 'nothing', but you're always doing something!"

"So? Why are you so nosey? Don't worry about what I'm doing. Worry about yourself."

"I'm not worried. I just want to make sure that you're not doing something that you shouldn't be doing." E16 ignored E15's statement.

Soon their Dad arrived with a fish. "Yay, Dad!" they cheered.

Harriet joined all of them in the nest and she quickly took the fish away from M and she started feeding E15 and E16.

"Okay... that's okay," said M. He turned and found the fish E16 was nibbling on before he arrived. M looked at the small bites taken out of the fish. "Gee, what happened here?"

Proudly E16 said, "That was ME, Dad!"

M looked at E16 with surprise. "YOU tried eating the fish on your own?" he asked.

"Yes, sir!" 16 replied confidently.

M looked at Harriet and Harriet smiled. "Very good, 16! Very good! Wow! That shows you are paying attention and learning! You are thinking like a big eagle! I'm very proud of you!"

In a sophisticated tone, E16 replied, "Thank you, Father." She turned her beak up and grinned at her sister mockingly.

E15 shook her head again, "Give me a break."

E16 conveniently positioned herself between her Mom and Dad to get the best seat at the "table."

"For you my love," M15 started feeding Harriet the leftover fish.

"Thank you, M, but I have fresh fish."

"I know, I'm the one that brought it in," M said and smiled.

Harriet started feeding E16. Then M started feeding E16. E16 was being fed by both Harriet and M as if each was determined to be the only one feeding E16. Back and forth they both took turns feeding their little girl while E15 just watched in disbelief.

"Please, please... Mother, Father, don't fight over me! I'm an equal opportunity eater." E16 looked at Harriet as she hesitated to feed 16. "Okay, Mama... it's your turn. Food please...!" But soon E16 realized that her Mother's fish was fresher tasting. She moved closer to her Mother which allowed M15 to move closer to E15 so he could feed her.

Belly and crop full, E16 moved behind E15 while 15 was being fed by their Dad. While M fed E15, he moved in the nest and hit E16 with his tail.

"Hey, Dad...I'm over here," said E16.

"Sorry, 16," replied M.

"It's okay," said 16 and she bit her Dad's tail.

"HEY!" said M.

"Oops," said 16. "It was just too tempting!" Harriet looked at her youngest and shook her head and smiled.

M went to the upper branch. Harriet finished feeding E15 and joined M. The two eaglets moved to the nest rails.

"After eating, do you know what a good thing to do is?" Harriet asked the two siblings.

E15 quickly answered, "Oh, I know! Bonk empty head over here like you're playing the drums?" E15 laughed at her own remark.

"I don't have an empty head! YOU have an empty head!"

"No, I don't!"

"Yes, you do!"

"Okay, ENOUGH!" demanded Harriet. Harriet dropped back down into the nest. "No, the best thing to do after you enjoy a good meal is to feak your beak AND preen yourselves."

Both eaglets whined, "Oh no, Mom!"

Harriet started to allopreen E15's feathers. "Okay, Mom. I'll do it," said E15, annoyed.

"Good, 15!" She then started on E16.

"Okay, okay... I can do it myself!" protested E16.

Harriet smiled and went back up to perch near M.

"Well you should be very proud of yourself and the kids," said M.

"Yes, I am!" Harriet replied. She smiled with pride. She was so pleased with the eaglets willingness to preen themselves. She started to preen herself. She looked down into the nest at her two angels. Her smile quickly disappeared. E15 and E16 were busy playing with nest material and teasing each other. She rolled her eyes and shook her head.

M saw the disappointment on her face. "Well you tried and it was a good first attempt."

"Yes, I know," she replied sadly. But when Harriet looked back down into the nest, she saw their two eaglets had worn themselves out. They were passed out exhausted near the nest rails as they cuddled each other. Harriet smiled and her heart melted as she gazed upon their two babies... their second clutch... their little Blessings.

Chapter 13 … Protecting Their Family And Territory

May seemed to start off as a peaceful month. Both Harriet and M15 were perched above the nest. Harriet woke up first. She stretched her wings and legs after a long restful night. M soon started to stir as he heard E15 and E16 as they woke up in the nest below.

"Good morning, little ones!" greeted Harriet.

"Morning Mama. Morning Dad," 15 and 16 replied.

"Morning kidlets," said M.

Harriet dropped down into the nest. M had brought a fish to the nest late the night before so Harriet fed the two siblings that fish. As soon as breakfast was over, Harriet went up to the attic and feaked her beak. She flew off and quickly returned with a pine bough, placed it the nest and went up to the outer branch. Both eaglets were standing and walking in the nest. They were getting bigger every day!

E15 enjoyed flapping her wings. "I'm a BIG eagle!" she cheered.

"You're a BIG pain in my..."

"SIXTEEN!" Harriet said abruptly. E16 stopped and just turned and walked to the nest rails... no bickering... just quiet.

M seemed agitated and flew off, but soon returned. He landed next to Harriet.

"Now don't go getting too upset, but there are two intruders on our power poles," said M.

Harriet leaned forward and her eyes narrowed as she zeroed in on the two intruders. "Who are they?" she asked.

"I don't know. I never saw them before. Harriet, don't let your blood pressure go through the roof over this. I'll take care of it."

"Oh no, this one is mine."

"Okay, but calm down first."

"Oh, I'll be calm and I'll make my point." And Harriet flew off toward the power poles.

"That's what I'm afraid of," said M as he watched her leave. M sighed. He knew that seeing these eagles infuriated Harriet.

E15 and E16 heard some of their parent's conversation. "Where's Mama going?" asked E16.

"She's just going to give directions to two eagles that are lost," M replied quickly. The two siblings looked at each other with concern. M watched closely, ready to fly off to the power poles if needed. In the distance, M could see the confrontation was about to escalate. "Oh Harriet, NO!" he said softly not to scare the kids.

"Get out of here!" Harriet screamed. "You don't belong here! This is OUR territory!"

"Yeah? And who are you? The Queen?" the one intruder disrespectfully asked.

"I'm not only the Queen, I'm your reality check."

Harriet chased the two eagles off of the poles. One of the intruders flew at Harriet, talons extended. They locked talons and at a fierce rate of speed they started to tumble in the sky.

"You can't tell us what to do!" the intruder yelled.

Mockingly, Harriet laughed, "You MUST be new here!"

Harriet's grasp on the intruder got tighter. They continued to spin toward the ground. The world around them swirled and became a blur. The intruder was getting scared as the ground was getting closer at an alarming rate. Harriet just continued to fearlessly stare into the intruder's eyes. Her eyes were blazing. As they were feet away from the ground the intruder struggled to get free from Harriet's grasp.

"Alright! Alright! We'll leave! LET GO!" he begged.

Inches from the ground, Harriet released the eagle. She quickly maneuvered her wings to gain height and she flew off victoriously.

M cheered loudly, "WOOHOO! That's MY female eagle!!! Yeah!"

E15 and E16 stood up at the nest rails and tried to see what their Father was cheering about. "What happened?" asked E15.

"Your awesome Mom just taught some eagle a very valuable lesson... Harriet style!"

E15 and E16 watched as Harriet flew toward the nest tree. "I'll be right back," she said.

The kids waved as she threw them each a kiss. Harriet flew across the street and perched on the Norfolk pine to regain her composure and to catch her breath. She soon flew back to the nest tree and landed next to M. They all cheered. She lifted her wing and "high winged" M15. They smiled at each other.

"That was some performance you put on," said M proudly.

"Ah, it was nothing. They needed to learn a lesson. Nothing like locking talons to get the point across."

"And you certainly got your point across! But you could have let me help, ya know."

"I know, but I needed to do this on my own. I haven't had a good skyfall like that in years!"

"Well, let's keep it that way."

"Oh, believe me I won't be rushing into anything like that again anytime soon. I am exhausted. I guess I'm not seven years old anymore," Harriet smiled.

E15 and E16 looked at each other. "Skyfall?" questioned E15.

"Locking talons?" asked E16.

They shrugged their shoulders and said, "ADULTS!"

"So, did you happen to bring back any food with you after your play date?" teased M with a smile.

"No, I was too busy goofing off." Harriet smiled too.

Harriet started preening. M could see she was pleased with herself and the outcome. Locking talons can be extremely dangerous. He was so proud of his Harriet! M watched her preen. They both noticed she had a few cuts on her feet. M looked at her as she looked at her wounds... the scars of battle for protecting their babies and territory.

"Are you sure you are okay?" asked M.

Harriet looked up and said, "Yep! I kicked his butt good!" She smiled a smile that made her look seven years old again... and it reflected in her spirit!

M looked at Harriet and said, "Come on!" And he flew off.

"Where are we going," Harriet asked as she followed him.

M climbed higher and higher in the sky. "I thought we should celebrate!"

"Oh, M! This is perfect! Thank you! What a fabulous idea! Soaring just rejuvenates the body, mind and soul."

They soared high above the nest tree as E15 and E16 watched from the nest rails.

"I'm going to do that someday soon!" said 15.

"Me too!" added 16.

"But I'll do it first!" claimed 15.

"But I'll do it better!" boasted 16.

"You will NOT!"

"Will too!"

"You can't even flap your wings yet!"

"Can to!" E16 stood up, tried to get steady on her feet and flapped her wings, which caused her to fall forward.

"See, I told you!"

"So, I'm younger, that's why!"

"Because you're a baby, that's why!"

"Am not!"

"Are too!"

"Am not! And I'm cuter!" E16 tilted her head and batted her eyes.

"No, you're not!"

"Oh yes I am!" She continued to pose.

Suddenly Harriet landed above the nest.

"You're a dork!" said E15.

"You're a dork!" said E16.

Harriet shook her head and rolled her eyes. "Oh, my goodness! Will the two of you please stop bickering! Your Father and I could hear both of you while we were soaring."

"E15 started it!"

"You started it!"

"Did not!"

"Did to!"

Harriet thought to herself that locking talons was less stressful than raising eaglets. "I don't care WHO started it. I want it stopped! NOW!"

"Yes, Mama," they both quietly replied. E15 pushed E16 and E16 pushed E15 back.

"Stop touching me," demanded E15.

"You stop touching me!" replied E16.

"I said STOP!" Harriet's voice seemed to echo through the pasture. The pasture animals all stopped in their tracks. No one made a sound or dared to move.

NutJob gulped as he stood still as a statue.

Waddles opened her eyes wide and asked, "How long do you think we have to stay still like this?"

The Commander laughed. "I don't think Miss Harriet was telling us to stop. I think she's disciplining her little ones."

"Ohhhh...." said all the animals in relief.

"Whew! That's good I was getting a cramp in my tail," said NutJob as he scurried on his way.

E15 and E16 moved to the nest rails and cuddled with each other. "There, that's better! Thank you!" said Harriet and she took a deep breath.

Now one month old, the two eaglet siblings continued to grow bigger every day. Both were walking better, sitting up better, preening better and flapping their wings better. Their days consisted of the usual eating, sleeping, watching, and growing... and doing things around the nest just like their parents did, sort of.

E16 found a stick and moved it around the nest, just like their Dad, except no one was getting hit with it. E15 found nest material and moved it around the nest just like their Mom and Dad. And just like their Mom and Dad, they had nest discussions. Each one had their idea of where the nest material or stick should go.

E15 moved the nest material to the side of the nest rail. E16 looked at the placement and picked up the nest material and moved it.

"No, it goes here!" said 16.

E15 picked up the nest material and moved it a few inches and said, "No, it doesn't. It goes here!"

E16 grabbed the nest material again and E15 tried to take it away from E16. A tug of war ensued until E16 let go causing E15 to lose her footing and landed on her tail feathers. E15 got up and moved the nest material to the middle of the nest. These were all playful times for the eaglets without them realizing it was all lessons being learned... and they learned well!

E16 flapped her wings and stepped onto the nest rails. E15 watched her sister and said, "Be careful, spaz."

"I know what I'm doing," replied E16.

"Well at least you know your name... Spaz!" E15 laughed.

E16 shrugged her shoulders, closed her eyes and took a deep breath as she enjoyed standing on the nest rails. She quietly whispered, "I don't care what she says."

The sun was hot and the nest was heating up. Without their parents to block the sun, they looked for some way to shield themselves from the sun's rays. E16 tried to get some relief under E15.

E15 frowned, shook her head and said, "What are you doing?"

"I'm trying to get under you for some shade."

E15 moved away from E16. "I am not your Mommy. So, get away from me." E15 walked away to the other side of the nest not knowing E16 was behind her wiggling her tail feathers, flapping her wings and making faces behind E15's back.

Just as E15 got to the nest rails, Jay the blue jay, landed on a branch above the nest. E15 watched closely.

"Hey, little eagle!" said Jay. E15 narrowed her eyes as she listened to the brightly colored bird. E16 walked over to get a better view of what was going on. "WHOA! Who's this? Your twin?"

"We don't look anything alike," announced E15.

"Yeah!" agreed E16. "I am much better looking!"

"Oh gross! You are not!"

"Am too!"

"Are not!"

Jay rolled his eyes and said' "Oh okay, I'm out of here. This sounds like a family issue so I better be going. You two can argue about it without me. I'm out of here." And Jay flew off.

"See, you scared him off," said E15.

"So, I don't care. Anyway, I don't think we're supposed to be talking to strangers."

"No, peanut head. We're not supposed to talk to humans," said E15.

"I don't have a peanut head. My head is perfectly sized for my body." E16 paused and added. "And you're mean!" E16 walked closer to the nest rails and cuddled next to her sister.

Next, Gladys the starling landed on another nest tree branch. "Well, aren't the two of you absolutely adorable!?" she gushed. The two siblings tilted their heads at the starling and blinked their eyes. Just in case E16 was right about not talking to strangers, neither eaglet spoke to the visiting starling. "Oh, you two are just so sweet and well-behaved… and shy." The two siblings smiled and looked at each other and quietly giggled. "Your parents must be so proud! Okay, I'm sorry for disturbing you. Go back to your nap, little ones!" And Gladys went to her nest nestled below theirs. E15 and E16 looked at each other.

"Who are all of these birds?" asked E16.

"I have no idea," replied E15.

Harriet soon arrived and landed on the branch above the nest.

"Mama, there were birds here and E15 was talking to them. I told her we're not allowed to talk to strangers."

"Tattletale!" complained E15. E16 grinned at her.

"No, it's okay to talk to most birds," said Harriet.

"Ha, ha! I told you!" said E15 smugly.

E16 stuck out her tongue at E15. "But we can't talk to humans, right?" 16 asked.

"That's right, 16," replied Harriet.

"HA! Who's the peanut head now?"

Harriet sighed, "No name calling!"

"E15 called me it first before," said 16 in her defense.

"I don't care! No name calling! So… who was here?" asked Harriet.

"Some bird that has a lot of blue on him and a pointy head that goes up and down," said E15.

"Ha, ha, ha… that's Jay. He's called a blue jay. He was sort of a friend to your brother, E9. You'll probably see a lot of Jay when you get older. Who else was here?"

"Some lady," E15 tried to recall something about the starling.

"She said I was adorable, sweet and well-behaved," E16 smiled.

"She said we both are," snapped E15.

"She meant it for only me. She was just being polite to include you," teased E16.

"That's Gladys Starling. She lives in a nest within our nest.

"That's allowed?" asked E15.

"Yes," Harriet laughed. "That's allowed. You know that beautiful singing we hear throughout the day?" The eaglets nodded their heads. "That's Gladys and her son, Jett. He was a good friend to E9. So, you two be nice to both Miss Gladys and Jett!"

"Yes, Mama," they both replied.

Harriet stayed above the nest and kept her eye on her two babies. E15 stood up and walked over to Stuffy. Like she saw her parents do at feeding time, E15 stood on the toy and started to pull on its fur. E15 tried so hard. She pulled on Stuffy's ears, nose and body.

E16 watched and asked, "You know that's not real, right?"

E15 ignored E16's question. Looking to outdo her sister, E16 walked over to a leftover fish and like her parents, she too stood on the fish and started to pull on it to get bites. E16 kept trying and as she did, she eventually got some bites of food. Not big bites, but they were still bites! It was a great attempt at such a young age.

That night everyone was getting ready for bed. The two eaglets were all tuckered out from a big day of growing, observing and doing. Harriet and M were on separate branches as they protected their eaglets.

But sometime after midnight, a great horned owl had flown into the pasture and had his sights on the eagle family and their nest tree. It is unknown if it was the same owl that was a problem earlier in the season or if it was a different one. It didn't matter either way. What mattered was it happened... again.

All sound asleep, suddenly M called out, "WHOA!" The silent flying owl hit into M15 and knocked him off of the nest tree branch. Harriet, E15 and E16 immediately woke up.

"M!" Harriet cried out.

M15 quickly returned to the nest tree. "I'm okay," M informed his family. "That annoying owl... or another one just like the other one... is back. I can't stand how they can fly so silently!"

Harriet flew off and landed in the snag tree. She called out into the night air, "You stay away from us! You leave our family and our home alone!" She returned to the nest tree.

"Mama? Daddy?" E15 and E16 were frightened.

"It's okay... we're both okay. You are both safe. Go back to sleep," said Harriet. The two siblings cuddled each other to keep each other safe.

Harriet looked at M and said, "He's gone for now, but this has got to stop." Harriet looked up at the sky and said, "Please Ozzie, watch over our little family."

Everyone woke up safe and sound in the nest tree and the day continued as usual... feedings, beakings, playing, watching, wingersizing... all of the usual. The kids still enjoyed watching their world over the nest rails.

E16 stood on the nest rails, spread her wings wide and flapped them. "See! I'm big too!"

"Yeah, you're big for a pip squeak!"

E16 ignored 15 and said, "Feel the breeze! Woohoo!" She closed her eyes and smiled and dreamed of days to come.

The evening came fast and Harriet flew to the pasture pond where she joined M. They both enjoyed some refreshing water.

"Wow, this has been some start to the month," commented Harriet.

"It sure has been," replied M.

"But we're strong," they both said at the same time. They looked at each other and smiled.

"What did you teach E7 and E8 that they used to cheer?"

"We're strong!" cheered M.

"Oh yes, now I remember... We're proud!" added Harriet confidently.

"We're eagles!" They both cheered and they held their heads high.

"We can do anything!" said M.

"Yes, we can!" Harriet agreed. They could hear E15 and E16 bickering in the nest. Harriet laughed. "AND... we're parents...!" They smiled and laughed. They knew this was the biggest job of any eagle. So, the loving parents both flew back to the nest tree to restore peace and tranquility. Even while their little ones bickered, Harriet and M15 just loved their E15 and E16.

Chapter 14 ... A Rainbow Of Love And Protection

E15 and E16 kept themselves busy on this special day. They rearranged some sticks and nest material. They stood high on the nest rails looking like big eagles. They stretched and flapped their developing wings to make them strong for the days soon to come. Of course, while E15 wingersized, E16 usually got hit by 15's impressive wings.

"Hey! Watch it!" exclaimed E16.

"Well don't sit in my way!" retorted E15.

"I was here first! Go flap your wings on the other side of the nest!"

"Well technically I WAS here first!" teased E15.

Of course, E15 didn't move, so E16 got up and searched the nest for some leftover snacks. She rummaged through the nest material and found only sticks and bones, but nothing to eat.

Suddenly, Harriet flew onto the nest tree. The two siblings quickly stood tall, side by side and cheered, "Happy Mother's Day, Mama!"

"Oh, my little angels! How sweet of both of you!"

The two eaglets smiled. Although they both pushed against each other as they stood shoulder to shoulder... they were always up to something... plotting.

E16 grabbed an intricate spine bone that she found while looking for a nestover. "Here, Mama! I got you this! I hope you like it! It is interesting and pretty... It has a lot of facets like a beautiful gem... just like jewelry and it reminded me of you! A GEM of a Mama!"

"Oh, 16! How adorable! Thank you, baby! I love it!" Harriet kissed E16 on the head.

E15's eyes opened wide and E16 grinned at her sibling.

"Mama's pet..." E15 mumbled.

"You're Daddy's favorite," snapped 16.

"Hey, hey, hey! What's all this nonsense talk about?" asked Harriet. Both eaglets sat silent. "We don't have favorites and we don't have pets."

"Dad does," E16 said quietly and sadly.

"What 16?" asked Harriet.

"Nothing," E16 said softly. But E16 quickly smiled and asked her Mother, "So do you like the bone that I found for you?"

"Yes, E16! I love it! And... I LOVE YOU!" Harriet and E16 hugged.

E15 swiftly looked around the nest and grabbed a clump of nest material. "I got you something too, Mama. And it reminds ME of you!" E15 smiled, proud of her gift.

Harriet and E16 both looked at the messy clump of nest material. They got closer and both said, "Yucky."

E15's smile turned into a frown. "You don't like it," she said disappointedly.

"You said this clump of... MESS material reminded you of Mama!" 16 said in a shocked voice.

"It does," replied 15. "It has grass and mud and feathers and pieces of fur on it. It is interesting and pretty like... like... what did you call it?"

"A gem?" E16 questioned.

"Yeah, that's it! Like a gem. So, it reminded me of you!"

Both Harriet and E16 stood in shock as they listened to E15's so called compliment. Harriet blinked her eyes as she tried to say something encouraging and positive about the gift... no matter how difficult it was to find the words.

"Well, thank you, 15! It is so..." Harriet paused and thought for a second as E15 listened intently. "I mean, it is so unique..." Harriet struggled as she spoke. "It is so... nice... that you look at this... this..." E15's smile got bigger as she anticipated her Mother's words. "And it reminds you of me... I mean that you... what I mean to say, 15, is thank you, sweetheart!" Harriet kissed the top of E15's head and E15 smiled and turned to look at E16.

Still in shock, E16 shook her head and said, "How are you Dad's favorite?" Harriet quickly responded, "Again, we don't have favorites!"

"You should now," E16 said under her breath.

Later that day, M flew in with food. He fed E15 first. "See, Daddy's favorite," E16 said sadly.

"Can you blame him?" teased E15.

E16 quickly grabbed the pelt that their Dad was feeding E15 from.

"No, not yet, 16," said M.

"Yeah," said 15 and she grabbed the pelt away from 16.

M took the pelt away from E15. "No, that goes for you, too, 15."

"Ha, ha!" said E16.

"Be nice, 16," demanded M.

"But…" and 16 quickly grabbed the pelt from her Father. Both M and E15 watched as little E16 swallowed the pelt. They watched in amazement. E16 smiled at her Dad and her sister and said, "BURP! Ahhhh! That was so good!" E16 smiled, turned and went to the nest rails to bask in all of her glory as her Dad and E15 stood there in disbelief.

The siblings were now six weeks old. They were getting bigger, stronger and smarter every day. Being E16 felt that E15 was their Dad's favorite, 16 had to work harder and learn faster than E15.

One day as M flew in with a fish, E16 quickly jumped up from the nest rails and rushed over to her Dad's catch. In a flash she grabbed the fish from M's grasp and covered the fish with a cloak of her wings. She mantled the food to hide it from view. An extremely important lesson for all eaglets to learn to survive in the wild.

"WOW, 16!" exclaimed M. "That is a very impressive mantle you have there! Who taught you that?"

"No one, Dad. I taught myself!" she said proudly.

"Very impressive!" said M as he smiled at his little girl.

E15 made a face and said. "I can do that too!"

"I'm sure you can, 15. I just haven't seen you do it."

E16 stood on the fish and she started to feed herself. M tried to take the fish from 16, but she was determined to show her Dad her abilities. Harriet flew to the nest and watched how focused E16 was. Harriet smiled with pride.

E16 was doing a good job, but she still wasn't ready to truly feed herself. Without making her little trooper feel bad, Harriet said, "That is wonderful, E16! We are so proud of you! But let your old Mom feed the two of you now. I have to have something to do." Harriet winked at her baby and E16 smiled and moved over so Harriet could feed them.

That evening, Harriet and M sat perched above the nest. They were both very impressed with E16's strong will and determination. Soon E15 would be doing the same, but right now she enjoyed being fed and catered to. But E16 showed her parents that she was learning to survive.

"Well, I think it's time," Harriet said loudly for the kids to hear her.

"Me too!" agreed M, also in a loud voice so the kids would hear him.

"E15 and E16… Your Dad and I feel the two of you are old enough to sleep in the nest tree by yourselves."

"You have been sleeping in the nest by yourselves for a while now," added M.

"So, we feel you are both ready for the next step of becoming big eagles and that is sleeping in the nest tree by yourselves. So... what do you think?" asked Harriet.

E15 and E16 looked at each other and shrugged their shoulders. They answered together, but their answer sounded more like a question than a decision. "Okay...?" they replied.

"That answer doesn't sound very convincing to me. Do you think you are ready to sleep in the nest tree without us?" Harriet asked again.

"I'm okay with it," said E15.

"Me too," said E16.

"Okay, good! We won't be far. So, there is no reason to be scared. If you need us just call out to us. We'll be right here! Goodnight my babies. I love you both. Sweet eagle dreams!"

"Goodnight, Mama! Goodnight, Dad!" the two siblings replied.

"Goodnight kids. I love you. See you in the morning," said M as he and Harriet flew off into the west pasture.

"WOW!" said E15. "We can do whatever we want!"

"YEAH!" agreed E16. She thought for a moment and asked, "Like what?"

They both sat in the nest and tried to think of what kind of mischief they could get into. And they sat... and they thought. And then just like big eagles, they preened and got ready for bed.

"Goodnight, 15," said E16.

"Goodnight, pip squeak," replied E15. And they fell asleep. Another milestone had been achieved and would continue until the next milestone. Which would come very soon.

On a rainy morning, the two eaglets waited for breakfast. While waiting they did typical eaglet behavior. They moved sticks, they preened, they wingersized and they did what most siblings do... they teased each other. While one was wingersizing the other would nibble at their sibling's wings. All in good fun.

They watched their world below and all around them. They saw their parent's friend, Gladys Starling and her little boy, Jett. The two starlings were perched on one of the nest tree branches and saw that the two eaglets were awake.

"Well good morning E15 and E16!" said Gladys. "This is my son, Jett."

"Hi Jett," said the two eagles. They stared at the little starling. They were surprised that he was so small.

"Hi guys! I was... well I always will be," Jett smiled, "...friends with your brother E9. You have the coolest brother in the entire world! We used to hang out together on that old snag tree in the pasture. If you two are anything like him, you'll be awesome! I hope we get to hang out when you two start flying!"

"Well we have to fly right now. Jett and I have choir practice this morning and we don't want to be late! You two have a good day and say hello to your parents for us. Oh, you two are just so cute! Come on, Jett."

"See ya!" said Jett as he and his Mom flew off the nest tree.

"He's so little!" said E15. "He's smaller than you!"

E16 ignored E15's comment. "He must be really nice if he was friends with E9. It seems like E9 had a lot of friends. I bet a lot of the pasture animals will compare us to him."

"I don't care what they do. I'm awesome!" boasted E15.

"Well I'm awesome, too," added 16.

"Why do you have to copy EVERYTHING I say... Oh! I know why... BECAUSE I'M SO AWESOME!" E15 laughed as she enjoyed her witty remark.

E16 rolled her eyes, "In your dreams!"

"No, in reality, pip squeak." E15 continued to laugh.

E16 shook her head. "Well I'm going to be me and everyone will like me too!"

E15 laughed, "Okay, you keep telling yourself that. They will know you as the eaglet related to E9 and E15."

E16 turned and said, "You'll see!" She lifted her head proudly and smiled as she stared out onto the pasture at all the animals.

While the two siblings "discussed" their future popularity, Harriet was out getting breakfast for them. It appeared the menu was going to consist of some roadkill that the vultures had located.

"Well I guess the kids would like that for breakfast." Harriet swooped down to the road and joined the vultures.

One of the vultures looked up from his meal and looked at Harriet as she landed. He thought and then realized who she was. "Harriet?" the vulture asked.

Harriet looked at the vulture uneasily. "Do I know you?" she asked.

95

"In a way. I know M15. I'm Vinny. Vinny the Vulture. I met up with E9 when he first soared."

"Oh yes!" Harriet smiled. "Vinny! How are you? M and E9 told me so much about you."

Vinny laughed. "All good, I hope."

Harriet smiled, "Yes, all good."

"I have to tell you, Harriet... your E9... he is some amazing eagle!" Harriet smiled as Vinny continued. "You and M should be very proud. You raised a gentleman, a warrior, a friend, just a majestic eagle. I am very honored that I got to know him and that I helped guide him when he started his new life. I get to see him every now and then. In fact, he was here a few months ago."

"Yes, he was here. And thank you! Our son is amazing! Thank you for being there for him!"

"My pleasure! Say listen, I'm sorry, I heard the news about your little eaglet..."

"E14... yes, thank you..." said Harriet quietly.

"But I see you have two other eaglets."

"Yes, we do! M and I had a second clutch."

"God Bless you guys. That's a lot of work."

Harriet laughed, "Yes. Yes, it is."

"So, what happens when these two grow up and leave? Do you and M take a season off or do you start a new season?"

Harriet stopped and thought. In a confused voice she answered, "Gee, Vinny... I never really thought of that. We could take a season off if we wanted to. But that isn't like us. But the kids won't be leaving until sometime around August. And we normally get the nest back in shape around October and start planning the next season." Harriet thought more. "Oh my... there's really no time to catch our breath."

"Oh, I'm sure the two of you will figure it out."

"Yes," Harriet said slowly, deep in thought. "Yes, we'll have to figure that out." Just then a truck's horn blared loudly. Harriet quickly got back in the moment as she saw all the trucks and cars speeding past them. "Hey! WATCH IT! Don't you see us getting food for our families?"

"People!" said Vinny. "They only think of themselves." And just as Vinny said that, they saw a car that was getting close to them. "Like this... what's this person doing? HEY!" Vinny yelled out.

Suddenly, Harriet and Vinny saw the vehicle's emergency flashers come on. Then the driver side window went down and they saw the arm of the driver come out. The woman waved the other motorists to go around her car to avoid Harriet and Vinny.

"Look at that!" said Harriet. "She's protecting us!"

"Well I'll be..." said Vinny. "That's a rarity if I ever saw one!"

"That's really very nice of her," said Harriet. "Well I better get back with the food. I have two hungry, GROWING eaglets to feed. Don't be a stranger. I'm sure M would love to get together and the two of you can tell some war stories."

Vinny laughed. "Oh yes we could. Maybe I'll catch up to him at the pasture pond someday. You take care of yourself and those two kids of yours."

"Thank you, Vinny. We will. See you around!"

"When your two rascals start soaring, you know I'll meet up with them and watch out for them."

"We appreciate that! Thank you! Be safe!" But just before Harriet flew off with breakfast in her mighty talons, she looked at the woman in the car and nodded her head to thank her. Harriet then turned and flew off to their nest tree. When she landed in the nest, she called out, "Yummy for your tummy!"

"Yay, Mama!" E15 and E16 cheered. Harriet fed the eaglets the food.

Soon M arrived with more of the same menu. "Looks like someone had the same idea," M laughed.

Harriet smiled. "Did you get to see Vinny?"

"Yes, I did. Hey, did you see that lady in the car protecting us?"

"Yes, I did!" Harriet nudged M and said, "See... I told you they aren't all bad."

"Yeah, yeah, yeah," said M. "Well, I'm going to go back for thirds while there is still some left. There's plenty there so we might as well stock up. Although these two little piglets..."

"DAD!" E15 and E16 objected with food in their mouths.

"Oh, I'm sorry, these two little EAGLETS don't let anything sit in the pantry," M teased.

"Okay, but be careful," said Harriet. "That road is dangerous. If that woman isn't there, don't get any."

"Okay, I'll be careful," and M flew off.

The two siblings took a few seconds away from eating and called out in unison, "Be careful, Dad!"

While he flew off the nest, M turned his head so the kids could hear him say, "I will." He then added, "Hey, look at the rainbow in the sky!" And he flew off.

Harriet, E15 and E16 all stopped and looked up at the sky.

"WOW!" said E15.

"That's cool!" said E16.

"That's Ozzie!" said Harriet as she smiled. "Thank you, Ozzie, for watching over us. I know you sent that lady to protect us today. Kiss E3, E5 and E14 for us. We love all of you."

"Who's Ozzie?" asked E16.

Harriet thought and smiled. She tilted her head and said, "Someone very loved and very magical. He watches over all of us. So, if you ever feel someone holding you and protecting you when no one else is around and you suddenly feel safe... that's Ozzie. Ozzie sends us a rainbow to say hello and to let us know he is near."

"WOW! COOL!" said E15.

"I'm going to be like Ozzie!" said E16.

"No, you're not!" whined E15.

"Yes, I am! I'm going to be like Ozzie and E9!" E16 smiled the biggest smile ever.

"No, you're not. I am!" announced E15.

"Now who's copying who?" asked E16. She knew she got E15 back for all the times 15 accused her of copying.

"You're a dweeb!" moaned E15.

"I don't care what you call me because I'm awesome like E9 and Ozzie and they wouldn't be mean. They would be sweet and adorable like me!" declared E16. E15 rolled her eyes.

They both quieted down and Harriet smiled. She softly said as she looked at the beautiful rainbow, "Yes, E16, both E9 and Ozzie are awesome. And you have their spirit, their fight and their love."

Chapter 15 ... Sibling Rivalry

Time was moving quickly. The siblings were getting bigger and stronger. Their appearance changed and their feathers had come in nice and dark. They were no longer babies. They watched their parents' actions... preening, eating, alerting. All lessons, valuable lessons. Even when they rested at the nest rails, they would look at the intricate placement of the sticks. They studied the importance of a strong foundation. They also studied the strong foundation of their parents' relationship and their love and devotion for their eaglets. It seemed so simple and matter of fact, but all of these lessons would be the basics of survival for when their new lives started. And their new lives were getting closer and closer to becoming a reality every day.

Typical of siblings, E15 and E16 were determined to prove they each had the strength, drive and spirit of true majestic eagles. So just as they started off in life together battling and competing with each other, they continued in eaglet competition. Each had their own strengths. E15 took pride in her impressive wings as they got stronger. E16 seemed to have complete control of the art of mantling. They both watched each other's attempt at self-feeding. Harriet and M continued to bring food to the nest and they would let the kids try to feed themselves. But Harriet and M also kept a watchful eye on the eaglets to know what they still needed to learn.

One day, while E15 watched E16 play with a stick, M flew to the nest with a fish. E16 immediately ran over to her Dad and grabbed the fish and mantled it, squeeing, "It's mine! It's MINE!"

M took the fish away from 16 and said, "Nice mantle 16, but let me feed the two of you."

E15 rushed over and said, "Yeah, pip squeak, wait your turn!"

E16 moved to the nest rails and waited as their Dad fed E15. Her eyes narrowed as she said, "NO! It is MINE!" and E16 stole the fish from her Dad. She moved it across the nest and M15 flew to the branch above.

"Hey! That's not yours! It's MINE!" demanded E15 as she quickly took the fish away from E16.

E16 had made a costly mistake by not holding the fish down with her talons which allowed E15 to easily take it away from her. E15 started to eat the fish. And typical of children, E15 was quickly distracted when a feather floated by the nest. So E16 quickly stole the unprotected fish away from E15.

"HA!" said 16.

"What the..." said E15 and she stole the fish back. She brought the fish to the center of the nest and walked in a circle with it.

E16 watched and asked, "What are you doing?" And, with great eye/beak coordination E16 grabbed the fish away from E15 as E15 passed in front of her. E16 mantled the fish. She thought this made her the winner, but E15 managed to get her beak close to the fish and stole it again. Infuriated, E16 bit the fish and held it in her beak. E15 and E16 both had the fish in their mouths. Both E15 and E16 pulled on the fish. Their eyes were locked on each other. The tug of war began as they circled around the center of the nest. E15 tugged hard on the fish just as E16 released it. E15 stumbled backward for a moment.

"Oops!" laughed E16.

"Mmmmm... yummy!" said E15 as she antagonized E16 as she ate.

E16 was determined and didn't give up. She slowly climbed onto the nest rails and as fast as lightning, she stole the fish away from E15. This went on and on and back and forth for quite some time and all under the watchful eye of their Dad.

Harriet joined M15 on the branch. "Have I missed anything?" asked Harriet.

M laughed. "I wish I had some popcorn to go along with the show these two warriors are putting on. I don't know if I should be exhausted or hungry from watching these two!" He laughed again.

Harriet smiled and asked, "Why? What's going on?"

"I brought in a fish and before I knew it, 16 was all over it and stole it from me. So, I came up here to wait and see. This fish has gone back and forth between the two of them for around fifteen minutes. First it looked like 15 was dancing with it in a circle. Then 16 climbed the nest rails to get it back. But back and forth the entire time. There was even a showdown with a tug of war. These two are fierce!"

"But are they eating any of it?"

Again, M laughed, "I have no idea!" He pointed and added "I guess they have been eating it because now all I see left is the fish tail."

Harriet's eyes opened wide and her mouth could taste the delicacy just by looking at it. "I can end it right here, you know, and solve any problem of who should eat it," said Harriet as she smiled.

E15 looked at E16 with the prized fish tail in her talons. "NO!" E16 whispered. Her eyes grew large.

"Ha, ha, ha! Yes, pip squeak, the fish tail! And it is ALL mine!" taunted E15. She smiled a devilish grin. E16's eyes saddened and she gulped as her mouth watered. But the feather floated by again and it caught E15's attention and E16 slowly made her way closer to E15 and snatched the fish tail away from her. E16 mantled the tail, lifted her head and with a victorious grin she swallowed the fish tail. "NOOOO!" cried E15.

"Burp!" replied E16.

M quietly laughed. "See? They are a comedy act! All that for the fish tail. Now they'll need a nap. Ah, youth."

"Sure brings me back to my youth," smiled Harriet. "It's so much nicer now to be able to get your own food and eat it without having to battle a sibling over it. And they are on their way. They just need more practice."

Both eaglets were now full and tired. The two siblings rested in the nest on Stuffy. E16 found a small stick, grabbed it and placed it on E15's back. Annoyed, E15 moved the stick away.

"No! I like it there," said E16 as she moved the stick onto E15's back again. They stared each other down. But they were too tired to argue over it. E16 stretched out her leg so that her foot was next to E15's head. At first E15 was going to complain, but then she realized she could use a pillow and she rested her head on E16's foot.

Harriet and M smiled and shook their heads. "Kids!" said M as he chuckled.

"Well you were certainly right. Watching these two made me hungry!" and Harriet flew off.

"Wait for me!" said M as he chased after Harriet. "I'm hungry too!"

E15 and E16 woke up and watched their parents as they flew from the nest tree. Just before the two siblings could go back to their nap, Gladys and Jett both landed on a nest tree branch.

"Hello, E15! Hello E16!" chirped Gladys.

"Hi!" said Jett.

"Hi..." replied the two eaglets in shy voices.

"Ready, Jett?

"Ready, Mom!" The two starlings started flapping their wings and then started to sing. The two eaglets got up and moved closer to the two singers. They stood side by side on the nest rails as the two starlings started to sing.

"Your feathers unfurl, oh what a girl. A voice that's piercing but fine. You're 15, you're beautiful and you're mine. You're all poop shoots and squees. You do as you please. Your talons are used when you dine. You're 16, you're beautiful and you're mine." E15 and E16 smiled and swayed to the music. The song came to an end as Gladys Starling and Jett finished with, "We love you and you're beautiful and you're mine... all mine... all mine!"

E15 and E16 flapped their wings and cheered, "BRAVO! BRAVO!"

"Thank you!" said the two starlings as they both took a bow.

"We have to go now," added Gladys. "Hope you enjoyed the show! Have fun!" and they flew off.

"Bye!" said E15 and E16 as they waved to their friends.

"My feathers unfurl!" boasted 15.

"And I do as I please," bragged E16.

"Yeah, but you're all poop shoots and squees," 15 laughed.

"And your voice is piercing," mocked E16.

"But fine," smiled E15.

The teasing stopped and the two eaglets kept themselves entertained in the nest until it was time to get ready for bed. Both Harriet and M returned.

"Goodnight, Mama! Goodnight, Dad!" they both called out.

"Goodnight, sweethearts. We love you both," said Harriet.

"Sleep well," said M.

E15 and E16 cuddled together. They started humming the song Gladys and Jett sang about them. Harriet heard the humming, but was unsure of where it was coming from. It sounded like it was coming from the nest so they both leaned forward to listen. They looked at each other.

"Are they humming?" asked Harriet.

"I think they are," replied M. "Catchy tune," M smiled.

"You haven't sung with E16 in a while."

M held his head down and said, "I know."

"Because of 14?" Harriet asked gently.

Quickly M answered, "Because when she leaves, she'll not only be out of our lives, but she'll take her voice and her songs with her. Now I don't want to talk about it. Let's go to sleep, okay? Goodnight." M kissed Harriet and went to sleep.

Sadly, Harriet just sighed and then looked down into the nest at their two babies. She loved them and M so much. She stared off into the night.

The morning was a busy one with food deliveries and the two eaglets fighting over the fish tails. Harriet and M left the nest and stayed away from the constant food time competition.

But early that afternoon, Harriet had returned to the nest tree. E15 was restless. She started flapping her wings and in a blink of an eye, she was out of the nest and on a branch. Not a high branch and not a flight to the branch, but she was officially out of the nest and had officially branched!

"I did it! Woohoo! Look at me! I DID IT!" E15 cheered.

Harriet looked at E15 while she sat perched above the nest. "Congratulations, E15! That was wonderful! You're becoming a BIG eagle now! Just be careful and mindful of your movements. You're not ready to fly yet."

"Thank you, Mama! I know. I'll be careful."

"Woohoo!" cheered E16. "Yeah, that's great! See ya around! Don't forget to write! Don't let the pine tree hit you in the..."

"Sixteen!" Harriet said sternly. "Don't you want to congratulate your sister on her branching?"

"Ummm? I guess?" E16 thought and then said, "Congratulations on branching and it was nice knowing you!" E16 smiled and flapped across the nest in anticipated celebration.

"I'm not going anywhere. I only branched, airhead."

"Oh," E16 said disappointedly.

Jett flew by the nest tree and cheered, "Congratulations, E15! You almost look like E9 up there!"

E15 held her head high and proudly sighed, "I look like E9!" E16 made a sour face and rested by the nest rails.

E15 enjoyed her new feeling of freedom... even though it wasn't very far from the nest. She was only fifty-five days old. The youngest of Harriet's offspring to branch.

That night Harriet and M whispered as the eaglets fell asleep in the nest below.

"That was very impressive today. Only fifty-five days old and already branching! That's MY namesake!"

"Well remember she still has to build up more confidence before going any further."

"I know, I know. But you have to admit that it is very impressive," M said proudly.

"I wish 16 would wingersize more. I know she has been more aggressive and she has a remarkable mantle…"

"Yes, she does," said M. He paused and added, "You have a soft spot for her."

"No, I don't! I treat them exactly the same! Unlike you!"

"What are you talking about?" questioned M.

"Oh, please! You just boasted, 'That's MY namesake!' Like you aren't partial to 15…"

"I am not!"

"Right," Harriet said annoyed. "Now, shush, they'll hear us." Harriet knew that M knew she was right. She knew it all was because of his heartbreak over E14. She knew that E16 reminded him of E14 so much. But it wasn't 16's fault. Why couldn't he get beyond this?

E15 didn't go back onto any of the branches right away, but eventually she did while E16 wingersized. Now when food arrived, 16 immediately grabbed it and mantled. E15 tried to steal it, but E16 was determined.

"Get away!" demanded 16 and she pushed her sister away with her wing.

"I want some," said 15.

"I don't care what you want. It's mine!"

"Come on… I'd give you some if I had food and you didn't."

"You're a liar! You just lied! You would never give me any food if you had some and I didn't!" E16 pushed E15 away again.

"Sure I would!"

"Stop lying! And get away from me!" E16 continued to push E15 away.

"But I'm really hungry…"

E16 ate and looked up at E15. E16 finally gave into E15's pity act. "Okay, you can have a bite."

"Thanks!" and E15 took what was left of the food.

"HEY! I didn't say you could have all of it!" yelled E16.

"Oops! I guess… I LIED!" E15 laughed. E15 finished the food and went to her branch. She looked up and saw their Mother above them in an amazing pose… a heraldic pose… a breathtaking, majestic eagle pose. "WOW!" E15 quietly said in awe. "That is awesome!" E15 studied her Mom's position and how she held her wings open. E15 then opened her wings and imitated her Mother and she too looked majestic.

"Oh, E15! You look magnificent!" said Harriet, her head held high. "I am so proud of you! You are advancing so quickly and you look so majestic! A TRUE big eagle!"

"Thank you, Mama," replied E15. She felt the wind all around her and although she hadn't fledged yet, her heart soared with her Mother's words.

E16 watched and heard everything. She turned away from her sister. This was another important and hard lesson. She had lost her food to E15 and now she felt as if her Mother wasn't proud of her because she hadn't branched and wasn't majestic like her sister. E16 sat on the nest rails and sadly looked out onto the pasture. She felt a breeze flutter by her face and heard a comforting whisper in the wind, "Don't be sad, E16. I am with you always. I watch over you and protect you. Your day is coming soon! You will be a majestic eagle! You are so loved!"

"Huh?" E16 turned around and looked to see where the voice came from. "Who said that?" she asked quietly so E15 wouldn't hear her. A tiny light gray feather floated past her beak and then swiftly beyond the nest tree. E16 had no idea who spoke to her or where the feather came from, but she did know that the voice brought her comfort and confidence. She smiled as she watched the feather happily float out of sight.

Chapter 16 ... Milestones

*E*15 and E16 were growing up so quickly. The weeks seemed to fly by. Harriet and M recognized that the two eaglets still needed to perfect how to grab, mantle and protect their food as it was brought to the nest. And as time went by, they got better and aggression was more intense. So much so that E16's beak had a small tear, nothing serious, but a battle scar from sibling nest rivalry. At feeding time when food arrived, E16 was quick to grab it and display a magnificent mantle. E15 learned how to go for the steal from behind E16. All lessons that needed to be learned. Even though food deliveries appeared to look treacherous, the two siblings were friends afterward and would cuddle together. That is when E16 wasn't wingersizing or E15 wasn't on the veranda. Harriet and M watched E15 and E16 very carefully and noted each eaglets' strengths and weaknesses. They saw that so far E15 had accomplished very much. They knew from day one that she was very aggressive when it came to food. They also knew she was the youngest of Harriet's children to branch at only fifty-five days old. And now she was venturing out onto more advanced branches and going further out on them.

"Remember when E15 went to the spike for the first time?" asked Harriet.

M smiled and chuckled. "She looked like a bull in a bullfight. She leaned forward and ran toward it, but knew she wasn't quite in the right spot."

Harriet giggled. "She backed up and tried again."

"And like a bull, I thought she was going to shuffle her talons in the nest as she zeroed in on the spike and charged at it and tada! On the spike!" They both smiled.

They saw that E16 was getting very good at wingersizing and was getting great lift. Her mantle display was beautiful. She was slowly getting aggressive at food time and when E15 wouldn't allow her to get the food, she was very, very creative in getting the steal. Harriet and M were aware of the fact that just because E15 branched very early that didn't have any reflection on E16. She would branch when she was good and ready. E16 aggressively came out of her shell swinging, but slowly. Slow and steady. So, in time she would branch when she was ready.

E15 went from the nest to the veranda to the spike and back and forth.

"Woohoo!" cheered E15. She looked at her sister and said, "HA!"

E16 looked at E15 and shrugged her shoulders. "So big deal! Mama and Dad do that all the time."

"So that means I'm a big eagle like them... not a baby like you!"

"I'm not a baby! I just know that if I stay in the nest..." 16 caught herself and suddenly went silent.

"If you stay in the nest what?" asked E15.

"Nothing..."

"No, you just said that you know if you stay in the nest you know something."

"Nope! I don't know anything!" E16 smiled.

"Well you're right about that!" jeered E15.

E16 couldn't let her secret out of how she knew she would get more food when it was delivered. She knew if she was the only one in the nest, she would always be the first to get the food. But Harriet and M knew exactly what she was doing and they knew they would have to entice her to want to branch. They saw that E16 was very smart. They also knew she needed food and she needed to eventually branch.

E16 enjoyed sitting on the nest rails while she watched the pasture below. She especially enjoyed watching the horses. While doing so she usually sang a made-up song.

"I'm gonna fly! I'm an eagle and I'll see what I can see! I'm gonna fly! I'm an eagle. I'm majestic and I'm free!" she sang.

"You have to branch before you can fly, featherbrain. And stop singing! You can't sing!" complained E15.

"I can too! You're just jealous!"

"Jealous? Jealous of what? You sound like talons on a chalkboard!"

E16 answered with another made up song. "J is for you are juvenile. E is for you are evil. A is for you are awful. L is for you are lethal. O is for you are offensive. U is for you are uncouth. S is for you are spiteful... put it all together and you are JEALOUS! Jealous! E15 is jealous!"

E15 rolled her eyes. "You are such a dork!"

"You're jealous! And that's why you gave my beak a boo-boo because you are also jealous that I'm so beautiful. But there is nothing you can do that can take away my beauty because my beauty comes from within... and you know what that does to you?" E16 sang the answer. "It makes you jealous!" She wingersized all around the nest happy with herself.

E15 shook her head and flapped her wings and went to the veranda. "You're exhausting..."

But while E16 went back to the nest rails and continued to sing to the horses below... or whoever would listen to her... E15 was eyeing the attic branch.

E16 looked at her sister. Her eyes got big and she said, "I wouldn't if I were you!"

"Well then I will because I'm not you!" And as if she had done it all of her life, E15 went up to the attic branch. "YES! Woohoo!" she cheered.

"You're gonna get in trouble. That's Mama's and Dad's branch."

"We're supposed to go to the branches, you knot head. Why are you so afraid? I'm not going to call you E16 anymore. I'm going to call you C16 for CHICKEN 16." E15 started clucking. E16 didn't respond and went back to watching the horses below.

The wind started to pick up and the sky had gotten ominous. "You better get down before you get blown away," warned E16.

E15 figured out how to turn around and went toward the veranda. She hovered over the branch, but it started to rain and just like a big eagle she easily directed herself to the nest instead.

No matter how much they bickered, E15 and E16 loved each other. And as the storm rolled in the two siblings cuddled for comfort and protection.

The coming days continued to be extremely hot, humid and very wet. Harriet and M continued to bring food to the nest, although some days were more bountiful than others.

One morning, while Harriet was perched on the attic branch, she carefully watched Brenda, the cormorant at the pond. E15 and E16 were busy starting their day with their usual agendas. E15 flapped her wings and went to the veranda, the spike, the porch and the nest. E16 wingersized and hopped around the nest while she searched for nestovers to eat. She moved sticks in the nest and she squeed the whole time.

Harriet remained focused on Brenda. Both E15 and E16 stopped what they were doing and they watched their Mother as she flew off to the pond.

Brenda saw Harriet flying right toward her. "OH NO!" Brenda cried as she dropped the fish and rushed back into the pond.

"Thanks Brenda! The kids have really worn us out. So, I really appreciate the fish." Harriet started to eat.

"Sure Harriet, I understand." Brenda was hungry herself, but she knew she could easily catch another fish.

Harriet flew to the snag and continued to eat. She could hear the cries from the nest for breakfast. Harriet flew to the nest tree. E16 quickly grabbed the fish, but Harriet didn't let go of it and the two of them had a tug-of-war over the fish. E16 got the fish away from Harriet, but quickly lost it to E15. Disappointed, Harriet went to the attic and watched. E15 warned E16 every time she tried to steal the fish. And every time E15 looked away, Harriet would quietly mutter, "Now 16, NOW!" E16 was determined and made slow moves to get the fish back. E16 pushed E15 and then backed into her. Then suddenly E16 stole the fish! Shocked, E15 tried to get the fish back, but E16 mantled her beautiful cloak-like wings to protect the food. E16 danced and squeed around the nest with her prize. Harriet smiled.

"Whatever," E15 said in a disappointed voice and she went to the veranda.

Throughout the day the two siblings went back to their usual routines. E15 went from branch to branch and E16 looked for snacks to eat. That's when it happened. E16 found the shell of the armored catfish. She put her beak and head into the shell searching for a tidbit to eat. E16 stood up.

E15 looked at E16 and laughed out loud. "Look at you! What a knot head! No wait...what a fish head!"

E15 could hear E16's muffled response. "I meant to do this!" E16 frantically shook her head and tried to get herself freed. "I'm making a fashion statement!" She tried hard to get free of the fish helmet. She shook her head again and it came off. She turned and looked at E15 and gave a defiant smile. "So there!"

"So there what? You know, maybe I bonked you too much when you were little because there has to be something wrong with you."

"Nope, I'm perfect the way I am! So, don't think you can take any of the credit!"

E15 sighed and shook her head.

The following day was like any other. The eaglets spent the morning and afternoon doing their usual routines... after all it is said that practice makes perfect. They both flapped their wings for hours and hours. E15 became more confident on going from branch to branch. And E16 took advantage of E15 not being in the nest during food delivery and her constant search for something to nibble on... all while she squeed.

"Do you ever stop talking?" asked E15 as she shook her head.

111

Suddenly, M flew to the nest with food. Again, E16 had positioned herself perfectly in the nest to grab the food and mantle. E15 jumped down into the nest and attempted to steal the food. E16 continued to mantle and protected her food. But E15 made a quick move and reached under E16 and grabbed at what she thought was the food and moved across the nest.

E16 looked over her shoulder while she ate. "Ha, ha," she laughed. "Enjoy your meal!"

E15 looked down and saw that she had grabbed Stuffy instead of the food. Some lessons are not just hard, but humbling. But E15 got over it quickly and continued to practice on the branches throughout the day which made her stronger and more confident. And all under the watchful eyes of her Mom.

But later in the day, E15 moved to another branch, an upper, outer branch. She looked around, but she wasn't sure if she felt at ease on the branch. She decided to go back to the nest. And that was when it happened.

E16's eyes opened wide in surprise as she and Harriet both gasped. E15 had missed the nest and landed on a branch below the nest.

"Uh-oh, that wasn't supposed to happen," E15 sighed.

"MOM!" cried E16.

"Are you alright, 15?" Harriet quickly asked.

"I'm fine!" said E15.

Harriet flew off to find M.

E16 started squeeing and cried, "E15! E15, speak to me! Are you okay? Can you hear me?"

"Yes, 16. I only missed the nest. I didn't leave the state. Calm down!"

"Well excuse me for being worried about you!" E16 turned away from where she could see E15.

"I'm sorry. I know you're only being nice and you are concerned about me."

E16 was shocked by E15's answer. "OH NO! Did you hit your head?"

"No, I didn't hit my head! Why would you ask something like that?"

"Because you are being nice and you said you were sorry."

Suddenly, M15 flew into the nest with a fish to try to entice E15 back to the nest, but instead E16 grabbed and mantled it. She squeed while she ate and M flew off.

"I can't understand what you're saying," said E15. E16 continued to eat and squee. "I still can't understand what you're saying! WAIT! Are you eating?" E15 asked in disbelief. E16 couldn't answer because her mouth was so full. "Oh yeah, you're worried about me alright, but not worried enough to lose your appetite."

"I stress eat," said E16 in between bites. "Besides, I don't want to upset Dad being he went through all the trouble of getting this great, BIG, delicious fish!" She continued to eat. "And I don't want it to go to waste."

E15 rolled her eyes. She looked down at the horses below as they walked in the pasture and then she looked up at the nest that was so close, yet so far away. E15 flapped her wings and moved around to see how she could get back to the nest. She went to another branch, a thinner, bouncy branch. She flapped her wings. "Uh-oh," as she saw a piece of the branch fall to the ground. "Oh no," another piece fell. E15 looked around to find a safer branch, but as she did the branch broke beneath her.

E15 heard someone yell, "JUMP!" She quickly flapped her wings and headed toward the nest tree trunk. She grabbed onto the hanging moss, but it slipped through her talons. She remained calm even though her heart was racing. She quickly and safely landed at the base of the tree. The grass was high and she could hardly be seen.

"E15! E15! Oh E15... I'm sorry I ate all of the fish! Please E15, oh please! God... please let her be alright! Please, I promise if she's okay..."

"If I'm okay what?" E15 called out.

"Who said that?" E16 quickly looked left and right.

"Who do you think brainiac?"

"E15? Is that you? Where are you?"

"I'm on the ground at the bottom of the tree."

"Are you okay?"

"Yes, I'm fine. Who knows what would have happened if you didn't tell me to jump?"

"I didn't tell you to jump."

"Sure you did when the branch started to break you yelled, JUMP!"

"As much as I would love to take the credit for saving your life, it wasn't me."

"So who?" Just then a tiny gray feather went past E15. She tilted her head and watched it float out of sight.

"So, what's it like down there?"

"Huh? Oh... It looks really different down here than how it looks from up there."

E16 tried to see where her sister was. E15 walked away from the tree. "I see you!" E16 flapped her wings and smiled.

E15 looked up and flapped her wings and smiled back at 16. She tasted some of the grass and weeds that surrounded her. "Definitely not eagle food and I'm an eagle, not a rabbit!" There was just so much to see and E15 was eager to see it all. And just like that she pushed off with the strong legs she developed in the nest. She flapped her wings and from the ground E15 flew! That was when it actually hit her! "I fledged! WOOHOO!" she called out to the world. It might have been an accidental fledge, but it still was a fledge.

"Hey! You're going the wrong way!" E16 cried. "Come back!"

E15 landed by the driveway fence and tried to take in all of her new surroundings. The horses that she had seen so many times from the nest tree walked toward her.

The big horse, the Commander, walked up to E15 and said, "Hey there young lady! I'm..."

But E15 was startled by the horse's size and said, "Whoa!" and she immediately flew off toward the pasture pond. She tried to land in the oak tree, but she didn't quite make the landing. But that was okay. E15 quickly made the adjustment and landed on the grass instead. This grass was different from the grass she landed in by the nest tree. This grass had been mowed and it felt good around her. She looked around this new area and said, "This is the pond with all the fish!" E15 said with joy. So E15 laid down in the grass and waited. She hoped either her Mom or Dad would show up or one of the fish would jump out of the pond so she could eat. After all she was starving. Suddenly, she could hear the frantic squees of E16 in the nest. E15 stood up and saw her Dad in the nest tree.

"And then she missed the nest and ended up on a branch down below," explained E16 to her Dad. "And then the branch broke and E15 grabbed the moss thinking she was Tarzan... but we all know she isn't... so she slid to the ground. And then she flew away. Make her come back, Dad. Please make her come back!" E16 pleaded.

"She'll be back, 16. Don't worry. Now... did you see where she finally landed?"

"I lost sight of her when she flew away from the horses. She might have gone by the pond."

"Okay, we'll wait a little bit and see if she comes to us first and if not, I'll go check."

E15 decided it was going to get dark soon so she knew she had to get off of the ground. With the grace of a seasoned eagle, E15 flew over the pond and toward the nest tree.

"There she is!" cheered E16. E15 flew past the nest tree and landed in the front pine. It was obvious that E15 was not going home this night. "No! Where is she going? Is she okay?"

M15 tried to calm E16 down. "Okay, okay. She's fine. That's what she is supposed to do. And that's what you'll be doing soon too."

"I don't know..." E16 said reluctantly.

"You will. You'll see. You won't be able to stop yourself. Here..." M fed E16 some comfort fish and she calmed down. E16 took full advantage of being the only eaglet in the nest.

E15 looked around the front pines. She landed on a sturdy branch. "I don't like those bouncy branches." She looked at the nest and saw E16 eating again. E15's stomach growled from hunger. She sadly looked down at the branch and then back up at the nest. She actually started to miss E16. The wind started to pick up and the weather started to change. E15's sadness turned to worry. She felt alone... and scared.

"Okay, 16. You are a big girl, so you're in charge of the nest tonight."

"So E15 isn't coming home tonight?" E16 sadly asked her Dad.

"Not tonight, 16. Not tonight." M kissed 16 on the head. "Sweet dreams, 16. I love you."

"I love you too, Dad."

"You'll see... everything will be just fine tomorrow. I promise."

E16 nodded and tried to smile. "Goodnight, Dad."

M15 flew to a tree in the front pine near the tree E15 was on. "Mind if I sleep here tonight?"

E15 smiled, "DAD! No, I don't mind at all!" E15 was so happy to see her Father.

M15 smiled back at his daughter. "I'm so proud of you, E15! You did great today!"

"I did?"

"You certainly did! You remained calm and applied the lessons you learned."

"I just hope I can get back to the nest tomorrow."

"Of course you will! You'll see!" M15 paused and said, "I have faith in you."

E15's heart started to beat faster with pride. "Thank you, Dad!"

"Now get some sleep. You have a big day ahead of you tomorrow."

"Yes, sir!" E15 said proudly. "And Dad... thank you... for everything."

"I love you, E15."

"I love you too, Dad."

E16 got settled in on the nest. She could barely see her Father and E15 in the front pine. She softly called out, "Goodnight E15. Be careful." She grabbed Stuffy and held him tight as she tried to fall asleep.

Although it seemed like an eternity, morning arrived and M15 brought a fish to the nest to try again to entice E15 to get back home. E16 grabbed the fish and ate. Harriet was in the attic and dropped down into the nest to give E16 incentive to be aggressive around food. Lessons continued. Even though one eaglet was learning a new lesson didn't mean the other eaglet had the day off. Harriet grabbed the fish and she and E16 had a tug-of-war with it. "Come on, 16! Work for it! Just because E15 isn't in the nest doesn't mean that you can take your time eating the food." E16 tried to be aggressive with Harriet, but she didn't do as well as Harriet wanted her to. Harriet went back to the attic. As soon as E16 finished eating. She held her head up high and suddenly branched to the veranda. Harriet's eyes opened wide. "Yes, 16! Yes! I'm so proud of you! Both you and 15 have achieved important milestones."

"Thanks, Mama!" replied 16. She looked over at the front pine where E15 sat perched by herself. "Don't worry, E15! I'll save you!" she cried out.

"You don't have to save me. I'm fine! Just save me some food, piglet."

"I'm not a piglet!"

"How many fish have you eaten between yesterday and today?"

"I'm a growing eagle!" E16 answered with a little sass in her voice.

"Yeah, you're growing alright," E15 smiled. "You're a piglet. And when you finally fledge, we'll know exactly what they mean when they say, when pigs fly!" E15 laughed.

"Ha, ha!" said E16 unimpressed with E15's wit. Instead E16 showed great balance on the veranda as she flapped her wings and of course... as she talked... and talked. E15 was very hungry and she knew she had to make an attempt to fly to the nest if she wanted to eat. She found a spike branch on the tree she was in and hopped onto it. She flapped her wings to build up her confidence.

E16 hopped down into the nest. M returned to the nest with a celebratory fish. "Congratulations, E16! I am so proud of you!"

E16 mantled the fish and started eating it. She managed a muffled, "Thank you, Dad," with a mouth full of food. This time she ate quickly like Harriet told her too. Harriet dropped down into the nest to share the gift with E16. E16 showed Harriet how capable she was and mantled and protected her food. That made Harriet happy and she went back up to the attic as E16 continued to eat.

E15 could hear that E16 was eating... again. She wanted to get to the nest quickly. Her mind was made up... She was going back home!

Done eating, E16 rested at the nest rails. She looked to her right and she saw E15 as she flew past the nest and circled around. E16 jumped up as E15 landed in the nest. She instinctively mantled and then she softly cried. "Why did you go? Why did you leave me all alone? I was worried about you."

E15 looked around the nest for some food. "Obviously, you weren't worried enough to leave me some food."

Embarrassed, E16 coyly replied, "Well, I didn't know if you were ever coming back." They both laid down in the nest by the nest rails. E16 quietly asked E15, "Were you scared?"

"No!" E15 quickly answered. E16 tilted her head and raised her eyebrows as she looked at her sister in disbelief. E15 continued, "Well, not scared... just unsure. Let's just relax, okay?" E16 nodded. "Oh, and hey... Congratulations on branching... finally!" E15 smiled at E16. "That's great!"

E16 smiled. "Thanks! You know... you fledged on the 15th and you're E15 and I branched on the 16th and I'm E16! Isn't that weird?"

"You're weird," laughed E15. But this time it was different. They laughed together and not at each other. The two eaglets had grown into not only beautiful young eagles, but they had become friends, sibling friends. There would always be the usual sibling bickering and rivalry, but they now had a closeness... a bond... another milestone.

Chapter 17 … The Town Bully And New Heights

T he eaglets were now eleven weeks old. They seemed to suddenly grow up in a blink of an eye. It seemed like just yesterday that they were bonking each other. But now they had matured. They still liked to play, but they had become more serious, more intense, more like... eagles.

Mornings continued to be the same. E15 woke up and headed to the attic. E16 continued to sleep in the nest and then would stretch and fly hop around the nest in search of nestovers... and of course, E16 would talk and sing the entire time.

Felix the great blue heron flew overhead. E16 looked up and said, "Whoa! Get a load of the size of that beak! It's bigger than yours, 15!" E15 ignored E16's comment.

M flew into the nest with a fish. E16 grabbed, mantled and started to eat it. M stood there and watched and sarcastically said, "Good morning, Dad... How are you today? I'm fine kids, thank you... My what a big, yummy fish you brought us Dad... You're a great Dad... thanks Dad... Oh it was nothing..."

E16 looked up from the fish as she ate and said, "Did you say something, Dad?"

"Me? No, nothing at all. Enjoy!" And M flew off.

E15 soon dropped down into the nest and the usual dance to steal the food began. They both got their fair share of breakfast. Just like her Mom, E16 enjoyed the fish tail and squeed with delight.

They looked up and saw their Mom fly off from a nearby tree. Harriet climbed higher and higher in the sky.

"WOW!" they both sighed. They watched and daydreamed of the day they would soar just like their Mom. Inspired as she watched Harriet, E16 flapped her wings and landed on the spike branch.

"Took you long enough," teased E15.

"I believe in quality, not quantity," replied E16.

The day went on as usual with multiple food deliveries, wingersizing and naps. But the eaglets were closer to the start of their new lives. They had made strides in their skills and lessons.

That evening, a beautiful sky around the nest tree was painted by the sunset. Harriet moved closer to M on the upper branch. "It's a beautiful night, isn't it, M?" Harriet said softly and sweetly.

M15 was exhausted. He had been so busy fishing and hunting for their two growing eaglets. The last thing that he wanted to do was to sit and watch the sunset. He wanted to go to sleep.

"Its's kinda humid," M replied.

"But it is so colorful… and tropical… and romantic."

M looked around at the sky and Harriet gave him a peck on the back of his head. He quickly turned and their eyes met. Harriet kissed M's beak and he kissed Harriet's.

Harriet gazed lovingly into M's eyes and then just like that M said, "Goodnight," and he quickly tucked his beak and pretended to sleep and snore.

Harriet just stared at M. Disappointed, Harriet said, "Goodnight." She watched the sun put out its light as the colorful sky turned to night. Then she saw M move his foot as he dangled it over the branch. Harriet's eyes narrowed. "You're not asleep!"

"Yes, I am!" replied M as he realized he spoke out loud.

Annoyed, Harriet added, "I guess you talk in your sleep now." Harriet's eyes got narrower as M lifted his head slowly. "You pretended to be asleep!"

M sighed. "Yes, guilty as charged. Harriet I'm exhausted. And as much as I love you, I want to go to sleep. I don't want to watch the sunset. I don't want to talk about the day. And I don't want to cuddle. I just want to rest my head, dangle my foot and think of nothing and then just fall asleep. I'm sorry, but I'm really tired."

Harriet looked at her M. She sweetly smiled and said, "I understand. I'm sorry. You have been doing so much. Sleep well, M. I love you."

"Thank you, Harriet. I love you, too." They kissed and M fell right to sleep.

The two E's watched and listened to their parent's conversation.

"What was that all about," asked E15.

E16 shook her head, "I have no idea."

"Adults are weird," said E15. E16 nodded.

They were all tired that night… after all it had been a busy week. Harriet and M slept peacefully on the upper branch of the nest tree. E15 slept on the attic branch and E16 happily slept cuddled up on the nest with Stuffy.

It was morning, but too early for the sun to rise. When suddenly… THUD!

E15 let out a cry as she descended below the nest and landed on a branch. "What in the world was that?" E15 asked, "Mama? Dad?"

"E15, are you okay?" Harriet quickly asked.

"Yes. But what was that?" E15 asked. Her voice sounded frightened.

M15 was furious, "That no good owl! Are you sure you are alright?"

"Yes, Dad." E15 paused. "I'm scared."

"Don't be scared, 15. He's just a bully and he wants you to be scared," said M.

"But I didn't even hear him coming."

"They silently fly, E15," said Harriet. "They are bullies and they don't fight fair."

"But I didn't do anything to him. Why would he hit me for no reason?"

"Because that's what bullies do," Harriet said sadly. "The main thing is you are okay!"

E16 had stretched her neck to look over the nest rails. "What are you doing down there?"

"Nothing. Go back to sleep," E15 snapped.

"Did you miss the nest again?"

"No, I didn't miss the nest again. Go back to sleep!" E15 demanded.

"Then why are you down there?"

"E15 got attacked by a bully... an owl... and he knocked E15 off of the attic branch," explained M15.

"A bully? I know what that's like!" said E16.

"Ha, ha. Very funny," said E15.

"Are you okay?" asked E16.

"I'm fine. You haven't gotten rid of me yet."

"Oh, okay. Well," E16 let out a big yawn and did a big wing stretch. "Goodnight," and E16 fell right back to sleep.

"Stay put, 15. Let the sun come up and then you can go back to the nest. You landed on a safe branch."

"Okay, Mama."

"Try to get some rest, 15," added M.

"I'll try, Dad."

But E15 couldn't sleep. She pictured an image of a monstrous bird silently coming up behind her. E15 flinched and looked all around to make sure the owl wasn't near her or watching her. Harriet and M didn't sleep either. They both kept watch for the owl. E16, on the other hand, slept peacefully, like a newborn hatchling.

When the sun rose and brightened up the pasture, E16 woke up and stretched. She fly hopped around the nest and saw that E15 was in the front pine. E16 went to the veranda and watched E15 as she planned her attempt of how to get back to the nest. E15 flew to the dead strangler fig tree that laid on its side on the ground in the pasture. E16 tilted her head as she watched and tried to figure out what E15 was doing. E15 moved from branch to branch as she assessed her situation.

A dove named Betty, landed on one of the branches near E15 and asked, "Are you okay?"

"I'm fine, thank you," answered E15.

"Okay," said Betty and she flew off.

Something high in the sky caught E15's eye and she watched with great curiosity. She leaned and leaned to get a better look and then she suddenly fell off of the branch and landed on the ground. E16's eyes opened wide and she couldn't help but laugh out loud. She quickly stopped when E15 looked in her direction. E15 couldn't decide what to do. So, she went back to the strangler fig tree and tried out more branches. Then she went back to the ground.

"Okay, this isn't working. I'm just going to have to take a leap of faith and go for it!" E15 flapped her wings and flew to the snag tree. "That's better!" But it still wasn't the nest.

Just then, M flew in with a fish. The only eaglet in the nest was E16 and she took full advantage of that fact. She enjoyed her breakfast as she squeed away and enjoyed every bite. M tried to entice and encourage E15 to map out her route to the nest tree. So, M flew in with another fish... and another.

"I like when E15 flies! I get to eat all the fish peacefully," 16 squeed.

E15 couldn't stand the thought of not being in the nest while her Dad delivered so many fish. The sound of E16's squees finally gave E15 the incentive she needed.

"That's it!" E15 decided and she flew to go back to the nest. But for some reason, she wasn't confident enough in landing in the nest. So, she headed toward the Church rooftop instead. She landed next to the steeple. She looked at the Cross and said, "Please God, Help me get back home..." and E15 flapped her wings and flew straight to the nest. E16 saw E15 as she headed toward the nest and she protected her third fish. E15 landed and immediately tried to steal it.

E16 looked at her sister and felt bad for her. "Here... you can have some. You've been through a lot and I guess I'm a little full."

"Thanks," said E15 and she quickly ate.

"Were you scared last night?" asked E16.

"No," answered E15 between bites.

"Yes, you were! I heard you tell Mama and Dad that you were."

"You know, if I didn't know better, I would think that you paid the owl to keep me off of the nest so you could get all of the food Mama and Dad bring."

"I guess we'll never know, will we..." E16 smiled and wiggled her eyebrows just like her Dad.

E15 continued to eat and then asked, "So do you really think that I'm a bully?"

"Only when I was little and you bonked me all the time when we ate. And also now when we eat... and don't forget you attacked my beak... and you make me flinch and intimidate me. But other than that, you're a pussycat."

"I'm sorry," said E15. "It's just the eagle in me. I don't mean to hurt you or bully you. I'm just being an eagle."

"I know. But I don't hurt you the way you hurt me. So that's when you're a bully. But I guess it is the same way for the owl. He's just being an owl."

The two siblings relaxed most of the day. It was hot and humid and they enjoyed the lazy summer day... especially E15.

The next day was Father's Day. The kids woke up early after a restful and peaceful night.

"Happy Father's Day, Dad!" they both cheered.

"Thank you both!"

"What do you want to get us for breakfast today," asked E16. "It is your special day. So, I'm thinking something special from our special Dad!" she smiled a great big smile.

M laughed and said, "Oh, I don't know... how about I surprise you?"

"Okay!" they both replied.

M laughed, shook his head and flew off to get his children their Father's Day breakfast.

"I hope he gets back soon. I'm starving!" said E16.

"Me, too," replied E15.

"Oh... great," sighed E16.

E15 and E16 moved around the nest while they waited. E15 perched on the veranda spike and then decided to go to the attic. But... it didn't go as she planned and once again, she ended up below the nest. "Oh no! Not again!" whined E15.

E16 went to look over the nest rails to see if her sister was alright. After seeing she was, E16 whispered, "YES! Come on Dad with the food!" She then leaned over the nest and commented, "You like going under the nest, don't you?" E15 ignored E16 and walked up the branch and then she flew to the attic.

"Darn!" E16 said under her breath.

"What?" asked E15.

"Nothing," replied E16.

E16 squeed with delight as her Dad landed in the nest with a fish. But E15 was quick and this time she claimed the fish and ate it. "Thanks, Dad!" E15 ate while E16 waited. E15 finished and then went up to the attic. E16 found some tidbits to nibble. When done, E16 wingersized and sang around the nest. Suddenly without any effort, E16 flew to the attic. E15 tilted her head until she could see E16 upside down.

"I can't believe it! Is it really you?" E15 said jokingly.

"You think you invented going from branch to branch?" asked E16.

"No, but I thought you were too afraid to come up here."

"Nope! I'm not afraid! You'll see what else I can do eventually."

Soon M flew in with another fish. Both eaglets dropped down to the nest. E16 grabbed it, but E15 stole it and warned E16 to stay away. But this time E16 was quick and stole the fish back. Then M flew in with another fish and E16 claimed that too! Still full from the earlier fish, E15 went back to the attic. M and E16 shared a few bites of one of the fish.

"I saw you on the attic branch, E16. That's great! And it is a GREAT Father's Day gift!"

"Thank you, Dad," E16 looked at E15 and smirked. She then added, "E15 didn't get you anything."

"That's okay... just having you both in my life is my gift."

E15 smiled at E16 and E16 narrowed her eyes at her sister. She then took the fish away from her Father and kept both fish.

M smiled. "Okay you two, enjoy the rest of your Father's Day," and he flew off to the pond.

Harriet soon arrived with more food. And right behind Harriet was M with even MORE food! They all ate and spent Father's Day together.

It was a great day in the nest tree. It was peaceful and relaxing. Food was bountiful as they all celebrated.

As the day turned to night, their happy voices were heard throughout the pasture.

"Goodnight, Mama," said E16.

"Goodnight, E16," replied Harriet.

"Goodnight, Dad."

"Goodnight, E16"

"Goodnight, Mama," said E15.

"Goodnight, E15," replied Harriet.

"Goodnight, Dad."

"Goodnight, E15."

"Goodnight, Harriet," M smiled.

"Goodnight, M," Harriet giggled.

"Goodnight, John Boy," M teased.

"WHO?" E15 and E16 gasped.

Harriet and M chuckled. "No one, goodnight kids," added M.

"We love you both. Sweet eagle dreams," said Harriet.

"I love you too, Mama," said E16. "I love you too, Dad. Goodnight, Mama."

"Oh, no. We're not starting that again, are we?" complained E15.

Harriet, M and E16 all laughed. E15 paused and laughed too...

Chapter 18 … Lounging Pondside

I n the days to come, E15 continued to practice flying and E16 practiced branching as she tried out all the nest tree branches. And of course, the teasing continued.

As E15 flew to the nest tree after a flight around the pasture, she attempted to land on the attic branch right next to E16.

"Gangway!" called out E15 as she crashed into E16.

"You really need landing lessons!" E16 complained as she brushed herself off.

"Did you see me fly?" asked E15.

"I see you fly all the time," replied E16.

"This was different! This was because I wanted to, not because the branch I was on broke and I had to fly... and not because an owl hit into me. This was because I wanted to fly!" E16 didn't seem impressed. E15 then asked, "So when are you going to fly?"

"When I feel like it!"

"You know you're an eagle, right?"

"I'm a BEAUTIFL eagle! Get it right!" E16 smiled proudly.

E15 rolled her eyes and flew off. She stayed away from the nest for a long time. E16 watched the pasture and surrounding area as she searched for a glimpse of E15. She didn't see where E15 was. Over two hours had gone by when E16 finally spotted E15 as she flew toward the nest.

"Did you miss me?" asked E15.

"Nope," replied E16.

"Yes, you did! I saw you looking for me!"

"No, I didn't! I was looking for Mama and Dad!"

"You missed me," smiled E15. E16 just stared at the pasture.

The eaglets were growing up quickly. Harriet and M knew they were suddenly getting closer to starting their new lives. There were still more lessons to be learned and E16 still had to fledge, but they knew the clock was ticking. Now was the time that Harriet would stay away from the nest more and let M take over. Although always in view of her babies, Harriet rejuvenated her soul. M, as usual, stepped up to the plate and was the great Dad he had proved to be. He now would train them to be more aggressive when food was brought in. He especially tried to encourage E16. He also knew they needed to learn a very important lesson. Right now they only associated food with the nest. They needed to learn that the nest was not the only place to eat. So, M brought a fish to the nest. E15 and E16 both battled to claim it.

As he watched, M grabbed a piece of the fish and flew to the snag tree. Both eaglets stopped to watch their Dad.

"What's he doing?" asked E16.

"I think he's eating the fish," answered E15.

"On the branch of the snag tree?"

"I think so."

"Why would he do that?"

"I don't know." They continued to watch. Both of them were unsure of what their Dad was doing.

"Do you think that maybe we're allowed to eat on trees and not just on the nest?" asked E16.

"WHY?"

"I don't know! I'm just trying to figure out why he's eating over there and not in the nest."

They watched and learned another lesson and it was a very valuable one.

The kids enjoyed their time and lessons with their Dad, but they also missed their Mom. Harriet had been away from them for a few days.

"Mama!" E16 softly sighed. "MAMA!" she cheered. Harriet flew to the nest. "Mama, I missed you!"

"I missed you too, sweetie. I'm so sorry, but I wasn't far and I was always watching you. But I also knew your Dad enjoyed spending time with both of you."

E15 flew to the nest, "Mama, you're back!"

"I saw that you've been flying around the pasture, 15. AND... you have been enjoying the pasture pond. You are really becoming a big eagle!" said Harriet. E15 proudly smiled.

The two eaglets were so excited to see their Mother that they spoke at the same time with excitement. "Mama! Mama!" they both chattered.

"Okay, okay," Harriet laughed. "Calm down. I'm excited too!"

E16 turned to her Mother and made big eagle vocals. Harriet's eyes opened wide in surprise. "E16! Listen to you! My big girl!" E16 smiled and turned and smiled at E15. E15 rolled her eyes.

So, every day the lessons continued. Then one special morning both eaglets were very active as they went from branch to branch on the nest tree. Suddenly E15 saw Harriet as she flew through the pasture.

"Hey, Mama! Where are you going?" shouted out E15 as she flew after Harriet.

And then... something happened that they had all been waiting for...

"WAIT FOR ME!" called out E16 as she flapped her wings and flew off of the nest tree. E16 finally fledged! FINALLY!!! She landed on the top of the snag tree. "I did it! I DID IT!!! I flew! I FLEW!!!" E16 cheered.

E15 flew back to the nest and called out, "Hey, pip squeak! You flew!"

"I flew! I flew! I didn't fall and I didn't get knocked off the branch by an owl! I did it when I wanted to! I FLEW!" replied E16.

"And until you figure out how to get back to the nest, I guess I'll be the only one eating!" E15 laughed.

"What?" E16 questioned as M flew past her and went to the nest with food. "Hey! Wait! Where's mine?"

"You have to come to the nest to get the food," replied M.

"But you showed us that we can eat on trees."

"Yes, you can, but you have to get the food first and then bring it to the tree." M dropped off the food and flew off as E15 ate.

Disappointed, E16 flew toward the nest tree. "Uh-oh!" she screamed as she missed the nest and headed toward a branch under the nest. "WHOA!" she cried as she dangled upside down on a branch before she fell to the ground. "This looked a lot easier to do when I was making fun of E15."

Harriet returned to the nest tree. "Congratulations, E16!"

"Thanks, Mama..." E16 paused. "Mama? How do I get back up to the nest?"

"You fly, baby. You just do it!"

"Not so easy, is it, pip squeak," asked E15 while she ate. M flew in with more food to entice E16 back to the nest. "Thanks, Dad, for more food," E15 said loudly for E16 to hear.

"Everything looks so different from down here," E16 said. She could hardly be seen in the tall grass. She flew off and headed toward the snag tree. E15 watched from the nest while she ate. E16's eyes opened wide as she screamed, "AHHHH!!!" and headed straight toward the trunk of the tree. She grabbed the trunk and tried to climb it.

E15's mouth dropped. "WOW! That was terrible! Who needs landing lessons?" E15 called out and laughed. "Even I haven't done anything that bad!"

Embarrassed, but trying not to show it, E16 flew to the west pasture and then to the driveway. A truck drove by and frightened her. "YIKES! What was that?" She flew to the building by the pond.

"Hey pip squeak! I flew to the pond on my first day of flying too! Still copying me."

M15 flew to the nest and had a quick bite to eat with E15. Done eating, E15 flew off of the nest tree to join her sister. The horses came out of the stables to see what all the excitement was about.

"I think the baby flew for the first time today," said the Commander. "Troops, watch where you step. There might be an eagle walking on the ground." The horses nodded and carefully walked through the tall grass.

Both E15 and E16 flew to the pond and sat at the pond together. They sipped the cool water and bathed. "It's about time you took a bath," teased E15.

"You don't smell like a bed of roses yourself, 15," replied E16.

"Look at the two of you!" said Harriet as she flew toward the nest.

The two eaglets spent the day together at the pond. E16 flew onto the rope railing hanging across the two pylons. She happily swung back and forth.

 E15 rolled her eyes. "What are you doing?"

"I'm having fun on my swing."

"It's not a swing."

"I'm swinging on it, so that makes it a swing. I found it first and I'm on it, so it's mine!" E16 declared. E15 shook her head and rolled her eyes.

Maria the anhinga sat on the pond fence rail as she dried her outspread wings. She greeted E16, "Buenos dias!" E16 tilted her head. "You must be E15's sister." E16 nodded. Maria giggled, "You're a quiet one!"

"Quiet one?" E15 laughed. "She hasn't shut up since the day she hatched. She even talks in her sleep!"

"No! Do you?" asked Maria.

"No, I don't. She's just mean."

"Ah, I have a sibling too. I know what you are saying. Well I wish you two a good day at the pond. My wings are dry now and I must go. I hope we will meet again! Adios, mis amigas!" and she flew off.

E16 flapped her wings and said, "Bye!" She turned to E15 and said, "She's nice!"

"Yes, she is and she catches a lot of fish for us to steal!"

A pretty little duck floated close to E16. "Hi!"

"Hello," replied E16.

"Congratulations! I heard you flew for the first time today."

"Yes, I did!" E16 said proudly.

"That's wonderful! Oh, where are my manners? My name is Quacks. I was good friends with your brother E9."

"You were?"

"Yes, he was such a wonderful eagle! I miss him so much."

"I've heard so much about him."

"That's because there is so much to tell!"

"Quacks!" A man's voice called out.

"That's my Dad. I have to go." Quacks then replied to her Father, "Coming Daddy!" She turned back to E16 and said, "I hope we get to talk again! See ya!" and she floated away.

"Bye!" said E16. "She seems really nice, too."

"I guess so. Anyway, are you going to sleep in the nest tonight?"

"I hope so," said E16 as she looked at the tall nest tree.

"Good luck with that," said E15.

E16 flew over the pond. Her wing tips slapped the water. She wanted to fly to the nest tree, but she just couldn't get the height she needed and she landed on the ground at the base of their home.

"Great, what am I going to do?" she asked as she looked around.

Harriet and M flew to the pond. They both sipped the cool water.

"Well she finally fledged!" Harriet said.

M heard the relief in her voice. "Yeah, now let's hope it doesn't take as long for her to get back to the nest." Harriet gave M a look of disapproval which M responded with, "I'm only kidding."

E15 flew to the nest tree and E16 flew to the dead strangler fig tree.

Harriet looked at M and said, "I guess it will be a sleepless night."

The morning didn't arrive fast enough. Harriet called out as the sun rose in the sky. "E16!" she cried.

"I'm here, Mama!"

"Where? I can't see you!" But the noise from the street muffled E16's response.

"Pip squeak!" called E15 as she looked for her sibling and flew to the snag tree.

Jay the blue jay landed on one of the branches near E15. "Hey, where's 61?"

"Her name is 16."

"Yeah, yeah, whatever, 61, 16... hey maybe I have dyslexia?"

"You have what?"

"Never-mind. So, where is she?"

"She's around."

"You know it's a lot quieter without her around the nest," Jay laughed.

E15 leaned toward the blue jay, opened her wings and narrowed her eyes and said, "I think it would be a lot quieter without you!"

"Geez! Someone woke up on the wrong side of the nest today. I was only kidding."

"Well maybe you should move along because I felt awfully hungry when I woke up this morning and I still haven't eaten yet."

"Okay, okay. I guess the friendly gene ended with E9." And the blue jay flew off.

M did a quick flight over the pond area to see if he could locate E16. The horses walked through the pasture.

"M! Have you located the young eaglet yet?" called out the Commander.

"No, Commander. No, not yet. I'm going to get some food for them now and that should bring her out in the open."

"Good idea! Let me know if there is anything I can do. Oh... and if we find her, am I correct in thinking her name is E16?"

"Yes, sir, you are correct. Her name is E16."

"Whoa. You two are up to 16 already. Time sure does fly," the Commander laughed.

"It sure does. Thanks, Commander," and M flew off.

"Okay troops, I understand the young eaglet has not yet been seen this morning. So again, watch your step and let me know if you spot her." The horses continued to walk through the pasture with their heads down as they watched out for E16. Suddenly E16's head popped up above the tall grass by the base of a tree in the pasture. The Commander and his troops stopped. "Well! Good morning there, little lady!" E16 tilted her head. "Ha, ha, ha. Why you just looked like your brother E9 doing that! Ha, ha, ha! Oh... I'm sorry. I'm the Commander. I'm friends with your Mom and Dad. You must be E16."

"Yes sir, I am." E16 was amazed by the size of the horse now that she was next to him.

"I understand that you flew for the first time yesterday."

"Yes, sir, I did!" 16 said proudly. "The sky is so much fun and the ground has so many things to see. It's like being in a toy store!"

"Ha, ha, ha! A toy store! Your brother E9 thought everything was a toy and that life was a toy. It's funny that you sort of said the same thing."

"Gee, I guess I did! You knew my brother?"

"Yes, little lady, I did! I had the honor to call E9 my friend. He was an amazing young eagle. He turned this pasture into a wonderland... fun, laughter and music."

"I LOVE TO SING!"

"You do? Well then you are certainly related to E9!" said the Commander. E16 smiled proudly. "Do you need any help, E16? Do you need me to call your Mom or Dad?"

"No, sir. I'm okay. Thank you!"

"Okay then. Carry on soldier, I mean E16." They smiled at each other. "I'm glad we got to meet today!"

"Me too, sir!"

The horses continued to walk through the pasture and E16 continued to look around while she was still on the ground. Jay landed near her and imitated E16's every move. He exaggerated her head movements. He laughed out loud when she started to walk. "You eagles have the funniest walk!" E16 turned and gave the blue jay a fierce look. Jay's eyes opened wide with fear. "Gulp... Bye!" The blue jay flew off and E16 flew behind the building at the pond.

M flew to the ground by the pond with a fish. E15 immediately followed him and grabbed the fish and ate it. M flew to a nearby tree and waited. One of the Commander's troops ran past E15. E15 spotted the massive horse as it ran in her direction. E15's eyes opened wide. "WHOA!" she yelled out and dropped the fish and she flew away.

Harriet flew down to the fish. "Well if no one else is going to eat this, I will!"

E15 flew over to her Mother. "MOM! That's my fish!"

"No, it WAS your fish. Now it is my fish!"

"But I had to fly away... there was a huge monster running toward me!"

"I'm sorry, 15. You have to learn when you have food you eat it and you eat it quickly. And if you have to leave, you have to take it with you." Harriet continued to eat the fish.

"Yes, ma'am," E15 said sadly and she flew off. She landed next to E16 at the water's edge. "Hey, pip squeak! You came out of hiding!"

"I wasn't hiding. I was just still checking out the place. Have you met the Commander?"

"The BIG horse? Yeah, he's scary!"

"Scary? I think he's cool! Did you know that he and E9 were friends?"

"I think E9 was friends with everyone."

"I'm going to be friends with everyone, too!"

"That's if they like you."

"What's not to like? I'm smart, beautiful, talented..."

"Conceited, you talk too much..."

"You're just jealous!"

"PLEASE, don't sing that stupid jealous song you made up!"

"J is for ..." E15 narrowed her eyes at 16 and 16 quickly stopped singing.

They both dipped their beaks into the water and had a refreshing drink. They then looked up at the nest tree and saw their Dad land in the nest with a fish.

"Oh, it's too hot to eat up there," said E15.

"Do you think he'll bring it down here?" asked 16.

"That would be great! It is too hot up there. It is so much nicer down here. Maybe we should wait and see."

And that is what the two siblings did. They waited until their Dad flew down to the pond with the fish. They both ran over to M. E16 claimed the fish, mantled and ate. M flew to the pond fence and E15 followed.

"Are you two enjoying hanging out together?" asked M.

"Yeah, it's better than being in the nest. This way when E16 annoys me I can fly away from her. Far away." M and 15 laughed.

The two eaglets spent the whole day together at the pond. They had squabbles that happened for no reason. But again, all lessons of eagle life and how to survive. Life on their own was not going to be easy. It certainly was not going to be lounging pondside and having their meals delivered to them. They had to stay strong and focused. So, their battles were lessons... needed lessons.

As the day was ending, E15 flew to the snag that she liked to sleep in. E16 was still at the pond and longed to get back to the nest. She sat perched on the pond pylon and decided to make the attempt. She flew across the pond and landed on another snag tree.

"Okay, I can do this! It is right there!" She flapped her wings and flew to the nest. She danced and sang as she made her perfect landing.

"Welcome home, baby!" said Harriet as she sat perched on the outer attic branch.

"Thanks, Mama!" said E16 and she searched for tidbits of food. She flew to the attic.

"You must be very tired after being away fom the nest for all this time. Maybe you should close your eyes."

"Oh, I'm okay, Mama," replied E16. But 16 was exhausted. She looked around the pasture as she caught her breath. As she relaxed, she started to get sleepy. She closed her eyes and abruptly caught herself as she started to fall asleep. "I'm awake! I'm awake!" she called out.

"What, 16?" asked Harriet, confused as to why 16 was announcing she was awake.

"Oh, nothing. I just wanted you to know that I'm not sleeping yet."

Harriet laughed to herself. She figured out that E16 was trying to act big and not let on that she was falling asleep. "Okay, sweetie. But if you start to get tired, just close your eyes. I'm sure you must be exhausted."

"Okay, Mama. Maybe I will. Goodnight. I love you."

"I love you too, 16." Harriet smiled as she looked at her baby and saw she was sound asleep.

Everyone woke up completely refreshed. E16 was eager to start her day at the pond. She squeed and hopped around the nest. She looked at the pond and said, "The last one to the pond is a rotten egg," and she flew off the nest.

"Hey! WAIT! I wasn't ready!" said E15.

"Then you're the rotten egg! But we already knew that!"

"Very funny, pip squeak!"

Harriet sat perched in the attic as she watched her two grown babies with pride. She looked at the sky and saw a rainbow. "Thank you, Ozzie! Thank you for watching over them. I feel you, E3, E5 and E14 with us all the time. I love and miss you all." She turned and watched the kids at the pond.

E15 and E16 had a wonderful time at their vacation home, the pond. They found sticks and palm fronds in and around the water and they carried them all over in their talons. They played with them, but little did they know it was just more lessons that they were learning... and they had gotten very good at it!

Felix the great blue heron landed near E15. E15 spread her wings and chased Felix away. "Hey, watch it little one or I'll tell your parents." E15 hid behind a palm frond that had fallen into the pond. "I see you hiding behind the palm frond," said Felix. "Kids!" laughed Felix and he flew away.

The kids spent the day playing, having mock battles and relaxing on the pond fence.

"I could get used to this," said E15 as she relaxed her foot over the fence rail.

"Me, too!" sighed E16.

"No hot nest."

"Nice cool shade."

"Having food delivered."

"Sipping cool drinks pondside."

"Yeah, this is the life!"

"Mmmm!!!" agreed E16.

That night E15 slept on her snag tree and E16 slept in the nest tree. They had no idea what day it was or what it meant. They certainly had no idea what impact they had as eagles on this special day or what they as eagles symbolized. The sky was dark as any other night... until...

BOOM! BOOM! BOOM!

"What the...?" they both exclaimed. The sky lit up with bright, twinkling lights... red, white and blue lights. "WOW!" they both sighed.

Yes, it was the Fourth of July. The Nation's Independence Day. Little did these two magnificient creatures know how much they meant to the Country. They had no idea that they were the living, breathing symbol of Freedom... the American Bald Eagle!

Chapter 19 ... Majestic Eagles In The Making

T he excitement of the night before had the two eaglets chattering away in the morning.

"Mama! Dad! Did you see the sky last night?" asked E15.

"It was amazing!" exclaimed E16.

Harriet and M looked at each other and smiled.

"Yes, we did," replied Harriet.

"What was that all about?" asked 15.

"Well that was sort of about the two of you... about us," added M.

The two eaglets looked at each other confused. "Us?" they both asked.

M chuckled, "Yes, indirectly. You have no idea of how loved and important you are to this Country."

"We are?" they both questioned together.

Harriet smiled. "Yes! We are the Nation's bird. We are the symbol of Freedom, Liberty and Justice. You symbolize strength, loyalty, and peace. You are the majestic ambassadors of all that is good."

E15 and E16 held their heads high, their shoulders pulled back and their chests were full of pride.

M added, "When you leave home and start your new lives, you will most likely soar to the Nation's Capital, Washington, D.C. and you'll see all the pride of the Country with an eagle symbol on it."

"WOW!" sighed E15.

"Wait..." said E16. "When we leave home?"

Harriet and M looked at each other. "Yes, E16. Both you and E15 will start new lives... BIG eagle lives," explained Harriet.

Confused, E15 and E16 looked at each other. They then looked at their parents. "But why?" E15 asked. They both stared at Harriet and M sadly as they searched for an answer.

"That is just the life of an eagle, 15. It is what your Dad and I had to do... what E9 had to do... and all of your siblings... 1, 2 , 4, 6, 7, 8, 10, 11, 12, and 13 had to do," Harriet replied.

"You said even E9?" asked E16.

"Yes, 16, even E9 had to leave home, too. And I won't lie to you, E9 had the same look on his face that the two of you have on yours right now. He asked us why he couldn't stay and why couldn't he live in one of the trees in the pasture."

"Well, E9 was right... why can't we?" asked 15.

M gave the two eaglets a comforting smile as he continued where Harriet left off. "We'll tell you what we told E9. It isn't us that doesn't want you to stay. It will actually be YOU that doesn't WANT to stay. You'll WANT to leave!"

"I don't want to leave," replied 16. "Do you?" she asked 15. E15 shook her head. They both had tears in their eyes.

"Now, let's not get upset over this. This is something that you will decide. You will tell us when it is time. It isn't something that we will tell you," added Harriet.

"Yeah, it isn't like we're going to throw you out of the nest one day," said M. Harriet nudged M with her wing. "Oh, I mean it is all up to the two of you. No pressure."

The two siblings looked at each other. "Do we leave together?" asked E16.

"Not usually. But again, it is all your decision," answered M.

"Gee, it seems that pip squeak has always been around. It would be weird without her," said E15.

"And I don't know what it is like not to have a bully... I mean someone bossing me around... I MEAN... I don't know what it would be like not to have E15 around. She's always been there since I hatched. She's always been with me. I don't know what it is like to be alone."

Harriet and M looked at each other unsure of how to explain everything without upsetting them. "I understand," said Harriet. "I was the youngest in my family. I never was alone." Harriet then smiled and her eyes twinkled. "But then suddenly one day something inside of me... I don't know what it was... a tiny voice?... my heart?... I don't know what it was, but it was pulling me away. Oh, how I loved my family, but something was calling me to start my own life. And that life would someday bring me to today where I have my own family." E15 and E16 tilted their heads as they continued to listen to their Mother. "I knew I might never see my parents or siblings ever again..."

"WHAT?" E15 and E16 asked, shocked.

"But I also knew where my parents lived. I imprinted everything around me as I grew up, like the two of you are doing. So, I knew I could always go see my parents when I wanted to. I sometimes ran into my siblings and we would catch up on each other's lives. We would always say how we loved and missed each other, but then we would fly off and continue on our way to our own lives."

"So... we can visit?" asked E16.

"Yes," said M. He glanced at Harriet and then he looked back at the kids. "You just have to make sure it isn't during nesting season and we don't have new babies in the nest."

"Why?" asked E15. "Why can't we meet our future siblings?"

"Have you ever seen the two of you eat?" said M as he and Harriet laughed. The eaglets were confused and had no idea what their parents thought was so funny. "You two are relentless when it comes to food! And until you have a family of your own you won't understand the importance of taking care of the new babies and keeping them fed."

"Well, 16 sure does make a piglet of herself when she eats," laughed E15.

"Me? At least I don't sneak under your tail feathers to eat your food... sneak!"

"But that is what your Dad is trying to explain to you. Babies need food to grow big and strong, like the two of you did when you were little. And we would have to chase you away if you came back when the new babies are here."

"You would chase us away?" asked E15.

"Would you even chase E9 away?" asked E16.

"Yes, we would have to chase you away and we would even chase E9 away," replied Harriet.

"Wow! Even E9! EVERYONE loved E9!" said E16. Everyone paused for a moment as the eaglets took this all in. "I guess that does make sense. And you know..." E16 blushed, "... all this talk of food is making me hungry."

"See! I told you she's a piglet!" E15 laughed.

"So, are we good?" asked M.

"Yes, Dad," the two replied.

"Now remember, when we leave you can't follow me," said E15.

"Why?" asked 16.

"Because you copy everything I do and I have to go without you."

"But... I'll miss you," 16 said sadly.

E15 looked at her sister. She gave her a little smile and said, "Well, maybe you can follow me for a little bit... but behind me."

E16 smiled. "Because you love me and you would miss me!" E16 started dancing and singing around the nest. "You would miss me, you would miss me. No one to tease me, no one to kiss me," she sang.

"Oh brother! You see what I mean? This is why you have to follow behind me... far behind me so I don't have to hear your silly songs."

Harriet and M laughed… and E16 continued to sing and dance. She then stopped and said, "You know, I think I'll have a spa day. Is that what you call it, Mama?"

Harriet laughed again and replied, "Yes, 16, that's what I call it."

"Great! See ya!" and 16 flew off to the pond.

"She is such a girly girl sometimes," commented E15.

"Well, I guess that is because she spent more time with your Mom and you spent more time with me. Although I like a good dip in the pond, too. And your Mom can be an awful fierce girly girl." They all giggled. "But you know you are both fierce and resilient, like an eagle should be… just like your Mom… beautiful and fierce… hmmm… fiercely beautiful!" said M. E15 smiled in agreement.

"Well thank you my handsome and FIERCE male eagle," said Harriet as M kissed Harriet.

"Okay, I'm out of here," said E15 and she flew to the pond fence to keep an eye on E16.

When she got to the pond, she found E16 in the water splashing away… and singing of course. E16 heard the conversation E15 had with their parents which inspired a song. "I'm fierce and I'm pretty. I can make up songs because I'm witty. E15 can't and that's a pity."

"Oh brother," said E15.

"This feels so good! You should bathe more often, you know."

"I take baths! I'm fine and I smell good."

"If you think so." E16 dunked her left wing and then her right and finally her head. She did it over and over again. "Ahhh… How refreshing!" She walked out of the pond. "Look at my beautiful feathers!" She smiled and flew to the pylon to dry off. She turned and looked at E15. "Whatcha doin'?"

"Just sitting," answered E15.

E16 flew over to E15 on the fence. "Well, then I guess I'll sit here with you." E16 paused. "So!... what do you want to talk about?"

"Nothing," replied 15.

"Nothing? There has to be something you want to talk about! We can talk about what Mama and Dad talked about, what your favorite food is, why you don't like taking as many baths as I do…" While E16 went on and on, E15 looked at E16 and turned her head upside down and watched her. "What are you doing? Stop looking at me upside down!"

"I'm trying to see if I can turn down your volume on your voice by moving my head upside down."

Ha, ha... very funny. So, did it work?"

"What?" 15 teased.

"I said, did it work?"

"Wait! I can't hear you, let me turn my head up so I can hear you better."

"DID IT WORK?" 16 said loudly. E15 laughed and E16 realized she was teasing her. "Oh... ha, ha, very funny."

"I thought so," said E15 and she flew to the pond's edge under a tree. While under the tree she found a palm frond. "Oh, I LOVE these! I wonder if these would be good to use in the nest for nest material or filler. Oh wait, when I was little there was one in the nest that we played with. Although this would just be filler, not what would make the best nest material. But something for the kids to play with. WOW! I am getting to be a big eagle! I can figure out what is good to make a nice nest and thinking of things for the kids to play with!" Proud of herself, E15 carried the frond in her beak and talons and enjoyed the solitude under the tree.

Tired of being alone on the fence with no one to talk to, E16 flew back to the nest tree. She hopped and danced around the nest. And then she started singing... "I'm your girl and you're my Dad. You're the best friend I ever had. Eagles may come and eagles may go, but my Dad's the best male eagle I'll ever know."

Harriet and M were in the front pine. "M! She's singing the song that you and she wrote and sang together." M slightly smiled. "Answer her!" said Harriet.

M watched E16 and sang out, "You're my girl..."

"Huh?"

"Try it again," encouraged Harriet.

"You're my girl," M sang out again.

"Ummm..." E16 paused. "And you're my Dad."

"My heart skips a beat and I'm so glad," M sang.

"I took your wing," added 16.

"And you stole my heart," and as he finished singing the line M flew to the nest.

Together they sang, "In your eyes I saw this love start." They smiled at each other and hugged.

"You remembered," M happily said.

E16 looked into her Dad's eyes and said, "Of course, I remembered! You know that's why I always sing... because of you Dad." M hugged his little girl.

E15 flew to the nest. "Hey, what's going on here?"

M started to sing... "You're my girl..." M and E16 looked at E15 in anticipation of E15 singing the next line. M sang the line again. "You're my girl..."

E15 looked at her Father and sister and hung her head and sighed... "You're my Dad..." M and E16 both cringed at the sound E15 made as she sang.

M quickly interrupted E15 from continuing. "Okay, okay! You do remember the song."

"Of course I do, but 16 says I can't sing."

"No, that's not true. I never said you can't sing. I said you should NEVER sing."

"Now, now," M attempted to avoid an argument between the two siblings. "Not everyone is a singer. Everyone has something that they are good at."

"Like what Dad? Tell me what I'm good at!" E15 eagerly waited for her Father's response.

E16 looked at M and asked, "Yeah, Dad! What's 15 good at?"

M looked at E16 with disapproval of how she asked her question. He turned to face E15 and said, "E15, you are good at so many things!"

"Like what?" 15 and 16 both asked.

"You are great at stealing food. You are great at flying..."

"She doesn't always land very well," interrupted E16.

"Excuse me, 16, I don't need your help, thank you. Anyway, 15, you are great at moving and carrying sticks and palm fronds."

"Oh! I know! I know!" E16 said excitedly. "You're really great at being bossy and mean to me!"

"Ha, ha. Very funny, pip squeak."

"See what I mean?"

"Okay, okay, you two. The main thing is your Mother and I love you both very much. You have grown into two beautiful, intelligent, majestic young eagles. We are so proud of both of you... and that means whether you can sing or not..."

"But singing is an added bonus," E16 whispered to E15.

"E16!"

"Sorry Dad," 16 said softly.

"It's what is in here…" M pointed to his head. "And what is in here…" and M pointed to his heart. "And both of you have it all!" M wrapped his wings around his two eaglets.

Harriet watched the entire time from the front pine. With tears in her eyes, she flew to the nest. They all turned to look at Harriet. "I love all of you!" she cried and they all hugged.

That night they all settled in to go to sleep. E16 slept on the attic branch. Harriet and M slept in the front pine, while E15 slept on her favorite snag. Everything was peaceful. Everything was quiet. Then suddenly…!

"AHHH!!!" screamed E15. She swiftly flew to the west pasture.

"E15!" called out Harriet.

"I'm okay, Mama! I'm safe!"

"Where are you?" asked M.

"I'm in a tree in the west pasture," replied E15.

"Good! Stay there!"

"I will, Dad"

M flew to the nest tree and landed near E16. E16 was sound asleep. M sounded the alert and startled E16 awake.

"I'm awake! I'm awake! What's up? What's going on?" E16 quickly blurted out.

"Your sister was just hit by the owl."

"Again?"

"Yes, again. I swear when I get my talons on that… owl."

"Is 15 okay?"

"Yes, 16, she is."

They all stayed on alert throughout the night. They slept, but with one eye open… and ready.

Morning came and all was well. The owl was another lesson. Owls would always be their nemesis. The silent flight of the owl wings made the longtime rival have an unfair advantage. E15, had now been the brunt of this lesson… twice. But she brushed off the attack and tried to learn from it.

Harriet called out to E15, "E15, are you alright?"

"Yes, Mama! I'm fine. This owl doesn't realize that his attacks only make me stronger."

The whole family heard the pride and conviction in E15's voice and they all stood proud and tall.

M flew off and within minutes, he flew to the ground near the pond with food. Harriet was right behind him. Immediately, E15 and E16 rushed to claim the food. E16 grabbed the food. Harriet flew to the pond oak tree and M went to the pond. The dance was on. E16 started eating and E15 started the attempt to steal the food. E15 finally did get part of the meal and they both moved away from each other and ate. M went back to the two eaglets to check on their progress. They both warned him to stay away. M moved closer to E15 and E15 quickly moved her food away.

"Stay away, Dad! It's MINE!" groaned E15.

M found a small tidbit of food. E16 saw that her Dad had something and she quickly left her food and rushed over to him and took it away from him.

"That's MINE!" E16 screeched.

Quietly, M continued to test E16 and moved to the food that E16 left behind. E16 looked up from the piece she stole from her Dad and saw he was going to take her larger piece of food. She ran over to M with her wings open, her eyes were fierce and she took the food away from her Father. "THAT IS MINE!" she screamed as she chased her Dad away.

"Okay, okay," said M as he tried not to look proud. M went to the pond as the two eaglets finished their food.

When finished, E15 flew to the oak tree to join Harriet. E16 walked to the pond and softly said, "I'm sorry, Dad. But you and Mama taught us well. I know you're my Dad, but I have to show you I'm an eagle... YOUR eagle."

M looked at 16. "Yes, you are my eagle and I love you." With pride in his heart and tears in his eyes, M flew to the oak and perched with Harriet and E15.

E16 bent over and took a sip of water. "I think I'll take a little bath." And E16 indulged herself in the refreshing pond. The whole family was together at the pond. Days like this would soon be over, so they took advantage of as many as they could.

The day continued with perfecting lessons. E15 enjoyed playing at the pond with sticks and fronds. E16 enjoyed dancing and singing... even though dancing and singing might not sound like a lesson. Dancing, especially on a branch in the rain, perfected balance and agility while strengthening muscles.

And the singing... hmmm... the singing... perhaps good practice on alerting potential danger.

The weather quickly changed. E15 flew for shelter and E16 flew to the nest tree.

"WOOHOO! Feel the rain on my face and on my wings!" E16 cheered.

The pasture animals heard E16's excitement.

"What's going on?" asked Waddles.

"What's all the excitement about?" questioned Sandy

"What is all that noise?" wondered Twitch.

'Don't look at me. I had nothing to do with it!" said NutJob defensively.

"No one said you had anything to do with it," replied Twitch.

"Oh... then what's going on?"

The Commander and his troops charged into the pasture. "Be prepared men! Keep an eye out for enemy infiltration."

And then it happened. E16 tapped her talons and flapped her mighty wings as she started to hum a tune.

Everyone gasped!

"Could it be?" asked Sandy.

"It couldn't be," said Waddles.

"Oh! Is it? Oh please, let it be!" prayed Quacks.

"Well, I'll be!" the Commander whispered.

The pasture was alive with music and fun. The pasture animals all joined in with E16 as they did years earlier with her brother, E9. They danced and sang as the rain washed away their cares.

When done, E16 flew toward the animals. "WOW! That was great!" exclaimed E16. They all stared at the young female eagle. "You guys sounded fantastic! We should all get together more often and sing and dance!" suggested E16.

They all stood there smiling... shocked.

"You look just like him," said Sandy as she tried not to stare.

E16 tilted her head. "Oh my! Even the head tilt," added Quacks.

"I knew it couldn't be," bragged Waddles.

"What are you talking about?" asked a confused E16.

"We're sorry, E16. We just can't get over how much you look and act like your brother E9," replied the Commander.

"Ohhh!" said E16. "Thank you! I hear he was amazing! And very good-looking, I might add." E16 smiled and batted her eyelashes.

146

"Well I guess the humble gene wasn't passed down," Waddles whispered to Sandy. Sandy nudged Waddles and quietly giggled.

"Yes, he was," answered Quacks.

"So, wait... E9 is your brother?" asked NutJob.

"Yes, he is! But I never met him," said E16.

"Oh, no..." sighed Twitch.

"Then who's that?" and NutJob pointed to E15.

"That's my sister, E15."

"But I thought you were related to E9?"

"I am!"

"How many siblings do you have," asked NutJob.

"Well... there is E1 and E2. And then there was E3 and E4, but E3 went to Heaven. Next there was E5 and E6 and E5 went to Heaven to keep E3 company. Then there is E7 and E8. And of course, E9! And E10 and E11. E12 and E13. And E14, but he went to Heaven too when Ozzie came to get him. And of course, E15. So that makes... let me see... 15 siblings. Three in Heaven and twelve that are here. But I never met any of them except for 15." E16 smiled. "Does that answer your question?"

Nut Job stood there with his mouth open and replied with, "I forgot what the question was." Twitch hit him in the back of his head.

"Anyway..." said Sandy. "E9 used to sing and dance in the rain. He brought so much happiness to this pasture. So you have given us such a treat today in reliving that all over again!"

E16 smiled. "Thank you!" She was so excited and proud.

"Does E15 sing?" asked Sandy.

"Ummm..." 16 carefully thought out her answer. "No. E15 has a lot of other qualities. We make a good team."

The Commander smiled. "Your parents certainly know how to raise wonderful eaglets! And they have raised you well! It is so refreshing to hear a sister speak highly of their sibling. Well done, E16!"

"Thank you, Commander, sir." E16 even surprised herself by not saying something... witty... about E15. M flew to the nest with food. They all looked up at the nest tree. E16 saw E15 as she flew toward the nest. "Well, I better go. That's the dinner bell."

"You better get going," said the Commander.

"Thanks again everyone for joining in! See you next time!" And E16 flew off to the nest.

"Bye!" they all called out.

"That was so much fun," said Sandy.

"It sure was!" they all agreed.

"A female E9," chuckled the Commander. "Outstanding! Ha, ha, ha! OUTSTANDING!" He strolled toward the stables as the rest of the pasture animals prepared to settle in for the night.

After E15 and E16 finished eating, they sat and talked. "What was all that about with the pasture animals?" asked E15.

"They were just telling me that they all had fun dancing and singing with me today. And they asked if you sang too."

"And what witty remark did you make about me? I know you had to say something to make them laugh at me."

"No... Actually, all I said was that you don't sing and that you have other qualities..." E16 paused and added, "And that we make a good team."

"Yeah, right," E15 rolled her eyes.

"I'm not kidding! That's what I said."

E15 looked at E16. "Really? You didn't make fun of me?"

"Nope! But if that bothers you so much, I'll go back down and tell them that your singing is like talons on a chalkboard."

"No, no need to do that..."

"Or maybe I should tell them that the only way you could carry a tune is in a bucket...

"No, 16... that isn't necessary."

"Or perhaps I can say..."

"Alright enough! Thank you for NOT saying those things!" E15 thought and softly added, "Thanks 16. You're a great sister... even for a pip squeak." They looked at each other and smiled. "Well... I guess I'm going to go to my snag tree and get ready for bed. Sweet eagle dreams, Sis."

"Sweet eagle dreams to you, too, Sis. Keep safe from that owl."

"I hope to. You too, 16."

"Thanks, 15... goodnight." E15 flew to the snag tree and E16 settled in on the attic branch.

"Goodnight, 15. I love you," said Harriet as she flew to join E16.

"Goodnight, Mama! I love you too," said E15.

"This is a nice surprise!" said E16 as she got closer to her Mother.

"Just making sure you are safe."

"Where's Dad?"

"He's in the front pine watching out for E15."

"Good. I love you, Mama."

"I love you, baby. Goodnight."

The morning arrived without incident. E15 flew to the nest tree and joined her sister. Suddenly, E15 flew off and went across the street.

"HEY! WAIT FOR ME!" called E16.

The two young eagles circled over the area as they soared higher and higher in the sky. "WOOHOO!" They both cheered out loud. They looked so majestic and free. They soared for quite a while and then they returned to the nest.

"WOW! That was amazing! Is that what Mama and Dad were talking about? About us wanting to leave?" asked 15.

"I don't know, but I want to do it again and again!" replied E16.

The two siblings were so excited. They flapped their wings, they beaked, they pulled each other's feathers... and then they hugged. They had been through this amazing journey together and it was soon going to end and they would both start their own new journey. They knew they loved each other and would always remember each other... the good and the bad... but they were beginning to feel that pull that their parents told them about. They knew their time together as siblings and friends would soon be a memory. So they held onto each other on that branch so they could always hold onto to that moment... and that memory.

Little did they know, Harriet and M were close by and they saw everything. They saw them soar... and they saw that familiar excitement. The type of excitement that will take them away from them... away from HOME. They looked at their two eaglets and smiled. Then they looked at each other and their smiles slowly faded away. They both took a deep breath and hung their heads. They knew that day was not far away.

Chapter 20 ... The Fierce And The Sweet

The days were rainy and stormy during Florida's hurricane season. The E's had gotten a lesson not all juveniles get to learn when growing up in Florida. Usually they would have begun their new lives on their own just as hurricane season started and they would have been venturing north. But as a second clutch, E15 and E16 got to learn all about the brutal Florida summer while still with their parents. The heat, the bugs, the rain, the lightning and thunder, and the wind were daily events that came out of nowhere… not to mention the threat of a hurricane. The siblings learned to endure the harsh weather.

While E16 was in the nest, she studied Stuffy. As the toy blankly stared off at nothing, E16 grabbed the toy in her talons and flapped her mighty wings. "Gotcha!!! Just like Mama and Dad do with food for us!" She continued to play and learn.

E15 joined her on the nest. "What are you doing?" asked E15.

"Just playing," 16 replied. E15 hopped to the veranda and then to the attic. E16 looked up and asked, "What are you doing?"

"I've been thinking."

"About what?"

"About what Mama and Dad told us about leaving and being on our own."

"What about it?"

"Well it sounds pretty awesome… but it also sounds pretty scary."

"I'm not going to do it," announced E16. "They said it was our decision. So, I'm going to stay here. Are you thinking of leaving?"

"Well I've been thinking that maybe I have to try harder at being on my own… you know, like doing things for myself." E15 stared off at the pasture.

E16 watched her sister and then hung her head and asked, "Do you think you can do it?"

"I don't know. But I think I have to at least try harder."

"Well let me know how it goes," E16 said sadly and flew off to the snag tree.

E15 followed her and asked, "Aren't you the least bit curious?"

"Nope!" E16 flew to the oak tree.

E15 followed E16 again. "Don't you want to see all the things they talked about and do things on your own?"

"NO! I like it here! I like the weather, the trees, the pond, the food and all the friends I've made… Quacks, the Commander, Jett… all of them."

"But you see, you and I are different. You're a social butterfly and me… well I'm an eagle!"

"Hey! I'm not a butterfly! I'm an eagle, too! I can't help it if I have a sparkling personality and that I'm irresistible and that others like to be around me and not you."

E16 flew to the pond fence and E15 followed… again. But this time she landed and twisted her ankle. "OW!" E15 cried.

"What's wrong?" E16 asked with concern.

"Just my ankle. It's nothing."

"Let me look."

"I said it's nothing!"

"Okay, no need to get nasty! Geez!" Just then M flew to the nest with food. "Oh yes! I'm starving!" said E16 and she flew to the nest tree hoping to get there before E15.

E15 started to push off of the fence, but her ankle made her wince in pain. She stayed perched as she watched E16 fly to the nest to eat the food. She tucked her foot and sat quietly on the fence rail.

E16 landed in the nest, claimed and mantled the food and started to eat.

"I'm in shock! Where's 15?" asked M.

"By the pond," answered E16. "Her ankle was hurting her so I guess she's not coming."

"What's wrong with her ankle?"

"She landed funny. You know how she isn't the best at landing."

M turned and looked toward the pond concerned about his daughter.

E15 was hungry. She tried again to fly, but it hurt too much to push hard off of the fence rail to get to the nest tree. She was able to do a short flight to the oak tree. "I think I should just relax my foot until it feels better. It will probably just be a few more minutes." So E15 relaxed on the oak… but not for a few minutes… for the entire day.

The next day E16 was as happy as she could be. She enjoyed every food delivery.

E15 knew she had to eat to get strong and healthy. The weather was stormy. Food was brought to the nest and E15 knew she had to eat. She stretched her leg and said, "It's now or never," and she flew to the nest and claimed the food.

But soon E16 arrived and stole the food from E15. E16 knew this was not like E15 at all. There was no fighting. But E16 wasn't about to give up food just because there wasn't a fight. So E16 ate. The wind started to blow. The nest tree started to sway. The clouds grew dark... and the rain poured down into the nest. E15 tried to hold onto the nest and protect herself from the storm, but her ankle was still too sore. She decided it was best to lay down in the nest to stay safe. E16 continued to eat. The wind howled and nest material started flying about... even Stuffy. Suddenly, a gust of wind blew through the nest area with great force and Stuffy flew out of the nest. The toy clung to the side of the nest through the storm. In eagle terms one could say that Stuffy "branched." But regardless, this wasn't good for the toy. Stuffy was doomed. E15 stayed low and E16 continued to eat as if nothing was going on. Neither seemed concerned for their childhood friend as he held onto the nest. It seemed they had now become mature eagles... juveniles.

Later in the day when more food arrived at the nest, E16 felt bad for E15 and she let her have some of the food. E16 flew to the attic and E15 gobbled down the food.

"You're welcome," E16 said sarcastically.

The next day E15 was feeling much better. She flew to other trees, the pond and wherever she pleased. "Ah! YES!!! Finally!" she said as she wiggled her toes and spun around on the oak tree limb. "I can fly and land without any pain!" And E15 seemed to come back stronger than before.

Both siblings flew to the nest. When they landed, E16 mantled as if she had food. E15 tried to steal it. She tried and tried, but nothing. Sooo...

"OW!" screamed E16 after E15 kicked her. "What was that for? What's wrong with you?"

"I want the food!"

"I don't have any food!" replied E16. E15 kicked E16 again. "I can see you are feeling better and you're back to your usual bully self... maybe even worse! And here I felt bad for you and gave you my food yesterday." E15 found something to nibble on and then flew to the oak tree.

Harriet flew to the attic. E16 flew to perch next to her. She could tell E16 was upset. "What's wrong, baby?"

"E15," E16 said sadly.

"What happened with E15?" Harriet asked although she knew.

"She's mean! She's a bully!"

153

"She's an eagle," said Harriet.

"But I'm an eagle too and I'm not a bully!"

Harriet looked at her sweet 16. "I know, sweetheart, but when you and 15 start on your new lives you will have to be a bully... I mean, an eagle to survive.

"But I'm not leaving!"

Harriet sighed and smiled. "My sweet 16. That's what you say now."

"Mama! You and Dad both said it was our decision... our choice... and my choice is to stay!"

"Okay, okay... BUT!... and this is only a but, you might want to get a little tougher. Let's pretend... When E15 leaves..."

"Good! I hope it's today!" E16 said bitterly.

"WHEN E15 leaves... what if E9 comes to visit?"

"Really? E9? When? I can't wait!" E16 said with so much enthusiasm.

"I didn't say he was coming. I said what if."

"Oh..." E16 said disappointedly.

"As much as you love E9 and he would love you, when it comes to food, E9 would not be looking to share. Remember he was an only child."

"No, he wasn't. He had Eggbert."

Harriet smiled. "Yes, he had Eggbert. But Eggbert didn't eat. So E9 was an only eagle child and Eggbert was an only eagle egg child. Okay?"

"Okay..."

"So E9 is not accustomed to sharing food with siblings and he would end up acting just like E15."

"No, he wouldn't! No one acts like E15! E15 is just mean!"

"I'm just saying that you need to get a little more aggressive... like 15."

"I don't want to be anything like E15!"

"You don't have to be like E15... you just need some aggressiveness when it comes to the food. Your Dad is aggressive and so am I." E16 stared into her Mother's eyes taking in every word she said. "Please, 16... for me. It is something you need to do."

"Even if I stay here?"

"Even if you stay here."

E16 paused and thought. "Alright... I'll try. I can't promise, but I'll try."

"That's all I can ask you to do, baby."

"Thank you, Mama. I love you." And E16 flew off to the snag tree in the west pasture.

Harriet watched E16 fly off and she softly replied, "I love you too, my sweet baby." She looked down at the empty nest and sighed with a heavy heart. She knew it wouldn't be long. "And I wouldn't doubt if you were the first to leave," sighed Harriet to herself.

E16 picked at small branches and broke the sticks and transferred them from her beak to her talons. Harriet watched and smiled.

That night the entire family slept together on the nest tree. Harriet slept with one eye open. She just felt like something was up. She saw E15 had woken up before midnight. Harriet watched E15 and saw she was restless and was moving around in the nest. E15 then went to the veranda and then to the porch. E15 stared out at the pasture and struggled to see where the trees were.

"E15!" Harriet said in a quiet, but firm tone.

"Yes, Mama?"

"What are you doing?"

"I'm watching the pasture. I can't see all the trees and the pond."

"Don't worry about the trees and the pond," Harriet replied. "I don't want you flying around at night so get it out of your head this minute!"

E16 heard the conversation between E15 and their Mother and of course she had to put her two cents in. "Yeah, what are you part owl or vampire or something? Go to sleep!"

"I'm an eagle, pip squeak. Mind your own business!" demanded E15.

"Okay you two, knock it off! Go back to sleep, 16. I can handle this myself."

"Okay, Mama. But let me know if you need me." E16 closed her eyes and went back to sleep.

"Now go back to sleep, 15. You need your rest!"

"Yes, Mama. Goodnight. I love you."

"I love you too, 15."

And E15 listened to Harriet and went to sleep.

The next day was like all the others EXCEPT... E15 was even more aggressive. The two siblings flew to the pond. E15 swooped down close to the pond and scared the ducks.

"INCOMING EAGLE!" said Lori the duck as she alerted everyone and they all scattered out of E15's path.

E16 flew to the pond and waded into the water for a bath. "Ahhh...!" exclaimed E16 as she smiled.

155

"Good morning, E16," said Quacks.

"Oh, good morning, Quacks! How are you today?" asked E16.

"I'm fine, thank you." Quacks glanced over at E15 on the pond fence. She narrowed her eyes.

"What's wrong?" asked E16 as she tilted her head.

"Your sibling is what's wrong," replied Quacks angrily.

"Oh... I know what you're talking about."

"She is so mean! If I could, I would... I would... ARGH! She gets me so mad!"

"You're not alone," said E16. "She's mean to me too and I'm her sister!"

"But I don't understand... You're so nice and you know how we all feel about E9... and all of your other siblings were always nice to all of us, too. But she's so... mean!"

"I think... I'm not sure... but... maybe it's because of her name."

"I don't understand," said Quacks.

"Her name is E15... 15 like our Dad. So, she thinks she's special."

"But your Dad isn't mean like her."

"I know. But I think it went to her head. She can be nice... sometimes." E16 paused and added, "I'm sorry she scared all of you."

Quacks looked at E15 as she snoozed on the pond fence. "I guess being mean takes a lot of work and makes her sleepy." Quacks and E16 giggled. "Thank you, 16. You are so much like E9." She turned and saw her friends were waiting for her.

"Come on, Quacks!" called out Rachel, Tina and Tracey.

"Those are my friends. I have to go now. You have a good day... and good luck!"

"Thanks, Quacks!" called out E16 as Quacks floated away. "I'll need it," E16 said quietly.

But E16 would need more than luck to put up with E15. The siblings seemed to argue more often and their squabbles became more aggressive. At first it was always about food, but now it became more frequent about... well about anything!

Both young eagles were in the nest when an argument started. Neither one wanted to give in. They both toppled over the nest and tumbled through the air. They managed to unwedge Stuffy from the side of the nest. Now Stuffy had "accidentally fledged" in eagle terms.

Later that day, E16 was perched on the veranda. For no reason, E15 pushed E16 off of the branch and then perched in the same spot. As E16 flew off she called out, "What is wrong with you? Leave me alone!"

But like her brother before her, E9, E16 didn't hold a grudge and the next day she was her usual happy self as she sang, danced and played on the branches of any tree she liked. She continued to practice picking up sticks in her beak and transferring them to her talons. Suddenly she flew off and on the fly she grabbed a branch, broke it off and carried it in her talons. She was so pleased and proud of herself! "Woohoo!" she cheered. "Like a BIG eagle! WOOHOO!" She flew through the pasture and like E9, she greeted her friends and anyone else in her path. "Good morning, Commander!"

"Well! Good morning there, little lady! How are you today?"

"I'm fine, sir! I broke a branch while I was in flight and I carried it in my talons!"

"Well that sounds like a big deal if I have ever heard one! That is outstanding!"

"It is, sir! My parents are the best nest builders in the whole wide world and I will be too!"

"I don't doubt that at all! Your parents are quite remarkable parents!"

"Yes, they are. Well, I better go. You have a good day, sir!"

"Thank you, Miss 16. You, too!" The Commander smiled and chuckled. "So much like E9."

E16 flew over the pond. "Good morning, Kelli! Hi, Amelia! Hi, Reid!"

"Hi, E16!" they all waved and replied.

"Hi, Miss Sandy and Miss Waddles!"

"Good morning, E16!" called out Sandy.

"Hi, 16!" said Waddles.

"Such a happy young eagle," said Sandy to Waddles.

"I'll say. Unlike..." Waddles motioned with her head toward E15 as E15 perched in the oak tree.

Sandy quietly nodded in agreement. "Maybe she'll come around."

"Don't hold your breath," said Waddles.

E16 landed next to E15. E15 was snoozing on the oak tree already.

"Hey! Are you awake?" E16 loudly asked.

"Not anymore," E15 answered in an annoyed tone.

"It is such a beautiful day, isn't it!?" There was no response from E15. "Smell that fresh air and feel that warm breeze."

"It smells like the stables and it isn't warm, it's hot."

"I love this time of day. Everything is fresh and new. But I also love the afternoon. Everything is active and busy... full of life and adventure." E16 stopped and thought for a moment. E15 closed her eyes. E16 continued. "But the evening... the evening is great too! Everything is winding down. The sky gets painted in beautiful colors as the sun sets and the moon rises. And before you know it... it is dark and all the stars come out and twinkle. Then all sorts of animals that we have never met or see during the day start their adventure. And then there's the crickets and the frogs! They all come out and sing their songs to lull us to sleep. Ahhh! Life is great!" E15 was sound asleep. "E15? E15 are you listening to me?" E15 woke up, shook her head and flew to a snag tree. E16 sighed. Suddenly, E16 sensed she wasn't alone. She noticed some movement to her left. She slowly turned to see what it was. "Hello!" The two small figures stood frozen with fear on the oak limb. "Don't be afraid," said E16. The two figures stood as still as statues. "Okay, I'll go first. My name is E16." Still nothing from the two statues. "Okay, this is where you two would introduce yourselves to me. You would say, my name is..."

One figure blinked his eyes, gulped and quietly said, "My name is NutJob and this is Witch, I mean Twitch." Twitch smacked NutJob in the back of his head.

E16 laughed, "Nice to make your acquaintance NutJob and Twitch." The two squirrels were unsure of what they should do. They both nodded their heads and stared at the young eagle. "Did you know my brother, E9?" The two nodded again. E16 looked at the two squirrels. She realized they were frightened. "Well, I'm glad we met. Maybe we can talk again some other time." The two squirrels nodded again. "Okay... Have a nice day!" said E16 and she flew off to the snag tree and joined E15. "Have you met NutJob and Twitch?"

E15 sighed. Annoyed, she replied, "No, I haven't. I'm not looking for friends. I'm looking for food." E15 then flew to the nest.

"No one wants to talk today!" said E16. She kept herself entertained as she hopped, danced and sang on the snag tree. She went to fly off, but she didn't let go. She hung upside down for a second. The pasture animals all gasped. She let go and flew back to the oak tree.

"Did you see that?" asked Waddles.

"I certainly did. It is uncanny!" replied Sandy. "Just like E9 did."

E16 kept herself occupied as she went from limb to limb on the oak tree. She heard a sweet little giggle. She looked to her left and she looked to her right, but she saw no one. "Who was that?" Suddenly a little light gray feather floated in front of her face. E16's eyes crossed as she focused on the feather. She smiled. "Hey! I know you. You floated by me in the nest!" She heard the giggle again and the feather happily floated away. "Bye!" said E16. "Hope to see you again!"

The day consisted of waiting for food, taking baths, and exploring. E15 was on the pond fence when E16 landed on a string of decorative lights hanging by the pond.

"What are you doing now?" asked E15 as she shook her head.

"Swinging" replied E16. E15 sighed and looked away. It might have looked like playtime and it probably was to E16, but it was an excellent display of balance, coordination and strength. E16 then flew to a tree stump and pulled on the plants and snapped branches. All lessons. E16 just couldn't sit still. She sang, danced, hopped, played, bathed, explored and talked... and talked. She looked at E15 and asked. "What are YOU doing?"

"Getting my beauty sleep. And don't get smart!"

"Well, I was just going to ask you what year we should wake you up?" she laughed and flew off.

That night in the nest tree, E15 was restless again. She moved from the attic to the veranda to the nest to the porch. She just couldn't get sleepy and she just couldn't stay still. She struggled again to see the trees and the pond. It was almost as if she needed to make sure they were still there. Only this time Harriet was not on the nest tree to stop her. Suddenly, E15 flew off toward a snag tree, but she didn't make the landing and she tumbled to the ground. "Uh-oh... Mama is NOT going to be happy about this!"

Hours later, the sun greeted the day. Felix the great blue heron flew above the nest tree as he headed toward the pond.

"Hey, Miss Harriet," Felix called out. "And little eagle," he added.

"Good morning, Felix," replied Harriet. E16 just waved.

"Where's the other baby?" Felix asked.

"We're not sure yet. She flew off of the nest tree during the night and we don't know where she ended up. She obviously didn't land on a tree. So we'll discover where she slept soon enough."

Felix rolled his eyes. "Kids! They think they know everything and we know nothing. They don't realize that's how we got to this age... by learning!"

"My Mama and Dad know everything!" E16 announced.

"E16!" Harriet smiled. "E16 doesn't fly at night. She stays on her perch."

"Smart girl! You keep listening to your Mama. Hope you find your little rebel soon. Y'all have a good day!" and Felix continued to the pond.

"Thanks Felix. You have a good day, too!"

"Mama, why does 15 fly at night?"

"I have no idea, 16. And she just doesn't want to listen! I wish I knew where she was." Harriet paused. "E15!!!" Harriet called out.

"E15!!!" E16 called out to help her Mother.

"I'm going to check on her, 16."

"Okay, Mama." E16 searched the nest for something to eat. "I'll keep calling for her, just in case." So E16 searched for food and found some to nibble on. In between bites, she would call out with a beak full of food, "E15! Where are you?" All done with nestovers, E16 flew to the snag tree. "There you are, 15!"

"Oh no! You found me," E15 smirked.

"I found you! I found you!" E16 repeated as she hopped on the snag limb. She then spotted M as he flew in with food. "And now I found Dad! WOOHOO!"

E16 immediately flew toward the nest to meet her Dad, but M flew right past E16 and headed to the pond instead. E16 had to put on the brakes and quickly turn around to follow him. M landed at the pond and both E15 and E16 surrounded their Father. They fought over the food he had for them. M ran to the pond to avoid the attack. He then went to the oak tree to observe how the kids interacted. First E16 claimed the food and then E15 stole it. M flew back down to the juveniles. Both of them warned their Dad to stay away. M flew off again and continued to watch their progress. He shook his head and flew back and landed near the two siblings.

"You must eat your food or someone else will! Someone like ME!" M attempted to steal the food, but both of the kids kept their Dad away. M flew off and out of sight. He soon returned with more food. E16 immediately rushed over to M and snatched the fish away from him. Pleased, M flew off.

Now both young eagles had food to eat. They both enjoyed their meals. E16 finished quickly and moved closer to E15. E15 warned E16 to stay away. E16 waited for an opportune time. M then landed nearby. E16 chased him away. She turned back to E15 and they battled over the food that E15 still had.

"It's mine!" screamed E15.

"I'm still hungry!" cried E16.

"I don't care!" yelled E15.

As the two argued, M saw that he could steal some of the food from them. E16 saw what her Dad had done.

"Hey! That's mine!" E16 screamed as she chased her Dad again. She quickly stole the food from M.

The kids battled again as M watched and then he flew off. An exhausting way to start the day. Food all eaten, E15 went to the pond fence and took a nap and E16 perched on the pylon at the pond. Tummies were full and the two siblings were quiet.

The days ahead were pretty much the same. They perfected their lessons. They took baths, they battled and sometimes they hung out peacefully with each other.

One morning as E15 and E16 sat perched on the nest tree, E16 saw something as it flew overhead.

E16 started screaming. "Get out of here! This is our home!" and she flew off of the attic and chased the large intruder. She quickly returned... and so did the large bird.

"What is that?" asked E15.

"I have no idea, but it is weird looking. At first, I thought it was some other young eagle, but he's funny looking. Certainly not good looking like me." E16 turned and looked at E15. "He looks more like you."

"Ha! Ha! You are a real comedian."

E16 smiled and continued to watch the large bird. She flew off again and chased it. "I said GO AWAY!"

"Okay, okay, little one. Cool your jets." The intruder laughed. "Seems like M15 has a real feisty one here."

"You know my Dad?" asked E16 as she and the intruder continued to fly around the nest tree area.

"Yes, yes I do. Your Dad and I go back a few years. I even know your brother E9."

"You do?" This bit of information impressed E16.

"I'm Vinny the vulture. You must be E12 and E13?"

"No, I'm E16 and that's E15." E16 pointed to E15 perched on the attic branch.

"That's right. Your Mom and I spoke about your little brother, E14. So, you're E16! Time goes by so fast. They are up to sixteen already!" Vinny shook his head in disbelief.

"You know my Mama?" asked 16.

"I just met her a while ago when she was getting you two some food." E16 listened as the vulture continued. "You know, I saw you had a couple of armored catfish heads as nestovers that no one was eating. I'm sure your parents taught you if you don't eat it someone else will. I KNOW your Dad taught you that. He never left a morsel of food for anyone when he was a young eagle like you. He learned the hard way like we all do. Once someone stole his food, they never stole it again." E16 knew the vulture was right. The vultures stomach growled with hunger. "Well, as my stomach just announced I'm hungry so I better keep moving along... for now. I'm sure I'll be seeing you and your sibling again real soon. Stay safe." And Vinny continued to fly away with empty talons.

E16 landed next to E15 and asked, "Do you know what a vulture is?"

"A what?" E15 questioned.

"A vulture. He said his name is Vinny and he is a vulture. He also said he knows Dad and E9." E16 stared at the sky.

"What's the matter?" asked E15.

E16 hesitated. "Nothing..." She paused and added, "He said he would see you and me again real soon. I wonder what he meant by that."

"He meant exactly what he said... He'll see us again real soon. It's a big sky and I'm sure that he'll be flying overhead again. Don't turn it into something that it isn't."

"I guess..." E16 then quietly added, "But it was the way he said it..." E16 broke her gaze from the sky and flew across the road. E15 followed. They met up with their parents.

"Hey, Dad... who's Vinny? Vinny the vulture?" asked E16.

Harriet and M looked at each other. M slowly answered, "He's an old friend of mine. Why?"

"He was flying over our nest and I chased him away. Then he came back and he told me that he knew you and E9. He also said he would see us again real soon. What do you think he meant by that?"

M looked at Harriet and then back at the two young eagles as they innocently waited for an explanation. Their eyes were wide as they searched for an answer. "He's been known to fly with our kids as they got older. So, he sees that you're both grown up now... so... I guess that's what he meant."

"Oh... okay!" replied E16. E15 and E16 were fine with the answer they got. They were content, but their parents' hearts started to break. The day was coming soon.

"I'll be right back," said M and he flew off.

"So, you know Vinny too, right Mama?" asked E16.

"I only met him once. This year in fact. He seems very nice."

M quickly returned with food. "Yay Dad!" the kids cheered.

"This is cool! We've never eaten over here before," said E16.

"It's sort of like going to a new restaurant," said Harriet as she smiled.

Both eaglets ate the food and soon went back to their pasture across the road.

They spent the day at the pond where they explored and rested. They both flew to the nest tree in anticipation of a food delivery. Eventually Harriet brought a fish to the nest. Both siblings opened their mighty wings and mantled as they rushed to claim the food. But in their eagerness, no one noticed that the fish fell out of the nest. E15 thought E16 had it and E15 kept looking under E16 so she could steal it.

"Stop it!" yelled E16 and she went up on the spike branch.

"Give it to me!" demanded E15.

"I don't have it!" exclaimed E16.

"You do have it because it isn't in the nest!"

"Well you're wrong because I don't have it!" And without any warning E15 pushed E16 off of the spike. "YOU ARE SO MEAN!" screamed E16 as she flew to the front snag tree. E15's aggression toward E16 seemed to have become a common daily occurrence.

Later as they both sat near the pond E16 asked E15, "Why are you so mean to me? Especially when there is food."

"You know how I get when I'm hungry," replied E15.

"I get hungry too, but I don't push you off of branches or the nest."

163

"Well you should know by now not to mess with me and my stomach when I'm hungry!"

"What?"

"It's like you're always trying to take a French fry off of my plate while I'm eating. Get your own!"

"I do have my own and then you steal the entire plate... French fries and all! By the way... what's a French fry?"

As the day was coming to an end, E15 napped on the attic branch. Harriet flew to the nest with a fish. She dropped it off in the nest and then went to the attic. E15 was full. She wasn't hungry at all, but she hopped down into the nest to claim the food. She didn't eat it. She looked around and waited for E16 to see that she had food. Sure enough E16 flew to the nest tree and landed under the nest.

Mockingly, E15 said, "Look what I have, pip squeak."

E16 yelled at E15. "You're not even hungry! I'm starving! You're just going to eat that fish because you know I want it!"

"Maybe," said E15 as she continued to guard the fish and then started to eat it.

Soon M flew to the nest with another fish. He dropped it off in the nest and he went to the attic. E16 followed her Dad and landed next to him.

"Thanks, Dad," said E16. She hopped down into the nest and claimed one of the fish. Both siblings ate. M flew next to Harriet and they perched together.

"That was very sweet of you, M," Harriet whispered.

"I know, but she has to get more aggressive! She reminds me so much of E9. Everything is a toy... everyone is a friend. She's just like him! She's too nice! She needs to be more like you." Harriet raised her eyebrows and gave him a look. "That didn't come out the way I wanted it to. I meant she is too nice... she has to be more aggressive like you are... you are nice, too... more than nice... but you have an aggressive side and she needs to have that too!"

"I understand, M. And she is very much like E9. But look how amazing he turned out. She will get more aggressive in her time. And she has gotten somewhat better. And just like E9, she has a hard time being aggressive with her family. Whereas E15..." Harriet grinned.

"E15's a beast!" M chuckled. Harriet gave M a look of disapproval. "I mean that in a good sense. She's fierce! Like you!" M gave Harriet one of his winning M smiles as he wiggled his eyebrows.

"Oh, your eyebrows! You haven't wiggled your eyebrows at me... gee, I can't remember when... did you even wiggle them this season?"

"Yeah, I think I might have once or twice." They both stopped, thought and laughed.

"It has certainly been some season." They hung their heads as they both thought of their E14. Harriet quickly changed the mood back to being lighthearted. "How can I ever resist those eyebrows and that smile of yours!" They kissed.

"They are both like you," said M. "E15 is your fierce side and E16 is your sweet side."

"They are like both of us," said Harriet. They continued to watch their two juveniles. "And just like E16 is developing a fierce side... you'll see... E15 will develop a sweet side."

"HA! Yeah, right!" M laughed. Harriet narrowed her eyes. "Oh... you were being serious. Oh okay, yeah, anything can happen." Harriet smiled, rolled her eyes and shook her head at her M.

E16 finished her fish first. She slowly moved closer to E15 and stole her fish. But it wasn't for long. E15 soon took the fish away from E16.

Then surprisingly, E15 said, "You can have it. I'm stuffed."

E16 quickly took the fish just in case it was a trick. But it wasn't and E16 ate the fish. E15 went to the spike and proudly displayed her huge crop for her Mom and Dad to see.

"Did you swallow a bowling ball, E15?" M teased. E15 just proudly smiled.

The nest tree was surrounded by a beautiful sky as the sun got ready for bed and the moon was waking up to shine.

E16 thought she finished the fish. Harriet didn't agree. So, she hopped down into the nest and started to eat the rest of the fish that E16 didn't eat.

"Hey! I was leaving that for a snack for later!" whined E16. She grabbed the fish with her talons and tugged.

Harriet held onto the fish with her beak and the tug of war started. "Come on, E16 take the fish away from me!" Harriet encouraged E16 to be more aggressive. But of course, Harriet won. "You have to learn, 16. The food is here now. I'm not worried about a snack later. I can have a crop drop later.

You have to learn to eat what you have when you have it and you have to eat it quickly... or someone else will."

"Yes, Mama," E16 said sadly.

Harriet felt bad for her baby so she fed E16 some fish. Tummy full, E16 then flew to the attic. She too had an impressive crop. Harriet finished the fish and she flew to the attic as well. E15 hopped down into the nest.

It was a beautiful sight to behold. Harriet and M perched side by side as their bodies formed a heart... their love for each other cradling their little ones. Their precious babies slept in the nest tree with them. Nights like this would end soon. But for this night, love surrounded the nest tree for all the world to see... their love and their HOME!

But little did they know the surprise that awaited them...

Chapter 21 ... Here I Come World!

*L*essons, lessons and more lessons. And each lesson was always being perfected. Each sibling showed off their skills to the other... that forever sibling rivalry.

E15 broke off a stick and transferred it from her beak to her talons. Then she carried it to the nest.

"See, I can carry things and build a nest too!" E15 said proudly as E16 watched.

Later on, M brought food to the nest. E15 immediately claimed it, but E16 stole it. E15 tried and tried to get it back, but 16 flew off to the snag tree with the prize and ate all of it. She too was proud of herself as E15 watched.

E16 started spending more time with Harriet and M. Moments spent with their parents were extremely important. All lessons were valuable, but these last lessons were the ones that taught them how to hunt and steal food to survive when they go off on their own.

One day, while the two siblings flew around the pasture, something was different. E16 landed on the snag tree and E15 followed. Immediately E16 flew to the pond and E15 followed. They both perched on a pylon. For a change E16 was quiet.

"Are you okay?" asked E15. "You seem very different today. You hardly said a word all day. THAT is NOT like you at all!"

E16 looked at the vast pasture and the endless sky and replied. "Do you really think there is more to life than just here? Do you think that the sky continues over other lands, rivers, trees... just more than just the pasture?"

"What are you talking about?"

"I can't stop thinking about Vinny the vulture."

"What do you mean?"

"I don't know... I just feel like I have to see what is over that horizon... past the tree line... beyond the ponds. I never thought I would say this, but I feel like something is calling me... like I have to soar to great heights and take on the world... that I have to start a new life... an eagle life!"

"You won't leave. You said so yourself. Besides, you're not tough enough."

"But I am, thanks to you. Because of how you treated me I am prepared. I know how to be around strangers. I know how to act and still protect myself and survive. I know when to fight and when to take flight. And it is all because of you, 15... thank you. I thought you were being a bully, but little did I know you were teaching me survival tactics. You made me stronger and wiser."

"Yeah, but you have Mama and Dad here... and what about all your friends?"

"I know... I know," E16 said with a heavy heart. Then she smiled and added, "But now something feels different. Talking with Vinny and feeling the thrill of soaring, I'm just..." 16 hesitated and sighed. "I'm just so torn! I love Mama and Dad... and you," E15 hung her head when hearing 16's words. E16 continued. "I'll miss you all! But I never dreamt I would feel this way." Tears filled 16's eyes and she flew to the snag.

E15 sat perched in shock with the echo of E16's words swirling around in her head. "No, she won't leave," she mumbled under her breath. "Will she?" E15's heart sunk to her stomach.

That evening, Harriet and M looked at their 16. They knew.

"You know you only leave when you are absolutely ready, right 16?"

"Yes, Mama... I know. I love you, Mama and I love you, Dad. I'll miss you both." Harriet and M looked at their little girl who wasn't little anymore. She had matured into a beautiful, smart and resilient young eagle. "I'll even miss you, 15. And remember Dad, I'm your girl and you're my Dad. You're the best friend I ever had. Eagles may come and eagles may go, but my Dad's the best male eagle I'll ever know." Tears filled everyone's eyes.

Choking back the tears, M responded, "You're my girl."

"And you're my Dad."

"My heart skips a beat and I'm so glad," M's voice cracked.

"I took your wing," added 16.

"And you stole my heart."

Together they sang, "In your eyes I saw this love start." They looked into each other's tear-filled eyes and hugged.

"I love you, 16," M whispered to his little girl.

"I love you, Dad... thank you... Thank you for everything." And with E16's words, M's emotions got the best of him and he flew to the pond.

Wiping away her tears, Harriet looked at their young eagle. "E16, when you come to visit it will be very difficult. We will have to chase you away if we have little ones."

"I know, Mama. You explained this to us. I know."

"But 16, please, when we chase you away, please turn and look at me. I will give you a wink. A wink that tells you everything... that we love you and miss you… and that every night we pray that you are healthy, happy and safe."

E16 smiled, "Thank you, Mama. That will mean so much to me. And I will wink back to say the same."

Harriet hugged her little baby as tears filled her eyes again. "Live a long, strong, healthy life, my 16." She was confident that their 16 was ready and mature enough to take care of herself. She also knew that one day she would make a remarkable mother to her own eaglets. It was difficult to let go of her 16, but she knew she had to. They looked into each other's eyes… a moment neither would ever forget.

In the morning, E16 was in the nest tree. E15 was at the pond. Harriet and M were perched across the road. Suddenly, a small light gray feather flew in front of E16. The same feather that had been watching over the nest guiding and protecting E16 and E15. E16 heard that familiar sweet giggle that accompanied the feather each time.

E16 smiled, flew off of the nest tree and called out as she started to soar high in the sky, "Goodbye everyone! Goodbye Commander, Goodbye Quacks! Goodbye Jett! Goodbye everyone! I love you, Mama! I love you, Dad! I love you, E15! You are all forever in my heart!"

"We love you, 16. You will forever be in my heart, too. Live a long, strong, healthy and happy life, my baby," said Harriet as her tears stained her beautiful, white feathers.

"I love you, 16… You're my girl that stole my heart," M tearfully called out.

Then the sweet little voice said, "Come on E16! I'll show you the way to start your new big eagle life! I will be forever young, but you will grow to be a remarkable and majestic eagle. I will always watch over you and protect you wherever you go! Fly high and free my beautiful sister… our E16!"

And E16's heart soared as she flew higher and higher to her new eagle life. "Goodbye! WOOHOO! Here I come world!"

The pasture animals all came out to watch E16 start her new life. "Goodbye!" they all called out.

"God speed, little lady," said the Commander tearfully.

"Goodbye, my friend!" said Quacks. "I'll miss you. Give E9 my love when you see him."

"Goodbye, E16. I'm so glad we met!" Jett said as he flew higher to wave to E16.

They could hear E16 singing a song as she soared higher and higher. "I'm on my way to start my life anew. You will always be with me and I'll always love you!" she sang. They all cheered and waved. E16's song danced on the wind. Soon both the song and E16 faded from their lives. They all looked at each other and slowly the smiles fell from their faces.

"It never gets easy," said the Commander as he turned and walked toward the stables.

E15 perched motionless on the pylon as E16 disappeared from sight. Tears rolled down E15's face. "Goodbye, 16. I'll miss you... I can't believe you left. Please live a good, long, healthy life! I hope we meet up again." E15 then yelled out... "I'M SORRY, 16. I'M SORRY I BULLIED YOU... I LOVE YOU... PLEASE COME BACK." Heartbroken, E15's tears fell into the pond.

Harriet and M watched and listened to E15's words.

"Well, I guess it won't be long until 15 decides to leave now," said M. "I can't stand this part. Sometimes it seems so hard and so much work to have eaglets, but it is all worth it. Then this day comes and it seems like it was just yesterday that they were eggs. It was just yesterday that 16 swung that wing of hers to get out of her egg. That one silly wing trying to break through. And then when she finally hatched, she was on top of 15 and ready to join in on the feeding time." M took a deep breath. "And now she soared out of our lives and into her own in the blink of an eye." Harriet and M hugged as tears fell from their eyes.

The days ahead were quiet. E16 had always kept the pasture busy and alive with her singing and constant talking.

E15 perched and just looked around the pasture. "IT JUST ISN'T FAIR! SHE WAS GOING TO STAY!" E15 cried out.

But as the days went by, life carried on at the nest tree. In fact, there were some unexpected changes. E15 started talking more. Afterall, she did have a wonderful teacher. M continued to bring food to the nest and soon E15 had become accustomed to being an only child.

One evening, Harriet and M flew to the pond for some adult eagle time together. The adults could hear E15 calling to them from the nest. But when they returned to the nest, E15 carried on like a spoiled little eaglet! E15 eventually calmed down as the setting sun illuminated her beautiful feathers.

The pasture became E15's world and E15 started to accept that others shared the pasture with her.

"Hello, E15!" said the Commander.

Shyly, E15 replied, "Hello."

"I'm the Commander. We've never been properly introduced." The Commander paused. "So E16 has started her new life! She must be so excited!"

"I guess so." E15 then slowly added, "It's weird without her."

"Oh, I'm sure it is. And I'm sure it is weird for her too not having her older sibling with her."

"Gee, I never thought of it that way. I guess you're right."

The conversation with E15 was a little difficult... after all talking a lot was very new to E15... especially with strangers. "Well," said the Commander after a long pause in the conversation. "I'm glad we finally met. If you ever need a friend to talk to, I'm always here."

E15 smiled. "Thank you, Commander, sir!" E15 was excited that she made a friend.

"You are very welcome, 15!" and the Commander turned and continued through the pasture.

"Gee, he isn't scary at all! I see why 16 liked him."

That evening M joined Harriet on the attic branch. E15 was nowhere in sight so it looked like the two adults had some alone time.

"Ah, my beautiful Harriet! It is such a lovely evening," said M. He went to kiss Harriet when suddenly they heard E15 flying toward them, squeeing loudly. Both Harriet and M nervously looked all around them to see where 15 was. Before they could even move, E15 landed right next to her parents.

"Okay! Okay, 15! Please calm down! Stop yelling!" said Harriet. But 15 continued to squee loudly and non-stop.

M moved closer to Harriet and whispered, "Let's remember all of this if we ever talk about a second clutch again." They both smiled.

E15 eventually calmed down. The sunset was beautiful and the family of three settled in for the night.

Days to come were filled with teaching E15 how to hunt and steal... and with providing E15 with food. E15 became very content with her new living arrangement.

Something amazing happened though... the days were full of rainbows. Harriet looked at M. "You know what all of these rainbows are telling us?" M nodded as Harriet continued, "Ozzie, E3, E5 and E14 are ALL watching over us and they are also guiding and protecting E16."

It was a welcomed sign and a comforting sign.

Something else was happening that was comforting. E15 became quite a character. Not only was E15 fierce, but now she became fun. Serious, no nonsense E15 had learned from E16 to stop and enjoy life and all of its beauty and wonder. E15 would watch all the little birds as they flew by, head tilted and taking it all in. And then E15 did something no one expected... SHE DANCED!!! She would fly from the nest tree to all the snags and then to the oak tree and she would dance. So as much as E16 learned from E15 being a "bully", E15 learned to have fun from E16.

"Are you seeing this?" asked Sandy.

"Yes, I am," replied Waddles.

"Hi, ladies," said 15 as she flew from tree to tree over the pond.

"Hi!" replied Sandy and Waddles.

"I guess some E16 sweetness rubbed off on 15," said Sandy. Shocked, Waddles nodded.

Then something caught E15's eye. Something very curious. E15 flew to the nest tree to get a better view. Unbeknownst to E15, a few years ago, Harriet and M started an alternate nest in the west pasture. The two adults brought sticks to that nest and placed them as if building a new nest. E15 watched with great curiosity.

"Hmmm... could they be building that for me? ...OR... is the nest tree mine and this new nest is for them?" E15 wondered out loud.

Jett landed next to E15 as E15 continued to watch Harriet and M.

"Hey, 15!"

"Hey, Jett!"

"What's going on?" asked Jett as he watched Harriet and M place more sticks in the partial nest in the west pasture.

"I don't know. I'm not sure if they want me to practice building a nest or if it is a new nest for them or maybe a new nest for me."

"For you?"

"Yeah, if I decide to stay."

"You can do that?"

"My Mama and Dad said it was up to us to make that decision."

"Wow! That's cool! Gee, I'm surprised that any of you guys ever leave."

E15 hopped down into her nest and moved some sticks around. "I'm not sure which tree I would want though... the new one or our home nest tree." E15 looked over at the new nest and then she looked around the nest tree nest. "Oh well. I guess we'll see."

It seemed E15 was quite content with the idea of staying home near Harriet and M... at least for now.

Chapter 22 ... A New Life, A New Season... Or Not

*E*15 enjoyed her extended stay with Harriet and M. She spent her time playing, dancing, making friends, and by taking an occasional nap. She carried sticks and moss to other trees. She broke pieces of bark from the snag tree all in fun and as a lesson. But E15 also SOARED! She loved the feeling of being free. What eagle doesn't? When she would return from the sky, she would search for her Dad. One day M15 was at Yonder Pond when E15 found him. They sat perched side by side on the pine tree and of course, E15 squeed away! Patient and well-trained, M just sat there while 15 carried on loudly. Occasionally M would respond to E15, but E15 did most of the "talking." E15 was relentless and moved closer to M. E15 got right up to M's face and while squeeing, she nipped at M's head.

M backed his head away from E15 and said, "What are you doing?"

But E15 didn't answer. She just squeed and complained in her Dad's ear and M quietly answered until enough was enough.

M certainly put up with a lot and showed his love for his babies. He would do anything for his family... and so would Harriet. But M just seemed to have so much more to tolerate.

There was one time that E15 flew to the nest with a fish that she stole from M15 over at the construction site pond across the street. Soon after E15 arrived at the nest with the fish, M flew to the nest with another fish. Immediately E15 stole that fish from M and kicked M out of the nest. E15 ate both fish.

One morning, as the family woke up, the pasture was full of morning vocals from all the pasture animals and of course the eagle family. E15 continued talking well after Harriet and M stopped. Funny how E15 developed characteristics of E16... mostly how to talk!

M15 flew across the street as E15 called out, "Bring back something yummy for breakfast! I'm starved!"

While waiting, E15 flew off to the snag tree. She watched all the little birds as they started their day and the ducks as they floated in the pond. As 15 bit at the tree's bark, she heard someone say her name.

"Good morning, Miss 15!"

E15 looked around. "Oh, good morning, Commander!"

"It looks like you're having fun picking at that tree today." E15 smiled and continued to pick at the bark. The Commander chuckled. "Well you have a good day. I have to get my troops to breakfast. Have fun little lady!"

"Thank you, Commander! Enjoy your breakfast!"

"Thank you, 15. I certainly will."

"Hmmm... gee, I wonder where Dad is with my breakfast," E15 thought out loud. E15 started hopping from branch to branch. Suddenly she ended up upside down. She hung onto the branch. "WHOA!" she cried.

The Commander and his troops, Sandy and Waddles all turned to see what had happened. They all saw 15 hanging upside down just before she flew off across the road to search for her parents.

"Did you see that? asked Waddles.

"Well, I'll be... Here we go again," replied Sandy.

A month had already gone by since E16 started her new life. E15 had now taken over the pasture and enjoyed the pine across the road and spent a lot of her time there.

"I wonder how 16 is enjoying her new life," 15 softly asked. "I know I enjoy being on this side of the road as if it is a new adventure. I wonder if she has found a favorite spot or tree." E15 stopped and looked across the road at the nest tree and added, "I wonder if she ever thinks of me and misses me... like I miss her."

Two adult white ibis caught E15's attention. They had a youngster with them. E15 tilted her head as she watched the little ibis follow behind the parents and learned how to get food for himself. "Look Mommy! Look Daddy! I caught my own food!" exclaimed the young ibis as the proud parents smiled.

"Gee, I guess all parents have to teach their kids how to hunt and feed themselves to survive." E15 had figured it out. Inspired by observing the ibis family, E15 flew to the west pasture. She grabbed a stick in her talons and brought it to the nest. "Woohoo!" she cheered. My stick will be a great addition to the nest!" E15 called out hoping her parents were nearby, "Mama! Dad! I can help with nestorations!"

Time had suddenly gone by so fast. E15 had become a beautiful, intelligent young eagle... and a demanding eagle... but also a fun-loving eagle... a well-rounded eagle.

Whenever Harriet and M flew to the nest tree, E15 would immediately join them. She would always question loudly why food was not provided. But E15 had now learned how to hunt and provide for herself. Although that didn't mean that E15 wouldn't try to persuade her parents to bring her food.

Both 15 and 16 learned well from their parents. One of their lessons was how to protect themselves from the elements. Being brought up in Southwest Florida that was very important, especially when storms suddenly pop up out of nowhere. And like her sister, perfecting lessons was extremely important... but so was fun time! E15 enjoyed the construction site across the road. She would play and hang out on the new rooftops as if looking to decide which house would suit her lifestyle. Yes, serious and focused, yet fun loving, E15 had certainly become a young eagle with dreams of her own.

Time was going by so quickly. The day started with E15 in the nest tree. But this day brought something special with it. It was a day of hope and promise. E15 looked up at the sky. Her eyes opened wide in wonder. "WOW!" she whispered in awe. From one side to the other a full rainbow arched over the nest tree. It was an amazing sight to see and it seemed to give a hint of what was to come... an Ozzie hint. That soft gentle giggle danced on the breeze as a feather floated by. Yes, wonder and love filled the air.

E15 spent the day flying throughout the pasture. At the end of the day, Harriet and M flew to the nest tree attic. They were soon joined by E15 as she squeed loudly, mantling as she landed near her parents.

Harriet and M knew something was going on. Harriet sighed and M said, "Here we go."

"Mama... Dad..." E15 paused.

Harriet and M looked at each other. "We know, 15... we know..." Harriet said softly.

"So, is it okay?"

"Oh, 15! Of course it is okay. It is what you are meant to do. Your Father and I will miss you and love you always. But this is what nature is calling you to do... IF you are ready."

"I am," 15 replied confidently.

Harriet gave E15 a soft smile. Her heart ached, but was full of pride at the same time. "And 15... I have to tell you something..."

"Is it about the wink?"

Surprised, Harriet replied, "Yes. How did you know?"

"I heard you when you told E16." Harriet and E15 hugged.

"I love you my beauty. You have grown to be fierce AND beautiful!"

"Thank you, Mama. It is all because of you and Dad." E15 paused and added... "And from E16. She taught me how to have a fun side and how to not take myself so seriously all the time."

Harriet's heart melted. "I love you so much."

"I love you too, Mama." E15 looked at her Dad. "I love you, Dad. And I'm sorry, but I'm not a singer. I can't sing the song."

"I love you too, 15. You don't have to sing. It's okay!" M smiled at his daughter.

"I'll miss you, Dad." E15's eyes filled with tears.

M's voice cracked as he spoke the words, "You will always be our 15 no matter what. There will never be another 15. You are my junior... my namesake. You have made me so proud. I love you..." M hugged his E15 and then quickly flew off to the front pine.

E15 moved closer to Harriet. Harriet looked at her young eagle. "Oh, my E15." Harriet sighed and hugged her baby. "Live a long, strong, healthy life my 15."

"I will, Mama..."

Harriet and E15 slept next to each other on the attic branch that night. When morning broke, E15 and Harriet were still next to each other. The long-awaited day had finally arrived... the bittersweet day they all live for. Harriet and E15 looked at each other and hugged. With tears in her eyes, Harriet turned and flew off of the nest tree. The morning sky was beautiful. E15 flew across the road to her favorite pine tree. And then... the area was quiet. No squees, no demands, no playtime, no fanfare... and no E15. Just like that... a young eaglet's life and lessons had been completed and a new life had begun. Quietly... but strong and confident.

Later, M sat perched on the attic branch when he heard Harriet as she called out alert vocals. She landed in the nest tree as she was being chased by an intruder.

"GET OUT!" yelled M15.

"This is our HOME!" warned Harriet. The intruder circled the nest tree and flew out of sight.

"Are you okay?" asked M.

"I'm fine," said Harriet. They looked around the pasture and across the road. "Has there been any sight of ..."

"No..." M quietly answered.

"It seemed like this season was never going to end," said Harriet. "And now it seems as if it has ended so quickly. I know it was time, but now it just seems so final."

"I know…"

"It not only starts E15's new life, but now it also brings back the day that 16 left and started her new life. So I can't help but feel the emptiness of the nest."

Harriet and M hugged and quietly cried. They were sad and happy for their babies now that they had both started their new lives. But they were also so exhausted. It had been a long, stressful and emotional season. Their resilient nature and their love for their eaglets had carried them through it all.

The reality that E15 and E16 had begun their eagle lives had started to settle in.

Harriet and M woke up on the attic branch. "Good morning," said Harriet.

"Good morning," replied M.

"It's so quiet," Harriet said softly as she looked around. M nodded, took a deep breath and flew off the nest tree. Harriet followed him.

Within minutes, M flew back to the nest with his first official stick of the new nesting season. No down time, no vacation, no rejuvenating the soul. They immediately started nestorations in preparation of the next season of eggs. M flew off again and returned quickly with another stick. He placed it and went up to the attic branch and assessed the nest from above. Harriet then flew in with a stick of her own. M hopped down into the nest to help with its placement.

"Here let me help," said M.

"I've got it. I'm okay," replied Harriet.

The nest discussions would start up again soon enough, but not just yet. After Harriet placed her stick, she flew to the attic. M laid down in the nest to get a feel for how much nest material would be needed. He grabbed a nest rail that was still in place and moved it. Harriet saw the look on M's face.

"M?" she asked.

"I'm okay. I just can't believe there are still a couple of nest rails in place. The nest went through so much this year. The annoying owl…" M paused and added, "E14… and then 15 and 16… and hurricane season."

"Thank goodness we were spared from hurricanes and major storms. I'm sure E14 was watching over us for that."

"I'm sure he was," said M.

"He'll always be with us."

"Yes, he will." M flew up to Harriet and they hugged.

Harriet and M worked on the nest throughout the day. The pasture animals watched the loving couple.

"Looks like they're thinking of having more eggs already," said the Commander in disbelief.

"No, they couldn't be. They just had two leave. They need to take their usual time off," said Waddles.

"I would think the same thing too, but they both just brought in some new sticks to the nest. And that means more eggs," explained the Commander.

"I'm exhausted just thinking of it," said Sandy. "Nest repairs, laying eggs, hatching them, feeding them and all the rest that comes with raising them. I mean they're cute little balls of fluff and all, but they're exhausting and demanding!" Sandy giggled.

The Commander laughed and said, "I'm glad I'm retired!"

They all chuckled.

The pasture always seemed so quiet and empty when all the young eagles left to start their new lives. They all brought so much life and excitement to the pasture.

Harriet and M flew to the pond area and greeted the small gathering of pasture friends.

"I don't know how you two do it," said Sandy. "You just sent off E15 and E16 and you are already getting ready to have more!"

"Do you two take super vitamins or something?" asked Waddles.

Harriet giggled. "No, it is just what we eagles do."

"To tell you the truth, I didn't think 15 was ever going to leave," added the Commander.

Harriet and M smiled and Harriet replied, "Well sometimes you just never know!"

"So, you're not going to take any time off? You're just going to go straight into a new season?" asked Sandy.

"That's the plan," replied M.

"God Bless you both! I'll say it again, I'm exhausted just thinking about it! I don't know... I must be getting old or something." As Sandy spoke, they all saw Twitch and NutJob running through the pasture. Sandy pointed at the two squirrels and said, "Look at them! Not a care in the world... young and so full of life... and fun! I used to be like that. But now for me, floating in the pond is my new speed."

"You're not alone, Sandy," the Commander chuckled. "You're not alone."

"Well we have busy days ahead of us. We have to get back to the nest, watch the sunset and get some rest. Goodnight everyone," said Harriet.

"Goodnight all," said M.

"Goodnight," they all responded as Harriet and M flew back to the nest tree.

Harriet and M perched on the attic branch and watched the sunset. They were happy for 15 and 16, but they missed them both. They looked at each other and hugged. They hung their heads and closed their eyes.

The days went by quietly... when suddenly...

Everything stopped in the nest tree pasture. EVERYTHING! All the pasture animals lifted their heads and stood completely still. Even the air seemed still.

"What was that?" asked Sandy. "Did you hear that?"

The animals all silently nodded. They all searched the area around them for the sound.

Harriet and M were by the pond. They turned their heads and they too searched for the sound. They looked at each other in disbelief. The sound got louder and closer and then... there she was! E15 landed on the attic branch squeeing away.

"I don't believe it," said Harriet. M only nodded.

The pasture animals whispered amongst themselves. "Is it her? Is she back?"

Harriet and M quickly flew to the nest tree.

"I'm starving!" exclaimed E15.

"E15! You're back! What happened?" asked Harriet.

"What happened? I got hungry! And then I thought about what E16 said to me... that she liked it here. The pond, the food. Why would I want to leave here when I have all the food I want with Mama and Dad. So, I decided to come home." Harriet and M looked at each other. E15 continued, "Plus I missed both of you."

"We missed you too, sweetheart. But didn't you like being on your own?" asked Harriet.

"It was alright. But I like it here better and I'm on my own a lot here. So... here I am!" E15 smiled.

"Yes, here you are," said M reluctantly.

"Aren't you glad to see me?" E15 asked sadly.

"Of course we are!" replied Harriet. "We're just surprised. That's all."

"Well I'm here!"

Harriet and M smiled and hugged their baby. Then they looked at each other unsure of what to do next.

But before anyone could say anything else, Harriet and M spotted an intruder. They all vocalized a warning. M quickly flew off to chase the intruder away. Harriet and E15 stayed on the nest tree and continued to warn the unwelcomed visitor.

"Looks like I came back just in time!" said E15.

Harriet smiled, "It is always good to learn more life lessons firsthand. You did great, 15!"

"Thanks, Mama!"

The next day everyone called out their morning vocals. E15 squeed nonstop, demanding food. One by one the family flew off of the nest tree. But soon Harriet returned with food with E15 following right behind her.

"Welcome home, baby!"

"Thanks, Mama!" E15 said happily as she claimed the food, mantled and ate. Harriet smiled and flew off.

M was in the pasture and found a stick worthy of being part of their nestorations. He grabbed the stick and flew to the nest to place it. Only E15 didn't realize her Dad had a stick. She thought M was there to steal her food.

"It's MINE! Mom brought it for me as a welcome home gift!" cried E15 as she flapped her wings.

M shook his head. "I don't want your food. I brought a stick." He left the stick in the nest and he flew to the attic. "Oh, I see this is going to be interesting with E15 back. I'm glad she's here, but how are we going to do nestorations?" M quietly asked himself.

It took a little time to adjust to having E15 back in the nest tree. E15 was now six months old and very demanding. Harriet and M would still look at each other in disbelief. But M being a great provider would always give in to E15's demands even though she also provided for herself.

E15 continued to perfect her lessons. Especially the lesson on how to protect their territory. Although having E15 back changed their plans, Harriet and M appreciated the extra help. Strength in numbers as they say.

One day while perched on the attic branch in a beautiful heraldic pose, E15 admired another beautiful rainbow. "Hi Ozzie! Hi 3, 5 and 14!" E15 called out. But as soon as she said those words a sub-adult flew over the nest. E15 immediately sounded a powerful alert. M flew in and chased the intruder away as E15 watched closely. This kind of lesson was priceless and E15 benefitted from being back home. As if the first part of her life was elementary school to high school and now she had graduated to college. These lessons would excel E15 onto her Master's Degree. Being back had its advantages for E15 and her parents. But there was one slight disadvantage... the upcoming new season. Harriet and M needed to prepare the nest for eggs. And something else very important... Harriet was accustomed to M bringing her food and treats at this time of the season. NOW Harriet had competition and M had another mouth to provide for. A mouth with an extremely LARGE appetite!

One evening, M flew to the nest with dinner. Harriet was right behind him, but E15 got to the nest before Harriet and E15 claimed the food.

Harriet looked at M and narrowed her eyes. "That was supposed to be MINE!" she said very displeased.

"I'm sorry, Harriet. I just get the food and deliver it. The two of you have to work that out," said M and he flew off.

M was right. This was going to prove to be very interesting. M knew he was going to have to please both of his divas... sorry, his ladies. He also needed to prepare the nest for eggs.

Anytime Harriet and M flew to the nest with food, E15 would be right there ready for the steal. One morning, M flew to the nest with a stick to show Harriet he was ready and eager to start the next season. E15 saw M land in the nest and she immediately went to claim the phantom food. M flew to the attic as E15 discovered the food was a stick.

"A stick? A stick, Dad? Are you kidding me?" E15 complained. She grabbed the stick and flew to the attic with it and mantled and squeed at her Father. Exhausted, M shook his head and flew off.

"WAIT! Wait for me! Are we getting food?" E15 called out as she flew after her Dad.

Poor M...

But Harriet had her fair share of E15, too. Whenever Harriet brought food to the nest, E15 would be there to steal it. E15 and Harriet would be very vocal with each other. Both being strong-willed females, neither wanted to give in. This was still new for Harriet and M. So Harriet would let E15 have the food... at least for now. E15 was an equal opportunity food stealer. It didn't matter if it was Harriet or M that she stole from. Food was food.

E15 continued to monopolize the food and Harriet had gotten to her breaking point. One night, E15 had a tremendous crop and yet she still demanded and claimed the food. Harriet watched her daughter as she mantled the food and just stood there not eating it.

"Okay, that's it!" Harriet said. She dropped down into the nest from the attic and immediately stole the food from E15.

"Hey! That's mine!" E15 demanded.

"No, it was yours and now it's mine!"

"Give it back!" yelled E15.

Harriet ignored E15 as she enjoyed her fish. E15 tried all of her tactics that she used on E16 to steal the fish from Harriet, but this wasn't E16... this was Harriet and Harriet wasn't hatched yesterday. She was able to keep the fish from E15. E15 made a great attempt to get the fish back, but without success. There was even a tug of war, but of course, Harriet won.

But remember, E15 is Harriet's daughter and she was taught by the best. Especially when it came to food. The next day E15 was in the nest eating. Harriet flew onto the nest with nest material and this upset E15 while she ate. She chased Harriet out of the nest. E15 almost fell out of the nest while yelling at Harriet, but she managed to catch herself in time and remained in the nest as Harriet flew off.

But there was more to E15's days than just eating. She was adventurous and she wanted to investigate. She discovered a parking lot light pole in the Church parking lot. She landed on the extended angled arm of the pole that held the light. She carefully walked up the arm to the light. As she reached it, she looked above it, below it, behind it... all around it. She was unsure of it and found it interesting. But just like that, she was done and she flew off.

Another day, she was determined to remove the nest tree webcam strap that held the webcam in place. She bit it and she pulled on it. At one point she had both feet on it and she pulled with all her might. She was having fun. Then she stopped and said, "Gee, maybe E9 was right! Life is a toy!" She giggled and stopped playing with the strap. Luckily, she wasn't successful at removing it, but she certainly was determined.

From there she flew to a pasture utility pole, different than the Church light pole. She sat on the pole as she looked around for more adventures. That was when she saw something small move in the grass below and she flew down to have a snack.

Then under the shimmering colors of another rainbow, E15 went to the driveway, looked both ways and walked across. Like her brother, E9, she showed a truck on the driveway who was in charge. "Eagles have the right of way!" she called out. She then flew up on the fence rail near the stables. The truck slowly drove past. E15 then heard a voice behind her.

"Well, well, well! Welcome home, little lady! There was a rumor going around the pasture that you were back," said the Commander.

"Thank you, sir! Yes, I'm back!" replied E15.

"It is such a nice surprise to see you again!"

"Not as surprised as my parents," E15 smiled.

"Oh," the Commander laughed, "I'm sure of that! But I'm curious, didn't you like it out there?"

"It was okay, but I like it here better."

"Well that's understandable. When it is your time to go off on your own, you'll know. Until then it is nice to have you back home again."

"Thank you, sir! It's good to be back!"

"Well I'm heading back to the stables and out of this sun and heat. I'll see you around, little lady."

"Keep cool!" said E15 and she flew to another new spot... the chimney on the building by the pond. "Wow! What is this? It has a hole in it. I think I should leave it alone so I don't get hurt or stuck. I don't know where that hole leads to." E15 flew off.

This was a very active time for sub-adults in the area. While Harriet and E15 were in the nest tree, a sub-adult tried to land near E15. E15 sounded the alert and almost fell off of the branch, but she was determined to maintain her spot and she held on. The sub-adult flew off and circled around. Both Harriet and E15 continued the alert. The sub-adult came back. E15 held her mighty wings open as the intruder approached and tried to land next to Harriet. Harriet scared the intruder and he then tried to land near E15. Harriet managed to chase the sub-adult off, but he was determined and made one more attempt. The intruder landed on the upper branch and Harriet immediately chased it away for good!

"Great job, Mama!" cheered E15.

"I couldn't have done it without you, E15. Great teamwork!" They both smiled.

E15 had grown up before her parents' eyes. She was a young eagle now. Even though it seemed odd that she was back, it was a Blessing. It gave everyone insight to a young eagle's life. No one in the pasture had ever seen any of Harriet's children at this stage and it was exciting to watch. E15 had developed into a beautiful, young eagle. Even her looks started to mature in front of everyone. She was now a confident, young eagle with a strong eagle attitude. With every day she learned more than her siblings before her. With every webcam view of her daily life, she gave all of the eagle watchers and experts insight to something they had never witnessed firsthand. E15 was now teaching her own lessons. The student had now become the teacher.

Chapter 23 ... All In The Family

The morning started with Harriet and M as they brought in sticks for the nest. But this was the OTHER nest. Not the nest tree nest, but the west pasture tree nest. The two eagles were determined to get the nest completed... any nest! E15 watched her parents from the snag... and she watched them very closely. The past few days she had moved some sticks in "her" nest by herself. But on this day after she watched her parents, she got her own stick and brought it to "her" nest.

"I'm over here!" she called out into the wind hoping her parents would hear her. "I brought a stick for the nest so we can start nestorations." She looked at the large stick M had brought into the nest. "Where does he find these big sticks?" she asked out loud. She tried to move it and place it in the nest, but it was a typical oversized M stick. E15 decided to move other "normal" sized sticks and rearranged them instead. "Sooo... maybe this will be my nest and the west pasture nest that Mama and Dad are working on will be theirs..." she said as she tilted her head in thought. And then just like an adult eagle, she laid down. But this time she looked like an adult female eagle protecting and caring for her eggs. She no longer looked like a young eaglet resting in the nest. E15 had matured and was thinking of her future. She smiled.

E15 was very happy and comfortable with the nest tree. To her it was HOME! But her home was also very attractive to other local wildlife.

One encounter was with a two year old sub-adult. The young eagle just flew to the nest tree and landed on an outer branch while E15 perched on the attic branch for the night.

"Hi!" said the visitor.

"Hi!" replied E15.

"I'm E13," said the visitor.

"I'm E15."

"Hi, 15."

"Hi, 13." And that was it. No alerts, no yelling, no drama. Each young eagle stayed on the nest tree until morning.

"Well, thanks for letting me stay for the night. Tell Mom and Dad that I love them."

"You're welcome. I'll tell them... bye," replied E15 and the young eagle flew off.

The next encounter was with a Great Horned Owl. Since E15 came back home, she had already had two encounters with this forceful owl. E15 was no stranger to this troublemaker. The first encounter since she had been home was very creepy. E15 wasn't even aware that the owl was there. While E15 was asleep on the attic branch, without a sound the Great Horned Owl landed across from E15. E15 woke up. She sensed someone or something was there, but she remained quiet. The owl just sat on the branch and stared at E15. Eventually it flew off. As it turned to fly away, E15 heard the movement of the branch and E15 jumped and opened her wings to scare whatever it was away. Both E15 and M alerted the area to ward off the owl. But not long after that night, the second encounter with the owl happened. Although this encounter wasn't like the first one. Again, while E15 was asleep on the attic branch, the owl silently flew to the nest tree, but this time the owl hit into E15. Somehow E15 managed to hold on tight to the branch. The owl flew off to the snag tree, but it watched E15 from there until it finally left for the night. E15 and her parents sounded the alert to warn the owl to stay away. E15 had learned well from her past experiences with this owl. She stood strong!

The days ahead were filled with Harriet and M doing nestorations and building the new nest while E15 watched.

"What are they doing?" E15 would ask herself as her parents worked in the new nest. She blinked her eyes to focus on them. "Are they building two nests in that one tree? A second floor? Or maybe a condo?" The tree did appear to have sticks in two areas, but Harriet and M concentrated on the one main nest.

"M, don't you think we have enough room in the nest without having to build a condo?" asked Harriet.

M heard the disapproval in Harriet's tone. Then he thought of something. This was the time for M to use the stuffed animal reference. The Get Out Of Jail Free card. He felt confident and sure of himself that he could use this AND get the condo he always aspired to building. "Well I thought it might be a good idea in case you wanted to bring home things to store. It can be a storage area for you to keep all of your..." M laughed, "...stuffed animal toys..." M smiled. How could this go wrong. It was true. Harriet did bring a stuffed animal toy to the nest thinking it was food. She knew she did it. He told the truth. Harriet looked at M. She was hurt. "Oh, no," M quietly said to himself. His plan had backfired.

Harriet looked down and softly said, "I felt terrible about that! Why would you bring that up now?"

Now M felt horrible. "I'm so sorry, Harriet. I didn't mean to upset you." M paused. "I was only kidding." Harriet lifted her head and looked at M lovingly. She kissed him on the cheek. M smiled. She grabbed a stick and bonked M in the head with it. "OW!" M exclaimed.

"And don't you bring it up again! And you can forget about building a condo!"

"But...!"

"Don't 'but' me or I'll bring up all the silly things YOU have done over the years."

"Like what?" asked M, although not a really good idea to ask... don't ask if you don't want to hear the answer.

"Do you really want me to go into my list of silly things that you have done?"

M hung his head and replied, "No..."

"Then let's not mention the stuffed animal toy again!"

"Okay... I'm sorry I won't mention it again."

"Ever?"

"I won't mention it again, ever."

"Promise?"

"Promise." M paused again and asked, "You really have a list of silly things that I do?" Harriet looked at M and smiled. In shock, M asked, "Really? A whole list?" M sighed.

Harriet saw the look on M's face and she felt bad. "M, we both do things that are silly at times."

"I guess... but you have a list!"

"Well I didn't say it was a BIG list."

"But you have a list."

Now Harriet felt terrible. "It isn't a big list. In fact, I can't even think of one thing on it."

"You're just saying that to make me feel better."

"No, I'm not!" Harriet moved closer to M. "But I do have another list about you." She smiled.

"Oh, great! What else do I do wrong?"

"Who said it was anything you do wrong?" She looked into M's eyes. "My list... my important list... is of all the things I love about you!" Harriet tilted her head and smiled lovingly at her M.

M smiled and wiggled his eyebrows the way only her M could. "Really?"

"Yes, really! And those wiggling eyebrows is one of the things on that list."

M puffed out his chest and held his head high. He smiled and then said, "Well they do have a certain charisma about them." Harriet nodded as M paused. "So...what else is on the list that you love about me?"

Harriet started to answer and then said, "Everything!"

"Oh, that's not an answer." Harriet narrowed her eyes at M. "But it is a great answer," he quickly said.

"Good! Now can we please get back to work on the nest? We have to get one of these nests done. Without knowing what E15's plans are we have to have a nest completed for our eggs this season... and it can't be a nest where E15 looks for food. We have no choice, but to finish this nest. So, let's get back to work."

"Yes, my Lady Love!" and they kissed.

E15 sat perched on the driveway fence rail and watched her parents.

"They sure are busy up there," said the Commander as he strolled past E15. "What are they doing?"

"I have no idea," replied E15. "They bring sticks to our nest and then they bring sticks to the new nest... and the new nest looks like two nests."

The Commander chuckled. "Ha, ha, ha... you are so right, little lady. Oh!" the Commander paused and sighed. "Sometimes... well most of the time... well actually, all of the time... your parents may have a difference of opinion on the placement of the sticks. So, you might not want to watch them too closely."

"Why?" asked E15.

"Why?" The Commander hesitated before he answered. "Well because ..." the Commander paused again and E15 blinked her eyes as she waited for the explanation. "Well just because, ummm, because..."

"They argue?"

"Well... yes... wait, no... it is more like spirited discussions."

"They argue," chuckled E15. "That's okay. I can handle it. E16 and I used to argue all the time, but it didn't mean anything. We still loved each other."

The Commander smiled. "That is exactly right, little lady. Even if they argue... I mean have spirited discussions, they still love each other AND they love you very much!"

"I know." Just then a truck pulling a horse trailer drove past. "WHOA! Did you see that? What was that? And where is he going?"

The Commander laughed. "That is one of the newbies we had here. He was just here for a couple of weeks and now he is going to his own home. So, they put him in what they call a horse trailer to bring him there."

"But he's a horse. Can't he just walk there?"

"Yes, he can, but it's pretty far and he has people with him so the horse trailer is more for them than for him."

"Did you ever go in one of those things?"

"A trailer? Sure, I have. That's how I got here."

E15 saw her Dad as he flew to the nest. Her eyes opened wide. "I'm sorry, Commander. I have to go now. My Dad just brought in food."

"Go, go, young one and enjoy!"

"Thanks! Bye!" E15 flew to her nest to meet her Dad. M left the food in the nest and he flew to the attic. E15 looked at what M brought and then looked at M.

"Go ahead, E15," said M.

Looking at the food, E15 asked, "What is it?"

"It's a turtle."

E15 inspected the item and said, "It's weird looking." The little turtle was on his back as he hid in his shell. "I don't know. It looks terrible."

The little turtle prayed inside of his shell. "Yes, yes I'm weird looking and I taste terrible! Please, please, let me go!"

E15 joined her Dad on the attic. "E, that's your food."

"But I don't want that."

"Well that's all you're getting."

As Father and daughter argued over the menu choice, the little turtle quietly flipped himself over.

"Yes, yes... Keep arguing," whispered the turtle. The little turtle stuck his head, arms and legs out of his shell and rushed as fast as he could... as fast as a turtle could... to the edge of the nest. He looked down at the long drop to the ground and then he looked up at the two arguing eagles. He focused on their large beaks and their sharp talons. He gulped, closed his eyes and stepped over the edge of the nest. He pulled himself back into his shell. He prayed as he tumbled through the air to the ground. He landed on the soft grass at the base of the tree. His eyes grew wide and they glowed from inside his shell. "I made it! I'm alive!" he cheered. He quickly popped his head, arms and legs out of his shell and ran as fast as he could back to the pond. "Kelli! I'm home! Amelia! Reid! Daddy's home!" They all rushed to hug him.

"Jon, what's wrong? Where have you been?" asked Kelli.

"You don't want to know. But I'm home now. Thank God!" The little family held onto each other and smiled.

"WAIT! Be quiet!" said M. He and E15 sat in silence.

E15 waited and then asked, "What are we waiting for?"

"I thought I heard someone saying something." They sat silent again and then M said, "Anyway, now go back to the nest and eat your food!"

Reluctantly, E15 looked down into the nest and saw it was empty. "Ummm... Dad?"

"Don't give me a hard time, 15. Go eat your food!"

"That's just the problem, Dad."

"What's the problem now?"

"It's gone."

M looked over E15's shoulder. "So that's what I heard," he laughed. "Well that's what happens when you don't take advantage of what you've been given."

After that, no matter what M brought to the nest, E15 immediately flew in to claim it. Unfortunately for E15, it wasn't always food. Occasionally M would bring in a stick to add to the original nest which always disappointed E15. E15 was always forceful in her approach. M15 was moved out of the way or pushed out of the nest many times. E15 was certainly not shy or bashful when it came to food.

One morning, while on the grass near the pond, a sub-adult landed near E15.

"GO AWAY! This is MY home!"

"I know. But it is my home, too. Well, it was my home."

E15 tilted her head. Then she recognized the visitor. "Oh, that's right! You're E13."

"I won't stay long, 15. I just wanted to see Mom and Dad." E13 turned and saw Harriet and M perched in the nest tree. "And there they are now! See ya, 15!"

"See ya!"

Harriet and M watched the sky and turned to get a good view of the young eagle visitor. They stretched their necks as they strained to see the sub-adult flying above the pasture.

"There! Over there!" Harriet pointed to the visitor above the nest tree.

"Yes, I see!" said M.

"Hi Mom! Hi Dad! I love you both!" called out E13. Harriet and M called out their usual warning to their amazing E13. E13 replied, "I know and I won't stay, but I needed to see both of you and I also need to see that something special. You know what I'm talking about Mom." Harriet smiled and let out a call of love. Then she winked at her baby. "That's it! That's all I needed to see! I'm fine. And thank you both for all you have taught me. I sometimes run into E12. She sends her love. Now she thinks she's the princess of ALL ponds." E13 laughed. "I love and miss you both. I'll be back again, but bye for now..." and the young eagle flew out of sight.

M looked at his beautiful Harriet. "Your wink brings the kids so much happiness."

"And it brings me so much happiness too... but it brings me even more happiness when I see them. I just wish they could all stay."

"I know... I do, too. But remember Harriet, you are right. Your wink says it all. It will always say, we love you, we miss you and every night we pray you are healthy, happy and safe... It says it all..." M's voice trailed off.

"The kids are my heart."

"My heart, too." Harriet and M looked deeply into each other's eyes. They hugged. Their love was so strong. They were happy and secure in knowing they always did their best for their family.

Chapter 24 ... God Speed

*E*15 was perched on the fence rail by the pond. She watched and waited for the right moment. She leaned forward, her eyes fixed on the water, and she pushed off of the fence rail with her mighty legs and flew toward the pond. She lowered her legs and extended her talons as she grabbed at what she hoped would be a fish, but it got away. She landed in the pond and swam back to shore and dried off her wet, massive wings.

"Next time!" she confidently told herself. She had become quite the hunter so this was not a setback.

As soon as her wings were dry, E15 flew to the utility pole. She watched what seemed to be the oddest thing to her. People were on the backs of the horses. She tilted her head unsure of what they were doing. She watched, but it just didn't make sense to her. She shook her head. But she had something more important on her mind. So she flew to the Church.

She landed on the Cross on top of the steeple. E15 quietly looked all around her surroundings. She looked at the nest tree, the pasture, the pond, the stables and the land, houses and Yonder Pond across the road. Although she loved her parents and her home, she knew there was more to life. E15 bowed her head and said, "Hi, Lord. I don't know if You remember me. I'm E15. You helped me get back to my nest once. I was hoping that maybe You could Help me again. I'm a little confused. I really need Your Guidance. You see... I really love my parents and I am grateful for all they have done for me and have taught me... but... I think it is time for me to start my own life... away from them and here. I tried it for a little bit a while ago... but I wasn't ready and I came back home. But... well, now I know I'm ready. But I think Mama and Dad are happy that I'm back home. You see, Lord... they're building a new nest for me to live in... or for them to live in and I'll live in the nest I grew up in... either way they are doing this for me... but... I want to start my life... and if I go it will break their hearts and they're doing all this work for me... I don't want to disappoint them or hurt their feelings... So, I am so torn on what to do. Do I stay and make them happy? Or do I start my own life like I am supposed to do? So please, Lord, Guide me to do the right thing and to say the right words... Oh... and Lord... please Watch over my parents and my sister, E16. Thank You... Amen."

E15 flew to the nest tree. She landed on the attic branch. She looked at the nest and hopped down into it. She tilted her head as she studied the nest. She laid down in the nest and she smiled as she remembered all the good times with E16. "E16 is the best little sister anyone could ask for. I miss you E16. I hope we get to see each other soon," she called out. She moved a couple of nearby sticks. She sighed and was content.

That evening, E15 perched on the attic branch. The moon was above her. A beautiful moon beam shone directly on E15. Her heart filled with joy and love. She looked up and said, "Thank You, Lord. My answer is clear... and my future is bright!" She smiled and dreamt of good things to come.

Morning came and E15 was full of joy and excitement. She watched her Mom and Dad as they continued to build their new nest. E15 flew closer to watch. Both Harriet and M flew off of the nest. E15 looked all around and smiled. She quietly flew to the new nest.

"WOW! This is REALLY nice!" E15 inspected all the sticks her parents had brought in and she gazed at all the big branches that supported the beautiful nest. Suddenly E15 sighed. "I hope Mama and Dad won't be disappointed that I won't be using the nests." E15 looked up and saw her Dad as he flew to the other nest with food. Quickly E15 flew off to claim it. Harriet got to the nest before E15. E15 quickly stole it from Harriet. She mantled the food, squeed and protected her meal while she ate. Her parents soon went back to the new nest and added more sticks. When E15 finished her food, she watched Harriet and M very closely. She moved higher in the nest tree to get a better view. She flew to the snag tree and then the utility pole. Harriet stopped working and looked at their beautiful E15. She quietly stared at their baby.

M looked at Harriet. "Harriet?"

"It's time," she replied as she continued to just stare at E15.

"Time for what?" asked M.

Harriet didn't answer. She just stared at E15. M followed the direction of her gaze. He looked back at Harriet and saw tears in her eyes.

"It never gets easy... no matter how many babies and no matter how many times they start their new lives... it never gets easy to say goodbye," said Harriet. M put his wing around her.

E15 looked up toward the sky. She took a deep breath, smiled a great big smile and let out a joyful squee. She flew toward the new nest.

"I love you, Mama! I love you, Dad! I'm sorry, but it is time for me to start my life."

"We know, baby... we know," replied Harriet.

"You're not upset with me?"

"Upset with you? Why would we be upset with you?" asked M.

"Upset that you're doing all of this work to both nests just for me and I won't be here to enjoy all your hard work." Harriet and M looked at each other, unsure of what E15 was talking about. E15 continued, "And as much as I really appreciate all the work you've done and that you want to give me my own nest, I really have to go."

Harriet and M smiled. They didn't have the heart to tell E15 that the nests weren't for her, but for the new babies that would be coming. They just couldn't tell her that they couldn't use the original nest because she was still in it and they couldn't restore it while she was still there, so they HAD to build a new nest. They just didn't want to break her heart that the nests weren't being done for her, but were being done *because* of her. E15 was happy with the thought that her parents did this for her. So they saw no harm in letting her continue to think that.

"We love you, baby!" Harriet and M called out.

"I love you, Mama! I love you, Dad! Thank you! Thank you so much! I'll watch for your wink, Mama!" Harriet smiled hearing those words. "Goodbye everyone!" E15 called out to the pasture animals.

"God Speed, little lady, God Speed!" replied the Commander. A tear fell from his eye. "I'm getting too darn old for all of these goodbyes!"

"Bye, E15! Bye!" the pasture animals said in unison.

"Okay, E16! Here I come!" And E15 soared higher and higher until she was out of sight.

Harriet and M watched as their baby flew off to start her new life for the second time.

M looked at Harriet as she stared at the empty sky. "She might return," said M.

"She might... but I think this was it. This was her time. This time was second nature for her."

Harriet and M kept busy in the days to come. At night they both flew to their nest tree, the original nest tree. They aerated it and added and moved sticks. And they always searched the area for their little girl.

M hopped down into the nest. Quietly, he laid down and shimmied.

"What are you doing?" asked Harriet in disbelief.

"I'm just checking it out."

"For what?"

"Just in case."

"Just in case, what?"

M stood up and replied. "Now that E15 has started her new life… most likely…" M smiled and continued, "We don't need to build a new nest." Harriet raised her eyebrow. M paused and in a bold and firm tone said, "I like this nest!"

"Well I like the new nest! Why do you like this nest? It sways in the wind. It has lost so many branches throughout the years. It's too close to the road with all the noisy cars. It's right in the middle of everything with no privacy. So what could you possibly like about it?"

M looked at Harriet and said, "I like that it sways in the wind. I like that it has lost so many branches that it makes it easy to fly in and out of it. I like that's it's close to the road because I like to watch the noisy cars. I like that it is in the middle of everything so we can watch over our territory."

Harriet laughed and shook her head. "But the other tree is so strong and sturdy. And who knows, maybe the owl won't be able to hit us so easily over there." It was a stretch of the imagination, but Harriet still said it.

"I guess," said M. He looked toward the new nest. "But it isn't home…" Harriet sweetly looked at her handsome eagle. M looked at Harriet and said, "It isn't where you brought me when we first started our lives together… it isn't where we had all the kids… it isn't where you and Ozzie had your six kids…"

"But M, home is wherever we are… It isn't the nest that makes it a home, it's us… it's our love."

M smiled at his Lady Love. "You're right, Harriet. Whatever you want is fine with me. A nest is just a nest, but with you it is a home."

Harriet tilted her head and smiled at M. They hugged.

"Good! Then it's settled! I want the new nest!" She kissed M and flew to the front pine for the night.

M just stood there. "Wait… what just happened?" He shook his head and smiled. "Who am I kidding? How can I resist my Harriet?" M flew to the front pine and landed next to Harriet. "I love you!"

"I love you too, M." They kissed. "How about we see how things go and decide as it gets closer which nest we'll use."

"Really?" asked M. "I like… no, I LOVE that idea!"

"And no matter what, both nests are ours. So one can be our vacation home!"

"WOW! Two homes! I like the sound of that! That could work!"

Then Harriet added, "And who knows… if E15 or any of the other kids come back, they can have a place to stay."

They looked at each other… and they laughed and laughed… and then they stopped laughing and they really thought about that… panic came over their faces… and then they just stared off into the night.

Chapter 25 ... Love Lives On

Harriet and M both flew to the original nest tree. They had another long day of working on both nests. They also had an extremely long and busy season and they were exhausted. They sat perched next to each other and preened. But even preening was exhausting. They couldn't keep their eyes open any longer. They couldn't even stay awake to watch the sunset.

"Goodnight, Harriet. I love you," said M as he kissed his Lady Love.

"Goodnight, M. I love you, too," replied Harriet. The two immediately fell asleep on the attic branch.

Meanwhile, the sun was still bright enough for the pasture animals to play or enjoy a leisurely walk and gather together to talk about the day's events. Twitch and NutJob were busy as they scurried across the pasture fence like two tightrope walkers. Twitch jumped off of the fence and grabbed some acorns while NutJob jumped down into the tall grass and ran aimlessly toward the original nest tree.

"Where are you going?" called out Twitch.

"I don't know," replied NutJob. Up ahead NutJob saw a pretty little feather as it floated teasingly, beckoning him to follow. He caught up to the feather and it landed on his nose. His eyes crossed as he focused to see it. He heard a sweet little voice giggle. "Huh? Who said that?" he asked as he looked side to side in search of someone.

"I'm over here, NutJob!" the voice answered.

"Where? Where are you? Who are you?" The pretty feather floated in front of him again. NutJob chased the feather hoping it would lead him to the sweet voice. He got to the base of the nest tree. The feather landed in front of him. NutJob rubbed his eyes as he looked at something hiding in the grass. He slyly smiled and slowly moved toward whatever it was. He realized it was a fluffy tail. His eyes opened wide with excitement! He smiled and as quick as could be, he grabbed the fluffy tail and laughed, "Gotcha!" But NutJob's laugh soon turned into a scream as he stood there holding Stuffy's tail... Stuffy's tail without Stuffy's body. "AHHH!!!" NutJob's eyes were full of fear and his heart felt like it would explode in his chest. He turned to run away although he screamed again as he saw that he was still holding the bodyless tail. "AHHH!!!" NutJob dropped the tail and ran back to his home.

The sweet voice laughed and laughed.

"Now was that nice, E14?"

E14 laughed again. "Well it might not have been nice, but it sure was funny! Did you see his face?" E14 continued to laugh. Ozzie looked at the little eaglet. He didn't approve of 14's prank on the unsuspecting squirrel. E14 stopped laughing. "I'm sorry... I won't do it again."

"Okay... Now come on, you know the drill. Take my wing. It's time to go home."

"Oh, just a little longer, Ozzie... *please.*"

"No, it's getting late. Your Mom and Dad are already asleep and it's past your bedtime."

Disappointed, E14 said, "Okay... But can I say goodnight to Mama and Dad?"

"Of course you can."

E14 nestled himself between Harriet and M so that he was close to their ears. "I love you both so much. Please don't be sad that 15 and 16 have left home. Ozzie and I and my other siblings made sure they flew safely to start their new lives! They are doing so well and that's all because the two of you are such wonderful parents. Remember... no matter where they are or where any of us are, love lives on. Love protects and watches over loved ones. It doesn't matter which nest you use, I will always be with you. I will never leave you. I love you, Mama... I love you Dad. You know the rainbows show Ozzie, E3, E5 and me are here for you. And now always watch for that little feather... when it appears you know I am near! I watch over you and I listen to you all the time. Watch and listen for me in the wind." E14 hugged his parents and gave them a kiss. "Goodnight... sweet eagle dreams," he whispered. He turned and looked at Ozzie. "Okay, Ozzie... I'm ready to go home now." E14 climbed up onto Ozzie's wing. He glanced over toward him. Shocked, he looked closer at Ozzie. "Was that a tear you wiped away?"

"No," replied Ozzie as he tried to conceal the truth from E14.

"I think it was a tear," the little smarty pants insisted.

"Well I think that you think you know everything!"

"Hmmm... well come to think of it..." E14 smiled and they both laughed.

"So, what do you say? Ready?"

"Home, Ozzie! HOME!"

Harriet and M abruptly woke up. They looked at each other, then they looked out at the pasture and then back at each other.

"Did you...?" asked Harriet.

"Did you...?" asked M.

"I heard him right by my ear."

"I did too."

Harriet hung her head and a tear fell from her eye. "I just wish I could hold him and tell him how much I love and miss him."

"He said he hears us," M said with hope in his voice.

"I know... Maybe we need to watch and listen for him more." Harriet lifted her head and the most beautiful little feather floated in front of them. Harriet and M smiled.

They called out, "WE LOVE YOU, 14! GOOD NIGHT!"

They hugged each other and looked toward the sky. They could see a glorious eagle with a little eaglet on his wing. The eaglet's wings were outstretched as if he was flying. They watched in amazement. And then love filled their hearts as the little eaglet turned his head, looked over his shoulder, smiled... and WINKED!

Harriet gasped! "A wink... he knows what the wink means." And just like Harriet's wink to all of her babies that started their new lives, E14's wink said it all.

Tears of joy filled their eyes and both Harriet and M winked at their precious baby... their precious E14... and 14 and Ozzie safely went HOME... for now. And as they watched this wonderous sight they could hear the joy of a sweet little giggle in the wind...

Love lives on!!!

Lauren Roberts

About the Author

Lauren Roberts resides in Florida with her Husband. She finds so much happiness in being surrounded by the abundance of wildlife that also call Florida home. Observing this well-loved eagle family has brought Lauren, along with millions of others, great joy. Trying to understand the animal's point of view through a human's way of thinking can be difficult at times, but Lauren hopes that it can bring enjoyment to the reader with a chuckle here and there. A volunteer for the Florida Audubon Society Eagle Watch Program, Lauren hopes that anyone that enjoys her stories might be inspired to volunteer with local wildlife rescues and rehabilitators. Something as simple as helping an injured animal or at the very least reporting and seeking help for an injured animal is a great way to start! Carry a shovel and gloves in your car and safely remove roadkill to avoid the dangers of wildlife getting hurt. But please do it safely. Don't hurt yourself trying to be helpful. Donate to those organizations that TRULY help animals. Not the ones that only claim to. Help and support your local wildlife hospitals. Be the voice of the voices that speak the wildlife language!

Please visit us on Facebook at Lauren Roberts Author
https://www.facebook.com/HappyAnimalTales/

See you there!